FEAR ITSELF

. . . See, Erica. No one is watching. No one is looking over your shoulder.

Turning, she walked back toward the house. Dense thickets of brambles seemed to close in on her, and she crossed her arms for protection.

The path was narrowing, shutting out the light. Spines reached toward her, stabbing at her bare calves and forearms, poised to rip at her eyes.

Panic crept up her legs and turned them to frozen stumps. Her head was caught in a violent tremor. Blood roared in her temples, making it hard to see, to breathe.

Stop it, Erica. Get a hold of yourself. The brambles undulated in and out of focus. One step. Two.

Shivering violently, she managed to continue. Another step. Another. Her breath came in short, hot gasps. Burning coals in her chest. Hot stabs of terror . . .

PRIME EVIL

Judith Kelman

BANTAM BOOKS
NEW YORK • TORONTO • LONDON • SYDNEY • AUCKLAND

*This edition contains the complete text
of the original hardcover edition.*
NOT ONE WORD HAS BEEN OMITTED.

PRIME EVIL

A Bantam Book / published by arrangement with the author

PUBLISHING HISTORY
Berkley edition published / September 1986
Bantam edition / August 1995

ISBN 0-553-56437-4

Published simultaneously in the United States and Canada

Bantam Books are published by Bantam Books, a division of Bantam Dou-
bleday Dell Publishing Group, Inc. Its trademark, consisting of the words
"Bantam Books" and the portrayal of a rooster, is Registered in U.S. Patent
and Trademark Office and in other countries. Marca Registrada. Bantam
Books, 1540 Broadway, New York, New York 10036.

PRINTED IN THE UNITED STATES OF AMERICA

OPM   0 9 8 7 6 5 4 3 2 1

To
Ed, Matt, Josh,
Bailey and Taylor

PROLOGUE

As the black van turned into the rutted drive, the two men fell silent. One, a large bearish fellow in blue denim work clothes and a baseball cap, lit a cigarette as he drove, the matchlight wavering in his trembling hand. The other, stern-faced and sallow, fussed over bits of lint on his black mohair suit and rummaged through the contents of his shabby briefcase.

The van was unmarked, the windows tinted an inky grey to mask any signs of its grim mission. "Around back," the passenger said.

Nodding, the driver swung past the towering stands of evergreens, curved around the immaculate stone-faced fa-cade and screeched to a stop behind the screened service porch. Squinting in the midday sun, he lit another cigarette and placed it next to the one already smouldering in the ashtray. Then, hoisting himself from the cracked vinyl seat, he craned his thick neck, searching for signs of life.

Humming a tremulous tune, the man with the briefcase nodded toward the house. There in the dense shade of a pin oak, a stooped, ancient manservant stood waiting to show them the way. Catching the driver's eye, he moved his gnarled hand in a slow, exaggerated arc toward the entrance to the porch. Then, without further ceremony, he made his creaky way back into the cool comfort of the house.

In unison, the two got out and walked slowly up the gravel path. Holding his briefcase like a shield, the first man opened the screen door and peered inside.

Once his eyes adjusted to the dim light, he saw the girl lying on the flowered cushions of the antique wicker settee; her long hair spilled across her back like fresh honey. She was on her side, legs drawn up in defense, pale arms embracing the soft swell of her girlish breasts.

A child, the man thought. A beautiful child.

Motioning for his companion to follow, the man cleared his throat and crossed to the girl. He could smell the soft lilac of her cologne. "Maryann," he said. His voice broke.

So many years, so many children. Still he felt the slap of death as if its icy sting was new to him. So many children. Such a hideous waste.

Clearing his throat, he rolled the girl onto her back. Her body was already stiffening, the limbs stuck in position, the shock of death frozen in a scream across her face.

On the right side, the skull was shattered, crushed like a used paper bag. Bits of bone and brain tissue clung to the golden hair in bloody clumps. One eye was closed, the other bulged from her face in eternal terror. With a trembling finger, he tried to close the eyelid but it slid up again like a broken window shade. The swelling, he thought. Massive cerebral edema.

A simple fall, the maid had said when she called to report the accident. Jesus. In any other place, the girl would have gotten off with a bump and a headache. But not here. Here a simple fall and the poor, pretty little thing looked like some maniac had taken after her with a sledge hammer. A fresh trickle of blood oozed from the wound. No luck in this place. He shivered in the heat.

Out of ancient habit, he pressed the metal mouth of the stethoscope against the icy swell of the girl's bosom. Then he glanced at his ancient Bulova and scratched the time of death on the official certificate. "Twelve-ten."

"You need anything?" The big man spoke in the frightened whisper of a child. You want me to dust for prints or anything? I got my stuff in the van."

"No. No point in that." He scratched "accidental" in the space marked "cause of death" and filled in the young woman's name. He would get the rest later when the family was up to it. "Nothing sinister here except this whole damned place."

The big man retrieved a large black plastic zipper bag from the van, placed it beside the dead girl and lifted her from the settee as if she were weightless. "C'mon Maryann. Time to go." He set her gently inside and smoothed the hair back from her forehead. Such pretty hair, like spun gold and sunshine. He could remember admiring her from a proper distance, could feel the old ache of wanting her, the sick pang of jealousy when he heard she was engaged to the Calvert boy. It was right, he told himself. Maryann and Ray Calvert were from a different world, a world with no place for the likes of him. They had a whole perfect life ahead of them, he thought. Now look . . . His thick fingers grazed the girl's breast and he pulled away as if he'd been burned.

Averting his eyes, he zipped the bag, lifted it in his massive arms, and followed the coroner back out into the sunshine.

"Let's get the hell out of this place," the coroner said. "Gives me the creeps."

After placing the body in the black belly of the van, the driver climbed in and started the engine. "Christ," he said shaking his head. "Why her? It doesn't make any sense."

"I know, Larry. I know." They drove around front in slow reverence to their tragic cargo. The coroner looked over the pristine estate, the soaring stone face of the main house, the manicured beds and shrubbery. With an ironic chuckle he remembered the first time he saw this property. How envious he was then. Lucky people, he thought at the time. Luckiest people in the world. To have all this—everything. On the first call he kept imagining what it would be like to trade his clapboard two-family house with the tiny kitchen and the big mortgage for such unimaginable opulence.

Then he had been back. Again and again, to claim beautiful young women and small children. Fresh lives full of promise snuffed out by some cruel whim of fate. Back at the office, where death was a fierce giant to be faced down, they made jokes. "Oughta change the name of that place to 'God's waiting room' or something."

"How about starting a club out there, you know, Corpses' Anonymous?" But the laughter was thin and tinged with frightened hysteria. Even the coroner hated to set foot on the place, hated to view the seductive beauty of that hellhole.

Once is an unfortunate accident. Twice, an unthinkable tragedy. But on that property the air was thick with unseen evil and the devil's fangs dripped poison over innocent lives.

The last time, Larry said it best. "They should pour kerosene over the whole goddamned place and toss in a match. Or blow it to kingdom come. You know, Doc. I'm not superstitious but something . . ."

Now even voluble Larry was at a loss for words, sucking at his filter tip like a child starved for comfort. The coroner put a hand on Larry's arm. "What say we drop her off and go get snockered?"

A tear dripped down Larry's stubbly cheek. "Good idea. Excellent."

They drove down the long driveway, bumpy now from where tree roots had lifted the paving and frost heaves spun a growing web of cracks. Couldn't blame anyone for letting the place go, he thought. If only it could go quickly, before anyone else was taken.

Back on the main road, the coroner felt a flood of relief. He rolled down his window and filled himself with new air. Larry's cigarette was burned to a dead stub but he kept it between his lips and stared at nothing.

The coroner patted the thick hand for comfort. Superstition had nothing to do with it. The evil was real. And anyone with sense stayed as far away as possible.

CHAPTER

1

Erica felt lost, disconnected. Just a few words, a few minutes and her entire world had changed, shattered in useless, unrecognizable fragments. She relived the scene again and again. Brian sitting across from her at Marco's, their favorite neighborhood restaurant. A platter of antipasto and a bottle of Chianti between them on the checkered cloth. His knee pressed against hers, their fingers and eyes woven in easy familiarity.

Then the words. "I'm pregnant, Brian." She knew there was no easy way, no perfect moment. Thinking about it, preparing, she had rehearsed endless variations on the scene but his reaction was not among them.

At first, there was nothing. Shocked silence. Then the slow, sexy grin yielded to an ugly sneer. "Pregnant. You've got to be kidding. What about your supposed problem? I thought you couldn't have children. Did you really think I was that stupid? That easy to trap? Nice try but you shouldn't have bothered." You're on your own with this one, Sweetie.

She had never really known him. Never.

Still numb with hurt and anger, she walked down the long, beige corridor at Prescott Press. Without stopping for the usual morning hellos, she passed the row of editorial offices, including her own cluttered cubbyhole, and paused

5

at the door to Mel Underwood's corner suite. Nothing was easy. Not even running away. If only she could cut away the pieces of her life that were causing the pain. A clean amputation. But she owed Mel more than that. Arrangements had to be made.

Seeing her, he clasped his thick hands on his paper-strewn desk and frowned like a worried parent. "What's up, Erica? You look awful."

Awful was probably an understatement. With no clear plan or place to go, she had spent the night walking and thinking. Still nothing was completely clear. Nothing decided but her need to make the right decision. This was not just another unplanned pregnancy, not some simple inconvenience to be dispatched and forgotten. For years she heard the same sympathetic pronouncement from several doctors. "I'm sorry, Miss Phillips. But based on your tests, it's highly unlikely that you will ever be able to become pregnant. Of course, there's always adoption . . . and new developments in the field offer several other alternatives . . ."

Sensible Erica. She had made peace with a childless future. No big deal. Plenty of people chose not to have babies. There was her career to nurture, and herself. If a permanent love arrangement was buried in her tea leaves, it would have to be with someone who could live without passing on the family name or the family flaws. If someone cared enough about her, he would do without children or find a way to deal with the "alternatives."

But now. The highly unlikely had happened. She was pregnant. And given the odds, she had to view it as a once-in-a-lifetime opportunity. Or was it a once-in-a-lifetime curse? Pregnant. The word passed through her in a chill of fear. Her mother had died in childbirth. Such things did happen to real people. So many things to consider. So much hung in the balance.

She had rehearsed her speech and she blurted it quickly before she could change her mind. "I have to get away for awhile, Mel. Personal reasons. I hate to leave things in the middle. There's the Davenport manuscript. And the Ipswich series but I'm sure Karen or Elizabeth can take over. They're both good. And they've been close to both projects."

"What is it, Erica? Can I help? You know I'm very fond of you." Mel was that rare industry blend—part hard-nosed, all-business barracuda, part soft-centered teddy bear.

"No . . . there's nothing you can do." She avoided his eyes. "I just need some time to think, sort things out."

"I don't mean to be nosy." His voice was soft as syrup. "But did things sour with your friend Brian?"

She flushed. "Sour is an understatement. Things turned rancid. But that's not all of it, Mel. It's complicated."

His smile was sympathetic. "I don't want to lose you, Erica. You're a terrific editor. Do you think you can work things out and come back?"

"Anything's possible, I suppose." Her throat was burning. "I hope so. I'll miss you."

"You too, Mel." She managed a half smile. "I've really enjoyed working here."

He rose and wrapped her in a clumsy, comforting hug. "You go take care of that personal business. Your job will be waiting."

Back in her own office, she shut the door and allowed the tears to bubble up and spill over. Mel's kindness made leaving that much harder. She wanted to believe it could be easily resolved, forgotten. But she couldn't imagine her life ever settling back to normal rhythms.

Her desk was full of memories. She took Brian's picture from the lucite frame, crumpled it and tossed the remains in the wicker trash basket. A stack of business cards followed: Erica Phillips, Associate Editor, Prescott Press. She had been so proud of the position. Prescott was the Cadillac of publishers. Mel, in his genius, knew just when to hold a temperamental hand, when to allow complete artistic freedom, when to stroke or mollify. As a result, Prescott had a strong, solid list, no fluff or sensationalism. Mel's wisdom was unassailable, and his authors had the rewards and stature to prove it.

Erica's calendar was full of meetings and lunch appointments. She would ask her secretary, Claire, to cancel. The last thing she wanted to do was a lot of explaining. Everyone would know the truth soon enough. The industry thrived on regular doses of really good gossip.

Next, she removed her framed certificates from the wall: *magna cum laude* from Cornell in English, Master's in American Literature from Columbia, several short fiction awards for her own work, *Who's Who in American Women.* Rising young star, Mel used to call her. She sighed. Falling star was more like it.

She had an urge to open the twenty-first-floor window and toss all traces of herself to oblivion. The briefcase Brian bought her at Mark Cross could go first. He was so pleased with himself when he gave it to her. "To celebrate your first best-seller." As if he cared about anything but himself.

She looked down at the anthill of humanity. How easy it would be to step out, let go—a clear, sudden, dramatic end. But that would not serve the critical purpose, punishing Brian, paying him back. She could predict his reaction. "Really? No kidding? She jumped out the window, did she? Wish I'd known. I would have sent a film crew."

There was a dull thudding on the door. Mel opened it a crack and stuck in a raised hand. "Can I come in?"

"Yes, Mel, sure." She straightened her back, smoothed her hair and assumed what she hoped was a look of mature composure. "What's up?"

He surveyed the rubble and shook his head. "Do you have any plans, Erica? I mean, do you know where you'll be? What you'll be doing?"

"Not exactly. Not yet, I mean. But you don't have to worry about me. A bright, independent young woman like myself won't have a bit of trouble putting things in order. Right?" The words dropped out of her mouth like dead balls.

"I'm sure you'll be fine. That's not it . . ." Mel looked like a weary, old hound. "I just thought . . ."

"What? Tell me, Mel. I'm wonderful at taking good advice and trashing most of the rest." It was fine if he wanted to take charge of the rubble heap of her life. Someone had to.

He sighed and seemed to brace himself. "I know of something that might work for you for a while. But . . ."

"Come on, Mel. I'm in no condition for suspense."

His eyes were foggy and he seemed to be lost in an argument with himself. It wasn't like him. Not at all.

"Mel?" she prodded.

Finally, he sat on the edge of the desk and folded his arms in resignation. "I had a call last week from a man named Hemphill. His wife is a writer and she's recovering from a stroke she had a while back. Until now, she refused to allow anyone to work on her papers. In addition to everything else, the stroke left half her face paralyzed and I guess she looks more than a little peculiar. She's been depressed, refusing to see anyone but the doctors and therapists.

"Anyway, according to the husband she's finally ready to let someone get her work in order. She used to work with Brown and McEvoy but her editor there left the industry. The husband was looking for a bright, young individual to come for a few months and get things in shape and he likes Prescott's reputation. He has a house full of papers to organize and there are some short unpublished pieces, that sort of thing. They have a big old place in Connecticut. There would be lots of room to think. And time to straighten things out. It might be the right situation for a person to work out some 'personal' problems. But . . ."

"But what? Not that I'm really interested. The last thing I need is a sick old woman and some moldy old manuscripts."

"That's not the issue here, Erica. I happen to know that this particular writer's work is anything but moldy. In fact, I happen to know she's something of an idol of yours."

"You don't mean it's Theresa Bricklin, Mel? Tell me you

don't. I heard she had a stroke. Then nothing. And I assumed she was completely out of commission."

Mel held up a hand for moderation. "Wait a minute. Before you dance on the desktop, I'm not so sure about this Hemphill character. He sounds like a candidate for the butterfly net." He could still hear the shrill note of desperation in Hemphill's voice. "Really, Mr. Underwood. I am counting on your assistance. You must help me. It's quite imperative." Mel almost expected the next words to be "a matter of life or death."

"I don't care. I can handle it, Mel. Look at the experience I've had with crazy genius. It's perfect, Mel. Perfect. You wonderful man!" She kissed him on the cheek with a loud, smacking suction. "Theresa Bricklin! I can't believe it. I think you've saved my life."

He looked suddenly preoccupied. "I don't know if you should take it, Erica. I know it sounds perfect but . . . Well, it's hard to describe. There's just something about Hemphill." The man was like an instrument in poor repair. Odd rhythm, dissonance. In an unsettling instant his tone had changed from entreaty to threat. "I trust you to handle this matter with the utmost discretion, Mr. Underwood. I will not have my personal affairs paraded before the prying eyes of a greedy public," Hemphill had said. "Good day." Mel had made a face at the receiver as he had hung up. And had felt an inexplicable sense of relief.

Erica waved away his worries. "I'm sure I've dealt with worse, Mel. Much worse. Anyway, if he's good enough for Theresa Bricklin, he's good enough for me."

Mel's grin was stiff and unconvincing. "Sure, I guess I'm overreacting. You go and straighten out the Bricklin papers and your own problems. Then come back to us."

"Stop worrying, Mel. Loony isn't contagious. Anyway, so what if he's a little difficult? I'll handle it."

"Sure, sure you will, Erica." He was looking past her. Off again in some personal haze. Funny. Mel wasn't a worrier. She tried to push the flawless Underwood instincts out of her mind. No one could be right all the time.

"Come on, Mel. I'll be fine. What's the worst that can happen?"

Mel shrugged. "Pay no attention to me, Erica. I think it's just another symptom of middle-age decline. Once your hair falls out, it's easier for the nonsense to seep in. I don't know why this Hemphill character spooked me. I guess you're right. What's the worst thing that can happen?"

He forced a smile and tried to leave on an encouraging note. "Forgetting about Hemphill, this is a hell of an opportunity. You work out well for Theresa Bricklin and it can lead to bigger and better things."

"Sure, Mel. I know . . . And thanks." She watched him leave. He shut the door carefully behind him, protecting something. After years in the business of recording human nature, he knew only too well how malevolent that nature could be. Walking back to his office, he felt the weight of it all. You're overreacting, Mel, he told himself. Getting old.

Erica went back to her packing. Just a few minutes ago, she felt like a kid with a new puppy. But Mel's concerns crept over her like a bad chill. He was no doddering hysteric. If he had reservations about this Hemphill character, she should probably run quickly in the other direction. But how could she? The chance was too tempting, the timing too perfect. She would simply have to hope for the best, focus on the incredible opportunity.

Theresa Bricklin. Erica had spent years studying Bricklin's work, dissecting it, wanting to crawl inside the woman's genius. Was it one of those events too good to be true? No, Erica. Don't let your morbid imagination run ahead of your good sense. An old woman and her eccentric husband. Eccentric but loving, concerned. How bad could it be, Erica?

She emptied the last of her things from the desk and looked around the office. Down the hall, she heard a door slam. There was something so final in the sound.

CHAPTER

2

The midday train was half empty and the car's rhythmic swaying eased Erica into a welcome fog of tranquility. She pressed her cheek against the cool blue vinyl seat and stared out at the speeding blur of spring green and industrial grey.

Her phone conversation with Hemphill played again and again in her mind. The man was peculiar. She could understand Mel's apprehension. Hemphill went on and on. The words gushed but the tone seemed somehow flat and hollow, like lyrics set to the wrong melody. "You don't know how much this means to me, Miss Phillips. And how pleased dear Tessa will be. Despite all her current difficulties, despite all the forces bent on thwarting her indomitable spirit, I sense her work remains uppermost in her mind. Your assistance comes at a most propitious time. Most propitious."

"I'm glad to help." Erica was tempted to put it another way. "I hope I can." The thought of touching Theresa Bricklin's prose was intimidating to say the least, a little like going at a rare diamond with a rusty hacksaw.

The conductor came through and clipped her ticket. She ran a comb through her hair, touched up her lipstick and patted some blush on her cheeks. Nothing showed, she kept reassuring herself. Same pale complexion and copper-streaked hair, same sharp freckled nose. Her eyes seemed a bit greener from all the crying and sleeplessness but she hadn't been branded with a scarlet "A" or anything like that. Her belly was still flat and she patted it absently. All of it was so hard to absorb. Pregnant. She closed her eyes and tried to picture the miniscule life swimming in her womb. A baby. Brian's and hers. No. Hers alone. Self-delusion had no place in this.

Why was she so surprised by his reaction? His carefree, little boy hedonism was what attracted her in the first place. She was so tired of being sensible and responsible, tired of planning and worrying about consequences. Erica was only twelve when her mother died. After that, everything was too serious, too confined and complicated. She burdened herself with an adult's share of the responsibility for her three younger siblings, one a newborn infant. The parade of housekeepers did little in her view to fill the need for a maternal presence. And when Dad finally remarried, Erica's hopes for a mother-substitute were destroyed for good. Monika, her stepmother, was bright, witty, charming, strong, adventurous. Plenty of good qualities, but no one would ever accuse her of being motherly. In fact, she had settled in the role of beneficent big sister, full of fun and mischief. At times, Erica felt that Monika was just another child for her to watch.

Life with Brian was so different. His was a world of cinemascopic fairy tales. The heady world of stellar personalities, cosmic undertakings, and grand openings. His first film venture was a blockbuster, touted as a contemporary *Peter Pan*, that netted over fifty million dollars for Continental Films and turned him from a near-unknown to wunderkind producer/director, able to write his own celluloid ticket from his own offices and sound stages on the Continental lot.

Erica met him when his agent approached one of Prescott's authors to co-write a novelization of his latest film. Mel entrusted the project to Erica. "Brian Bregman is a sure thing," Mel told her. "You just don't turn him down."

Prophetic. Before their first meeting was over, Brian had

Erica in his hip pocket. He was everything her life seemed
to lack. Within two weeks, she had moved into his East Side
penthouse. In a month, she all but forgot life before Brian
and could barely imagine any sort of a life without him. He
was fun and foolishness, spontaneity and surprise. What
more could she possibly want? she had thought at the time.
Now, too late, she had a few sensible answers. Looking
back, the whole episode might have been the script of a
light romantic comedy with a sad twist ending. Lucky Erica,
leading lady. Curtain going down.

"Greenwich . . . Greenwich station . . . ," the conductor
chanted. Erica pulled her canvas duffel from under the seat
and retrieved her stuffed suitcase from the overhead rack.
Once more, she checked her reflection in the window.
Nothing showed. At least nothing had changed on the surface.

She hauled her things down the station steps and waited
in front of a darkened movie theatre marquee. A silver
blonde woman stood in the ticket booth, cracking a wad of
gum and leafing through the *Enquirer*. A stooped old hag
with long silver braids and a faded beige stocking cap
passed by pulling her worldly goods in a rusted shopping
cart. On the corner, a group of young boys stood eating dou-
ble-dip ice cream cones. They joked and pushed each other
affectionately. The air was tinged with lilac and the aroma
of fresh-baked bread.

A chauffeured, black Bentley rounded the corner and
pulled to a stop in front of her. "Erica Phillips?"

"Yes, are you Mr. Hemphill?"

"So sorry to be late. The traffic was dreadful."

Scanning the nearly deserted street, Erica smiled. Dreadful was stretching the point to say the least. "It's fine. I just
got in a few minutes ago."

While the chauffeur loaded her bags in the trunk, she
slipped in beside Hemphill in the rear seat. He offered a
clammy, slack handshake and the stilted smile of someone
unaccustomed to gaiety. "Welcome, welcome, Miss Phil-

lips. Your arrival brightens the day immeasurably." His
ivory linen suit was ill-fitting and blanched his complexion
to the watery white of skimmed milk. Dark mirrored sunglasses masked his eyes and he sported a pencil-thin mous-
tache and a cheap black wig. "Tessa was so enthusiastic
about your impending arrival, she could barely contain herself. Truly, I have not seen her so engaged since her unfortunate illness. A positive sign to be sure."

"I can't wait to meet her, Mr. Hemphill. Your wife is my
favorite author."

"I'm pleased to hear that, Miss Phillips. Tessa's work
must proceed while she is recuperating. That is the glorious
burden of true genius."

"I'll do my best, of course. But I must admit it's not a
simple matter to step into an author's shoes, especially one
as talented as your wife."

"Now, now, my dear. False modesty is a veil of burrs on
a gentle flower. Most unnecessary, I assure you. Your cre-
dentials are unimpeachable and your Mr. Underwood at-
tests most fervently to your familiarity with Tessa's work.
You are, he assured me, something of an expert in the matter of my darling's astonishing talents. Precisely the sort of
individual we sought. We look forward to the fruit of your
efforts. I will hear no words of compromise or surrender."

Erica bit back a grin. Hemphill's speech was a pompous
flourish from a bygone era, his gestures the overblown rav-
ings of a bad actor. Strange man. Almost a parody, though
she could not figure out what the original might be.

She settled back. The Bentley had soft burgundy leather
seats and a warm woody smell. Through the tinted window,
she watched as they left the center of town and followed a
stretch of winding, narrow road northward. Prim downtown
Victorian houses yielded to sprawling contemporaries faced
with natural cedar and broad expanses of glass. The houses
became progressively grander and more isolated as they
drove away from the center of town. Tudor mansions and
ivied Southern colonials. Federal and brick Georgian repro-

ductions and a sprawling pink adobe with a slate roof that
could have been housing for an entire Mexican village.
Tucked farther and farther back, Erica spied a clone of the
White House and a strong second for the main branch of
the New York Public Library, complete with great stone cats
and a mountainous granite staircase. Finally, the houses disappeared altogether behind masses of ancient evergreens
and pillared fences.

The car took a sharp right off the main road and snaked
through a maze of small, winding streets that confounded
Erica's sense of direction. Massive estates, their property
lines marked by the change of fence from brick to stone to
wrought iron, stood sentry over the casual passerby.

She saw few people. A fresh-faced couple zoomed past in
a vintage red convertible; so close together they appeared
to be a single two-headed driver. An old man made slow
passes with a straw rake at the meticulous expanse of green
fronting an electric gate. A security guard in an unmarked
vehicle tipped his hat as he made his rounds of the neighborhood. To preserve the sanctity of such places, Erica
thought, the world was kept at a careful distance.

As they drove past, she tried to make out the names on
the ornate brass plates. "Bolton, Silver Meadows," one read.
"The Hilliards at the Elms." "Van Aken—The Mill." Properties vast enough to merit titles and histories. It occurred
to Erica that she would be living in such a place, at least
temporarily. Life, it seemed, was full of bad jokes and startling surprises.

"We have arrived," Hemphill said at last.

They turned into a long, private road marked by a worn
bronze plaque, a dented mailbox and two turreted gate-
posts. The rutted, bumpy path slowed their progress. "A
great deal of work is needed here," he said as if reading her
mind. "At one time, it was the most elegant of estates. But
the owners allowed the property to deteriorate and it was
seized, at last, for taxes. Tessa was quite taken with the
grounds and the obvious potential. She is a woman of most

impeccable taste, you'll find. And she convinced me with her most irresistible charm to purchase it at auction shortly before her misfortune. Plans are underway for a complete restoration."

His expression was clouded; his fingers tapped a nervous rhythm on the leather armrest. Something about Hemphill reminded Erica of a sky at sea, clear and tranquil one minute, then suddenly filled with great puffs of grey menace.

"This is a beautiful area. I've never been to Greenwich." Brian had talked about spring picnics in New England but that was in a future that was not to be.

"Green Witch," Hemphill spat. "The demon greed resides in her base bosom and all the populace of this bucolic hamlet stands in turn to suckle like children starved by long famine."

Erica's skin prickled at the image. "You make it sound so ominous."

"Do I?" He allowed a dry chuckle. "You must not darken the innocent intent of my comments, my dear. That would be a grave error."

They were driving through thicker and thicker foliage, a twilight of dense leaves, seeking vines, and tall brambles. As they scratched the sides of the Bentley, Erica tensed against an odd, threatening sensation. In the false dusk, the brambles were masses of witch fingers, their spiny talons poised to injure. She felt as if she were being swallowed, sliding down the throat of a separate existence. Silly Erica, she chided herself. You must control that runaway imagination.

"I was sorry to hear about Miss Bricklin's stroke," she said to divert herself. "How badly is she affected?"

"She suffers from a paralysis of her right extremities, temporary to be sure. And a most unfortunate perversion of her lovely features, also temporary, though Tessa does suffer so for it. Vanity, I fear. A deserved flaw for one so lovely but a burden under the circumstances. For a time, she refused all callers. My gregarious darling played quite the recluse de-

spite my most ardent persuasions. A trial, to be sure. Still,
her speech difficulties are the most problematical. It is so
very difficult for her to communicate at the moment. Such a
criminal irony for a woman like Tessa. Words are her life, the
window to her gentle soul. Naturally, she will improve . . . in
time. All things in time." His words were calm and measured
but his hands worked in nervous kneading motions.

Erica shuddered. "It must be so awful for her, to be
trapped inside her own mind like that."

"Yes. It is frustrating. But she must not be coddled. Must
not. That is imperative, do you understand? I will not have
it!" His tone and color rose and his mouth narrowed to a
tight seam. Erica could see her own startled expression in
his mirrored lenses. "Tessa's spirit must be nurtured and
prodded. With daily work and consistent effort, she shall be
well again. I intend to see to that." As quickly as his annoyance flared, it flickered and dimmed to a kind, sheepish grin.

"I'm sure such determination is important for any recovery, Mr. Hemphill," she managed.

"You must call me Goody, a diminutive for Goodwin. I
know we are going to accomplish so much together—you
and I."

"And Theresa," Erica said.

"Of course. And Theresa."

The Bentley turned through an ornate wrought-iron gate,
rusted nearly through in spots, and onto a worn, circular
drive set with faded brick chevrons. The mansion loomed
before them, a massive stone structure burdened with tangled vines and ivies. There was a carved granite fountain,
now cracked and littered with dead leaves and cigarette
butts. The border beds were overrun with scraggly weeds.
A web of cracks ran through the leaded panes in the massive
mahogany door. And a large tarnished brass knocker hung
at an odd angle from a single corroded nail. Neglect. Such
awful neglect.

She shivered in the cold spot cast by the shadow of the
forbidding facade. "It reminds me of a medieval castle," she
said.

"You put entirely too much stock in appearances, my dear. An unfortunate tendency you would do well to correct."

She suppressed a flicker of anger. Why react? The man was a world-class oddball, nothing more. He was laundry flapping in a capricious wind. She had managed to deal with worse. A certain headstrong, self-centered lover came to mind. Anyway, there were bigger issues here than Hemphill's unpredictable nature and unsolicited comments. She had come to work, to think, to decide what was right for her and this baby.

"Come along, Erica," he said as if she were a tardy school child. "There is much to be done."

Managing, coping. All part of being a grown-up. Much to be done. True. No use putting it off any longer.

CHAPTER

3

A stooped, sallow, expressionless old man took Erica's bags. Moving in creaky slow motion, he returned to open her door and Hemphill's before shuffling back toward the house. She shook her head. "Somehow, I feel as though I should be waiting on him."

"He's quite capable, I assure you," Hemphill bristled. "Finding competent help is a trying challenge nowadays. Age is quite irrelevant."

"Of course. I was just kidding."

"You manage to find humor in the oddest situations, it seems," he sighed. "Then, I suppose that is of value in this uncertain world."

"I don't think it's a good idea to take things too seriously, if you can help it."

"Perhaps some of that easy nature will rub off, my dear. I confess to a tendency to brood."

"We are the way we are, Mr. Hemphill." She followed the servant through massive wooden doors to a marble-floored foyer. The walls were hung with faded silk and lined with oversized portraits of somber ancestors rendered in poor perspective. The Hemphill clan, Erica noted, tended to squat bodies, sour expressions and small wormy hands.

"Yes, my dear," Hemphill spoke at last. "We are the way we are indeed, though that is not always fate's ultimate intention. 'Tis far nobler to strive to one's optimal circumstance than to whine and whimper at the capricious offerings of a merciless fate."

Inside, the house was dim and musty. Grandeur's imprint was everywhere, on the sober antique furniture, the worn oriental runners, the elegant tapestries, the cascading crystal chandeliers. But it was stale grandeur at best, a teasing suggestion of the elegance that was before the priceless pieces lost their rich patina and the ornate grandfather clock ticked its last at some nine twenty-two in history. Erica's impulse was to tear down the heavy draw drapes and throw open the windows. The air was heavy with worn majesty and the acrid scent of neglect.

"Such a sin how the former owners permitted this magnificent home to fall to ruin," Goody sighed. "I have had to employ dozens of craftsmen to repair structural damage before certain rooms can be refurbished. In the meantime, I have shut down the east wing altogether. I should caution you against venturing there, my dear. The floors are unstable, I fear, and there could be a nasty accident. For the time being, I've moved my studio to a tack room in the stables. Painting is my meanest vice, I fear."

"I used to do a little myself, mostly watercolors, before my mother died."

"Then you must return to it, my dear. One must search carefully through all one's possibilities."

All one's possibilities, even the most threatening and difficult. "I suppose that's true, Mr. Hemphill. Goody, I mean." The first name felt funny on her tongue but it seemed to put them on a more equal plane. "May I see where I'll be staying? I'd like to get my things organized and wash up."

"Certainly. Mrs. Ohringer will show you to your quarters." He moved his foot almost imperceptibly and a thick, moon-faced, platinum blonde woman in a starched, white-aproned uniform appeared. "Yes, sir?"

"Show Miss Phillips to 'The Fallen Angel' room, Mrs. Ohringer. And see that she is comfortably settled."

"*The Fallen Angel*? That book was a favorite of mine," Erica said. "Are all the rooms named after Miss Bricklin's novels?"

Hemphill nodded briskly. "All the bedrooms. *Solomon's Child*, *The Debtor*, *Belinda* and so on. And we do more than affix a name, my dear. As each room is restored to its former state of elegance, we strive to match the decor to the mood of a given novel. It's quite an enjoyable undertaking. And a fitting tribute to my darling's considerable talents. I do believe it lifts Tessa's spirits as well. That's an essential element in her recovery, I believe."

"Hers and everyone's." Odd, Erica thought. Of all Theresa Bricklin's novels, she could not imagine a single one that would translate into comforting surroundings for anyone seeking a peaceful rest. Bricklin was brilliant but her subjects were anything but tranquil. She explored the starkest horrors. The vilest, most malevolent evil. Her themes were the most disturbing elements of human possibility—mindless rage, pure hatred, blood lust.

The house was a maze of steps and passages. Erica followed Mrs. Ohringer down a series of densely shadowed corridors and short, uneven flights of stairs. "I think I'll need a road map."

"Isn't it ridiculous?" the woman said. "I never seen a place like this. Walk so many goddamn stairs in a day my feet like to fall off." She clapped a hand over her mouth. "I shouldna said anything. It's none of my business. I'm sorry. Please, don't say anything to Mr. Hemphill. This is a real nice job, real nice. My Philly'll kill me if I get myself canned on account of my big mouth."

"Don't worry, I'm not working undercover the management or anything. Anyway, you're right. There are a lot of stairs."

"Yeah. Thank God they closed off a few rooms." She pointed to a boarded corridor off to Erica's left. "Place is like a big old hotel as it is. Can hardly count all the rooms. I tried a couple of times but I got lost after the first twenty,

twenty-five. Unbelievable what some folks got when others got nothing but the clothes on their backs. Or not even. Amazing just the two of them rattling around in this big old place. I told Philly they could take in roomers, make a bundle."

"I'm sure they could."

The Fallen Angel room was papered with tiny blue flowers on an ivory ground. The moldings were gloss white and the steel blue carpet was thick as unmowed grass. A deep billowing canopy fluttered gently over the brass four-poster bed. There was a plump eyelet coverlet and oversized goose-down pillows tucked into eyelet shams. Appointments for a child of privilege.

Erica's bags had been unpacked, the clothing hung with military precision in the small dormered closet, her cosmetics set in neat formation on the maple dresser.

"It's Hillary's room," Erica said marvelling at the detail. The book's child heroine might have stepped through the door and lived out the final chapter of her tragic odyssey.

"Yeah. Gives me the creeps. I tried to read that awful book but I couldn't get through it. That poor little Hillary. Such a sweet, pretty girl. Why would anyone want to hurt her? Crazy lunatic."

"It was just fiction, Mrs. Ohringer. Miss Bricklin did a brilliant job of exploring the coexistence of good and evil in ordinary lives." Erica shivered remembering her own reaction to the story. A soft, vulnerable child, protected by doting but fearful parents. Hillary was the center of her confined world—lovely, bright, charming. The canvas of a perfect future with silken hair and pale, curious eyes.

"Fiction, schmiction. For a week, I made Philly check under all the beds before I'd close my eyes. Scared me to death, I'll tell you. And I don't scare easy."

"It was frightening," Erica admitted. She could still see Hillary at the end. Tortured by a faceless, mindless, unstoppable force. Bricklin gave the creature no humanity. Nothing for the reader to repel or run from. By contrast, insanity seemed appealing. It was a wickedness that seemed to grow in response to the child's goodness, as if such goodness threatened some universal order.

"That was the whole point. To show the ultimate terror— pure evil. It wasn't meant to be taken literally." Erica hoped she could follow her own advice. Think of it as a story, a clever, disturbing invention. Otherwise, she faced a number of long, difficult nights.

"You only say that cause you got no children. That Hillary reminded me of my Lynnie when she was little—pretty, thin, even the way she wore her hair tied back and stuck a flower through the barrette. My Lynnie used to do that when she played dress up. Just like that little girl in the book."

No children, Erica fixed on the phrase. Not exactly. There was a new life growing inside her, her child. Erica could picture a little wide-eyed, freckle-faced girl. "Miss Bricklin wanted you to feel that way. She really knows how to draw a reader into the story. Hillary was the universal child. Every mother and father identified with her tragedy." Everyone did, Erica wanted to say. And everyone searched under the bed.

"I'm telling you she looked just like my Lynnie. Gave me the creeps."

"If you wouldn't mind, Mrs. Ohringer, I'd like to change before dinner."

Through the multi-paned window, Erica saw the vestiges of a sculpted garden. Weed-strangled beds formed a brick-bordered fleur-de-lis. A topiary elephant trumpeted through a wire trunk barely covered with dead ivy. The former owner must have had a British passion for formality.

Beyond the garden was the metal vent of a large exhaust fan, the sort that might serve a commercial kitchen. She saw the shadow of a cottage roof. For guests, she thought. Or servants. And the spare skeleton of an ancient greenhouse, the roof sagging in the center, the panes webbed with cracks. Horses whinnied in the distance.

Checking through the dresser drawers, Erica located the rest of her things, neatly stacked and folded and flanked by delicate packets of herbal sachet. The maple writing desk was stocked with fountain pens, ivory linen papers with flowered borders and small bottles of ink in a rainbow of shades. One drawer held a bright profusion of ribbons and costume jewelry. A leather-bound Bible sat on the bookshelves, surrounded by bisque dolls in period costumes. Every inch Hillary's room. When she had read *Fallen Angel*, she pictured Hillary as the image of her sister, Meg, same wavy brown hair and trusting expression.

The universal child. If Erica were superstitious, she might have viewed this as a sign. Some fates trying to remind her that good is inextricably linked with evil, future with past, promise with hopelessness. Nothing was simple. Nothing clear and definite. Loss could mean gain and happiness could be bought with sorrow. And the most chilling— birth and death. Her mother had died having Meg. It could happen to her, to anyone. She could trade her life for a possibility. Or she could trade a singular possibility for a foolish fear. If only she could be sure. If only anything were certain.

She dressed in a soft grey woolen skirt and white silk blouse and wrapped a patterned scarf around her neck. Frowning at her image, she realized how anxious she was to impress Theresa Bricklin. Talent of such magnitude made her feel awkward and inadequate.

Retracing her path through the maze of corridors, Erica found her way back to the front hall. Mrs. Ohringer was dusting the ornate frame of a portrait in oils Erica had not noticed before. "Is that Miss Bricklin?"

"Yeah, so I'm told. If you ask me, it don't look much like her at all. I guess it's because the stroke really did a number on her face. Pity it is. Her own mother wouldn't know her, all twisted up like that."

"The hair . . ." Erica said.

"Can't miss that. Never seen hair just that color. Reminds me of an old Raggedy Ann doll Lynnie used to have. So red you'd think her hair was on fire. Supposed to be natural too. At least, that's what I read in some magazine. Not that I believe it for a second. Woman her age must be all grey."

Erica stared at the portrait, trying to match the features with the image she still had from the time Theresa Bricklin came to speak at a Columbia commencement. Seated near the back of the auditorium, Erica could barely see though she heard the commanding voice reverberate through the public address system. And she remembered the words: "We are precisely what we make of ourselves—no more, no less. You face a world of choice and temptation. Face it willingly, openly and with the courage to take risks and make mistakes. From the distance of years, I can assure you that the worst regrets are the ones you do not allow yourself to have."

Hemphill came up soundlessly behind, startling her. "There you are, Erica. How very charming you look. My darling Tessa is so anxious to meet you. Come, she expects us in the music room."

She followed him down a long corridor, past the living and dining rooms, the formal parlor and a sun-drenched solarium, out through a covered courtyard with an irregular stone path that turned her footsteps to thunder. An odd musty smell made Erica wince and she detected the distant trickle of an untended leak.

"Through here, my dear." Following Hemphill, she ducked under a bower of scraggly purple clematis and followed him through a narrow, multi-paned glass door. Two concert grand pianos formed a giant black butterfly in the center of the room. Stiff groups of antique music stands held sheets of faded parchment.

"Here she is at last, my darling. Erica Phillips, may I present my wife, Theresa Bricklin." The wheelchair squeaked rhythmically as he moved it nearer Erica. Hemphill motioned her to sit on the beige loveseat and placed the old woman directly in front of her. Locking the chair brakes, he leaned and kissed his wife's papery cheek. "There, you see? I knew you'd take to her right away, darling. That's wonderful, simply wonderful."

Erica sat on the edge of the loveseat and folded her hands, trying to hide her reaction. Theresa's appearance was horrifying, the bold shock of flame red hair stuck out in knotted puffs, the face—two faces really—one side soft and expressive, one warped and set in a perpetual grimace, the lip curled, the eyelid drooped nearly shut, the brow peaked in permanent surprise. Her right leg was withered to a fleshy stick and her right arm was caught in an invisible sling against her chest.

"Hello, Miss Bricklin . . . I'm so glad to meet you," she managed. "I'm quite an admirer of yours. In fact, your work was the subject of my Master's thesis." So hard to connect this twisted wisp of a woman with Theresa Bricklin's luminous career.

Erica watched in horror as Theresa's mouth flew open like a door in a wind and her body stiffened as she emitted a burst of guttural gibberish. "Aach angh, uh . . . gah!"

Goody stroked her head. "Yes, darling. I know you're so pleased Erica is here. How fortunate we are to have her with us to look at your papers and help set things in order. Here, Erica." He held forth a tiny velvet box. "Tessa and I would like you to have this small token of our gratitude for your arrival."

Erica opened the box and found a lovely antique cameo on a gold chain. "It's beautiful. But not necessary, really."

"No matter. Tessa wants you to have it, to wear it always."

Erica put it on. "Thank you, Miss Bricklin." It felt heavier than she expected.

"Kikk . . . aaah!" The twig finger gestured with no meaning, the face contorted with anger and frustration.

"She is a lovely young woman, isn't she, my dear?"

"Can she . . . can she understand what I say?"

"Certainly she can. Her faculties are quite intact. And her speech has improved markedly. Hard work and practice. Before long, we shall have our darling well again, isn't that so?" He patted her slack arm.

"Kkkk . . . aah."

"There now, darling. You must be patient. Some things simply cannot be rushed. Time and patience. Everything in turn. Now is the time for us all to get acquainted. Then, we can have dinner and tell Miss Phillips our little surprise."

Erica fiddled with the cool face of the cameo. Enough of the unexpected, she thought. Her world had been turned over and shaken until the floating particles left her blind and dizzy. She was not ready for yet another surprise.

CHAPTER

4

Erica sat opposite Goody and Theresa at a polished antique mahogany dining table large enough to seat thirty. Her place was set with embroidered white linens, cut crystal wineglasses and goblets and handwrought silver flatware in a parade of shapes and sizes. The old man served dinner from an ornate silver tray, bowing and nodding in broad pantomine, and retreated in unbroken silence. A grey crocheted panel was draped over the front of his neck.

"Several years ago, Mr. Flumacher was stricken with laryngeal cancer," Hemphill explained. "After his voice box was removed, all attempts to teach him to speak again were unsuccessful. It seems that rendered him unemployable for a time. An absurdity to be sure. He's quite the most pleasant fellow. Loyal. Reliable. Unfailingly industrious. When we learned of his dreadful predicament, Tessa and I engaged him at once. And we feel most fortunate to have him in our employ. The communication is quite irrelevant. So many words float without substance until the air resounds with foolishness and baseless noise. One can appreciate the thought contained and held precious. Personally, I think Flumacher enjoys his silence. Don't you agree, Tessa dear?"

Her mouth was agape but no sounds emerged. After a few seconds, she seemed to surrender to the tug of a private reality.

"Tessa, on the other hand, struggles against limitation of any sort. Don't you, darling? That spirit is the key to her rehabilitation. What is it you always said, dear? 'Life is strife and death surrender'? Something in that vein. When Tessa regains her powers of speech, I intend to tape-record every syllable she utters. Each one a priceless jewel. Each word a treasure." He chewed a tiny piece of the rare meat and carved the boiled new potato into paper-thin slices.

"I agree. She was . . . is a remarkable talent." Erica bit her tongue. Each word a booby trap.

Hemphill grinned broadly and clapped his pale hands together. "Then you will be as excited as I am with our news. Shall I tell her, darling? Yes, of course, I must. That is the true purpose of her coming, after all."

Theresa's face drew into a deep, chiseled half frown. "Beckah . . . gab." Hemphill put a proprietary arm around her stooped shoulder.

"What would you say, Erica, if I told you I have found a nearly completed manuscript Theresa has written, all but a few chapters? From what she told me before she was stricken, I have reason to believe the book was completed."

Erica's mouth went dry. "I don't understand."

"It has to do with Tessa's way of protecting her work. Some years ago, when she was working on a short story, her sole copy of the manuscript disappeared. I suspect it was stolen by servants, though Tessa was too generous in her nature to make accusations. After that, she took precautions to avoid such an occurrence. She would hide portions of a work in various parts of the house. Reference was made within the book itself to where the next section could be found, and the next, and so on. But the code was known only to Theresa herself. Even I lacked access . . ."

"But she must have trusted you?"

Hemphill bristled. "Certainly, she did. Trust had nothing to do with it. Tessa has always enjoyed her little games, a rather charming childish quality. This was one of her little amusements. Quite harmless, we thought, until her illness . . ."

"Didn't she keep more than one copy?"

"You see, darling? The young lady is saying precisely what I always have. With work as valuable as yours, copies are essential. When you are well, we shall make extra copies of everything you do and secure them in a fireproof vault. I shall not hear any further arguments." He sliced another bit of meat and held it to Theresa's twisted lips. "There now, chew well, darling. That's a good girl."

"How long have you been married, Goody?"

He smoothed Theresa's cotton-candy hair. "Nearly three years now, isn't it, darling? My word. We shall have to make plans for an anniversary celebration before long. Perhaps that cruise we discussed if you are well enough. Three wonderful years. How fortunate I have been, my dear Tessa. How happy you have made me."

Anniversaries, celebrations, solidity. Erica wondered if she would ever be blessed with such permanence. She raised her glass. "I look forward to seeing what you've found. To you both."

Hemphill clinked his glass against hers with an excess of enthusiasm. "To Tessa . . . and to you, Erica. May you find all things lost and lose all evil encumbrances."

"You're quite the poet yourself, Goody."

"I admit to borrowing Tessa's words quite freely, Erica. My own pale so by comparison."

Theresa grew suddenly agitated. She pointed at Erica and made broad chewing motions. "Aagh . . . aaack."

"Clearer, darling. You can do it. Say 'Thank you.' You try it. 'Thank you for coming, Erica. We are so pleased to have you with us.' " He formed the words with dramatic exaggeration.

"Aah . . . asg . . . shit!"

Hemphill managed a benign smile. "Those words are somehow retained. One of the mysteries of the affliction. Tessa was quite the gentle woman. Never one to utter profanities under the direst circumstances. But now . . ."

"Now she had reason to curse," Erica said. "I mean . . ."

Hemphill raised his hand. "I understand perfectly. No need to explain yourself. Tessa's glorious gift has been taken from her. But it's only temporary, my darling. Goody will see to that."

Hemphill's devotion was obvious and touching. Maybe she had been too quick to judge him. Not many men would be so single-minded about such devastating illness. Hemphill was willing to place the full force of his efforts behind his wife's recovery, even though recovery seemed so distant and unlikely. Another man would have given up, turned Theresa over to the medical machine to be warehoused as a hopeless case. Not Goody. If Theresa Bricklin was to get well, it would be because of him. The same unreasonable passions that made Hemphill so difficult might be Theresa's best hope and therapy.

Love could do so much, Erica thought. Or so very little.

CHAPTER

5

The rush of morning light pulled Erica up from a dense, dreamless sleep. A horse whinnied in the vague distance, its message muted by the determined drone of a vacuum cleaner. Looking in vain for a clock, she dressed quickly, eager to see the manuscript.

Downstairs, Mrs. Ohringer was polishing the oiled balustrade in the foyer. She spoke in the fluid rhythm of her work. "I see you're an early bird. Good. You'll fit right in. Bunch of early birds in this place, I'll tell you. Mr. Hemphill is up and prowling before I ever get here at eight. Has his coffee already and everything. Have to leave it ready before I go, so he just plugs it in and takes a cup. Me, on the other hand, I love to sleep. Wouldn't see me till eleven if I had my druthers. Maybe twelve. My Lynnie's the same way. Loves to sleep in when she gets a chance. Needs her beauty sleep, she says. Not that she does, mind you. Girl's pretty as a picture if I do say so. I may be her mother but I know pretty when I see it."

"Where would I find Mr. Hemphill now?"

"You won't." Her eyes widened in warning. "He's gone to his precious studio already. Goes first thing every morning. You don't bother him there if you like your head. Once I went after him to ask a question and almost had mine handed to me. He's gone, that's it for the morning. Left you a note though."

Hemphill's writing was round and replete with feminine flourish. "The manuscript portions I've found to date are in the library. You may begin your review whenever you please. As we discussed, I have secured this work by making a copy so that you may feel free to mark the papers as you wish. May your endeavors be productive and pleasurable. All best, G."

Again Erica thought of the odd Hemphill-Bricklin alliance. There was the age difference. She guessed he was twenty years younger or more. But that was the least of the incongruity. Before her stroke, Theresa Bricklin's career had placed her at the social center of the creative world. Her wit and intellect were legend and lent her an aura of desirability equal to the most beautiful actresses or noblewomen. Bricklin had her pick of men: high-level politicians, screen stars, the rich, famous and powerful. It was rumored that she left several society marriages in tatters and cast off her own used husbands like last year's fashions. Erica remembered a cartoon in one despicable tabloid that had Miss Bricklin sitting at the breakfast table, cutlery in hand, napkin tied around her bejeweled neck, about to dig into a plate filled with miniature heads of state and Hollywood heartthrobs. Such portrayals made Erica furious. Miss Bricklin was no conniving user. Her attraction was a matter of true genius, charm. Nothing was more an aphrodisiac, it seemed, than genuine respect. Strange that she would settle on a peculiar soul like Goody Hemphill. There had to be more to the man than Erica could see.

Mrs. Ohringer directed her to the library, a damp cavernous room with soaring ceilings and shelves burdened by thousands of volumes: rare first editions, reference materials, a collection of classics and contemporary works to satisfy the most eclectic literary appetite. A single broad shelf held Theresa's own work and her vast array of prizes and honors. Among the spare furnishings was a worn green leather chair, a small sofa draped with a faded beige chenille spread and a large mahogany desk topped by a black blotter. A sheaf of crisp white pages sat squarely in the center. Erica lifted them with reverence and went out to the garden.

She sat for hours on a stone bench, heedless of the sun's ascent or the insistent sounds of enterprise nearby—the roaring of a large mower, a hammer pounding, the worried neighing of the horses. She read slowly, savoring Bricklin's firm voice and riveting vision. Artful, commanding. The prose elements balanced and manipulated with the casual dexterity of a master juggler. And then the pages ran out.

Restless, Erica tapped the papers into an orderly pile and returned them to the library. With several blank hours to fill, she decided to walk the grounds.

Hemphill's assurance was inadequate. What if no more of the manuscript were found? Theresa had drawn a haunting image of an old woman, the Grey Lady. She sat in a bare room, staring at an image beyond the reader's eye. Something in that unseen image triggered a flood of stored pain and memory. Theresa's words haunted Erica and the voice of the Grey Lady played over and over in her mind:

For what sin? For what crime of evil intent am I here? Bound but unbound. Forced to bleed the blood of my soul until the parched center of my earth is left in bleak abandonment—empty. The night is solid, unyielding; the day drifts in dreamy mist past my yearning fingers. All is taken: my liberty, the light of day, my name. I am nothing. The Grey Lady. Nothing more. I am held with the power of nonexistence and forced to hear the cries of all inhuman pain. I struggle against my bondless bonds and grasp—sorrow, emptiness, nothing. I know this must be the thing called death. Or worse than death, a thing whose name transcends all human tolerance and defies all human definition.

Who was this woman? And why was she in this dread isolation? Bondless bonds? The power of nonexistence? The mystery would continue to disturb Erica until she could learn the secret and the outcome. That was the effect Theresa Bricklin always managed to have on her.

Hemphill said he happened on the manuscript by chance. The first chapters were secreted in a dusty chest in his studio where he kept his personal souvenirs: old letters and clippings, pictures, fragments of his past. One day, seeking solace from the pain of Theresa's illness, he opened the chest to read the letters she wrote him early in their courtship and there were several chapters of an untitled manuscript. A few weeks later, he found several more hidden in the frame of a large canvas in the master bedroom. It was a childish, clumsy landscape from his earliest forays with the brush. Theresa knew he intended to paint over it. Hemphill thought she had placed the chapters where he would be likely to find them. If his theory were correct, the remaining pages would turn up eventually.

Beyond the formal garden, Erica followed a worn footpath through a ruined orchard. Misshapen fruit and nut trees, neglected and scarred by disease, were forcing their first, meager blossoms. A frantic bumblebee darted from tree to tree, overwhelmed by the futility of its task.

She came upon several dilapidated tennis courts. Two sides of the green wire fence were down and the gnarled roots of an ancient oak poked up through the weathered surface. According to Goody, the original owners had several estates and built Bramble Farm as a summer retreat. Erica could almost hear the light banter and laughs of youthful self-indulgence. She pictured the Highbrows and the Uppercrusts, the most pampered summer locals, sipping iced drinks at courtside after a few vigorous sets. There was an enormous pool, now cracked and littered with dead leaves and branches. The poolhouse was boarded, the windows broken, the crisp yellow paint faded to the beige of parched earth.

"Touring the property, Erica?" Hemphill had a feline's gift for unexpected appearance. He cocked his head and pursed his lips as if she were an interesting specimen under a microscope.

Erica looked away. "It must have been quite something . . ."

"And shall be again. I have contracted with a prominent firm of landscape architects. They are currently in the process of drawing plans for a complete restoration. I suspect the end result will be even grander than the original. A complete renaissance. Elegance reborn, the restoration of a noble legacy. Beautiful surroundings will surely have beneficial effects on my darling Tessa, don't you agree?"

"What is the prognosis? If you don't mind my asking."

His face darkened. "I do not concern myself with gratuitous predictions. Wellness springs from the human spirit, not the physician's bag of tricks and poisons. Tessa will recover because she must. I will not let it be otherwise." He bit his trembling lower lip.

"I'm sorry. It was a stupid thing for me to ask. No one really knows. You're right."

He inhaled deeply and the knots of his tension seemed to uncoil. "I cannot surrender to the bleak pronouncements of strangers. Tessa is my life. My future."

They walked side by side. Goody's stride was stiff and uneven as if he carried an invisible walking stick. "Over there, beside the elm, will be a solar-powered hydroponic greenhouse and a large potting shed. I have read extensively about the therapeutic value of horticulture. Tessa was always fond of gardening."

"Where did she ever find the time?"

"The drive of genius could power the world, my dear. Tessa has the ability to fragment her attentions so that one hand can be occupied with craft while the other tends to nurturing; all the while one foot seeks safe purchase in starkest reality and the other taps the rhythms of life. And none of that interferes with her complete concentration on the scene she is creating. The drive of genius."

But now . . . Erica thought. Then, she chided herself for

her pessimism. Maybe Hemphill's attitude was the correct
one. Maybe some indefinable force was responsible for miraculous recoveries. Bullheadedness and devotion seemed
as powerful a therapeutic program as any.

He gestured in grand sweeps as he spoke. "Over there,
beside the bath house, I have ordered a special hot pool
with exercise bars and whirlpool jets. We will have a therapist come for daily sessions until we have my darling back
on her feet. Dear Tessa should not be subject to the indignity of physical dependence."

Again she was touched by his devotion. "Miss Bricklin is
lucky to have such determination behind her. Where did
you two meet?"

Hemphill smiled. "A breath of pure good fortune, my
dear. Tessa was touring in Europe after the publication of
her last collection of short stories, *Midlife Vices*. I was on
holiday having finalized the sale of my import firm. I was
frankly weary of devoting my entire life to the pursuit of
affluence. My enterprise was highly successful but so all-
consuming I had no time left for personal pleasures. I had
never married or settled in a permanent home. The future
stretched before me in bleak stretches of lonely regret. A
solitary old age seemed a dire sentence to serve for the sin
of youthful self-indulgence."

"So you were ready . . ."

"Most assuredly. And fate was at her most generous. I
was in Paris, dining alone at Maxim's, toasting my retire-
ment with a bottle of Perrier Jouet, when Tessa happened
to sit at the next table. She noticed my solitary celebration
and offered to join me. We found a wealth of common phi-
losophy and purpose. The rest is a lovely, gentle fog of discovery and attachment."

Erica smiled at the easy sentimentality. "Nice story."

"On irrepressible impulse, we married three months
later, in a tiny chapel in Madrid, before returning to the
States and settling in at Bramble. Our union was entirely
blessed until darling Tessa's unfortunate illness. Still, I
know we appear an odd merger."

Erica thought of the odd couples in her life: Dad and Monika, Mel and Jeannie Underwood, Brian and . . . Brian and anyone. "But appearances are not to be trusted, are they?"

"Precisely. You are indeed a clever young woman, a woman with rare insight. The important issue is the dimension of our mutual feeling, our mutual need and devotion. And I intend to make the most of every moment we have together. I am determined to do so."

They were nearing the stables, a long, low, barn-red structure in far better condition than the rest of the property.

"Tessa has always had a passion for horses. In addition to her beloved old bay, she invested in several prize Anglo-Arabians in the last few years. The finest Arabian stock scrupulously crossed with top thoroughbreds to produce animals combining the best characteristics of both. Arabians with the size and stature of the thoroughbred. They are quite valuable as you might imagine. We had the stables upgraded immediately to make them worthy of such an investment."

"Painting and riding. Interesting coincidence. I used to love riding, until . . ."

"Come then. I shall show you the horses."

Prickles of fear crept up her spine. "No, thanks. I think I'll pass. I'm sure they're beautiful but I'd rather not. I had a bad experience and . . ."

"All the more reason. One most forge beyond the strangling bounds of one's fears and suspicions." He tapped the center row of buttons to disarm the security.

Painted a stark white and illuminated by cool white fluorescent tubes, the stable had the antiseptic atmosphere of a surgical suite. The air was filtered through a series of spotless ducts and circulated by muffled fans. At intervals, a whirring sound heralded the spray of a fine mist that cleared any stray dust particles and kept the space insect-free. "Magnificent animals, but quite temperamental and fragile, I'm afraid."

When she hesitated at the door, he took firm hold of her elbow and led her inside. Erica scanned the long double row of immaculate stalls. A single white giant was tethered in each beside a polished brass plaque inscribed with its name and pedigree. They were somber, arrogant names befitting the animals' value and carriage. Most stood motionless as statues. She breathed deeply and quipped to hide her tension. "Do you boil their hay?"

Goody chuckled. "Dear Erica. You do have an extraordinary sense of humor. They are quite fragile as I said. In fact, I must limit visitors to particular times when their presence will not upset the various systems we've installed to protect the animals. Thus the security."

She looked past the stalls, trying to think of something, anything else. "Where is your studio?"

He tensed at the question. "There are several tack rooms beyond the loft. Someday, we intend to show our horses and involve other enthusiasts. For now, I confess to appropriating one of them for my work. The room is spacious, and the light, perfect. At times, I feel the need for . . . distance."

"I understand. Everyone needs personal space. Room to think. May I see what you're working on?"

"No. You certainly may not!" he rasped, then he folded his hands and pursed his lips to gain control. "Forgive my outburst. I fear I am quite superstitious about the effect of extraneous eyes on work in progress. I allow no one to enter my studio. No one."

"Of course, that's your privilege. I'll be glad to wait until you've finished."

His earlier jocularity returned. "Humor and understanding, we are indeed fortunate to have you with us, my dear— indeed blessed."

She walked outside again, grateful to have the visit finished. "And I feel fortunate to be working on this book. I read the manuscript . . ."

His brow raised. "And?"

"You must find the rest." Her eyes clouded with distraction. "You must find it . . . soon."

Soon. Time was running out for her to make a decision about this baby. If she decided to go through with the pregnancy, this book would mean security, a future, a chance for a solid, settled career. Mel was right. Being associated with a successful Theresa Bricklin novel was the opportunity of a lifetime.

Could she decide not to have the baby? Was abortion a possibility? More and more she saw this tiny abstraction as a real child—her child. A child with a face, a future, tiny fingers to weave into hers. But there was more, she knew. Demands, responsibilities, her entire life rewritten.

And so much of that new life depended on this place, this book, these people. How would they react to the pregnancy? Which doors would be open and shut in the unpredictable wake of her decision? She felt overwhelmed by the jumble of possibilities. And her own future seemed to slip further and further from her meager grasp. The ropes connecting her to Hemphill, Theresa Bricklin and Bramble Farm seemed to be drawing tighter and tighter. And she felt powerless to stop them.

CHAPTER

6

Bramble Farm was rich in space and solitude. Erica found her place in the particular rhythms of the estate, filling her days with Theresa Bricklin's vast sea of papers.

When she was not at work, she explored every corner of the vast acreage. As the weather softened, she took to walking barefoot, feeling a part of the scented spring breezes and nature's continuous showings of bloom and surrender.

Each of the estate's occupants seemed to exist in a separate capsule. Hemphill awoke early and worked at his studio until lunch. On the stroke of twelve, he appeared on the rear veranda, sat in the white wrought-iron chair facing the solarium, crossed his legs delicately and waited for his meal to arrive. He ate without visible opinion, chewing slowly and, after each bite, patting his pursed lips with a linen napkin.

Afternoons, he worked with Theresa, continuing her rigorous program of speech and physical training: exercises practiced in firm order, limbs stretched like strands of pliant taffy and moved through every conceivable plane, meaningless sounds and syllables repeated in a patient, determined drone. "Say 'ah,' darling. 'Ah.' Watch my lips, Tessa dear. 'Ah.' Open wide, wider. You can do it, darling. There, that's a good effort."

The work was endless. Practice in dressing, hair combing,

face washing, using utensils; every action difficult, frustrating, exhausting. "Hold the cloth, Tessa dear. Now you don't want the dampness to stain your blouse, my darling. Firmer, Tessa. Make sure you have a good grasp. Better, that's better. We are making progress, aren't we, darling?"

He was the most unpredictable man, sometimes open and effusive, sometimes dark and intractable. His moods could swing on the narrowest fulcrum—a single word, a gesture. But his devotion to Theresa was unwavering.

Over several weeks, he found another missing chapter folded in a cotton sweater in his armoire. Mrs. Ohringer happened on yet another, placed behind the drapes in Goody's study. "See that. Lucky thing I'm so thorough. Philly always says, 'Lorraine, you're crazy clean, just crazy.' See, even crazy has its good side."

Still, the Grey Lady remained in the dim, eerie room, locked in her own mind and misery. And the story seemed to shift slightly out of focus, as if Theresa had allowed herself to wander off the central path and somehow lost her way:

> Thoughts, visions sheer as dreams pressed between the firm hands of reality: slim, frightened children pumping their restless energies toward a laughing sky, young men climbing the flimsy vines of their ambition, women with dry, empty breasts and hands roughened by the endless abrasion of rebuked affections; all are my lost link with hope and future. All lost.

Erica felt even more compelled to see the rest of the manuscript, to see where the story might lead. More than once, she was tempted to peek in a drawer, rummage through a spare closet. But her curiosity was cooled by an icy prickle of warning on the back of her neck, the feeling of being watched, and she turned, expecting to find Goody behind her. He seemed to be everywhere.

Work began on the property. One morning, while Erica

was reading in the topiary garden, a trio of trucks arrived, clattering over the stony path. There were five men—tanned and shirtless. The foreman approached Erica with an outstretched hand. His fingers were stained and he smelled of sweat and pine needles. "Rich Standeval. You Mrs. Hemphill?"

"No, I work here. My name's Phillips. Erica Phillips."

"Oh." His eyes walked slowly over her body. "I just figured . . ."

Erica flushed. "Mr. Hemphill is in his studio. He usually breaks for lunch at twelve. I suppose you can just get started."

"We sure got our work cut out on this place." He scratched his stubby chin. His face was coarse, his features spread as though they had melted from too much sun. "Seems we get all the tough jobs. Last month, we turned a rats' nest into a park for the kiddies in Norwalk. Every place we went to clean up, those suckers came running out screeching like crazies. Got so Barry over there could grab one by the tail and mash him with a shovel before the poor little rat knew what hit 'm, couldn't you, Bar?"

Erica shuddered as the hero in question smiled and flexed his muscles. She had a dread of rodents in any form. The tiniest field mouse could freeze her in terror. It started when Meg was just a few weeks old. It was three in the morning and Erica was holding the baby for her night feeding. As Meg suckled on the rubber nipple, Erica settled in the dreamy fog of her own exhaustion. Perfect, dreamy peace. A soothing wholeness she hadn't felt since the birth and her mother's death wound together in black horror. Sweet little Meg. Erica would protect her, help her grow. Dreams of Meg, tall and lovely . . . then, the jolt of horror as something ran across her dangling, bare foot. The scream. The baby's frightened wail. "Just a little mouse," Dad said. "Jesus, Erica. You didn't have to wake the whole house!" And he took a straw broom and bludgeoned the hapless creature until it lay in a bloody, mangled heap. Strange how certain events stayed with you, changed you permanently.

Sandeval noticed her reaction. "You scared of rats, lady?" He shrugged. "My wife's the same way. Funny. Listen, we got two dozen azaleas going in over here and a coupla pink dogwoods. We gotta bring in a load or two of topsoil, so you better move. You gotta be careful in your condition."

She turned to the sound of Goody clearing his throat for attention. "There you are, my dear Erica. And you must be Mr. Sandeval. I am so anxious for you to begin your work. As you mentioned, the undertaking is considerable."

As he mentioned. Erica wondered how long Goody had been listening, how much he had heard. Too late, she thought. Words could not be retrieved, not fully.

Without further comment, he walked her to the terrace for lunch. "A lovely day, my dear. Nature at her most immodest. My senses are overwhelmed and I fear my contentment shall spill where it is not necessarily welcome."

She managed a vague smile. "Who could object to that?"

He clicked his tongue. "There are those who enjoy their anguish. One does hate to impose."

In the yard, a rusty yellow backhoe took giant bites of clay-ridden earth. She rested her chin in her hand and stared at nothing. "Would you say that an end always comes before a beginning or is it the other way around?"

"So, my dear. I see you wax philosophical. Is it your intention to solve the ancient riddle of the chicken and the egg?"

She straightened and brought herself back in focus. "That one is easy. The chicken came first. Then, it was dipped in the egg and deep-fried to a crispy, golden . . ."

Hemphill folded his hands like a lecturing professor. "Let us return to the serious side, Erica. Life cannot be circumvented on a raft to levity. I do believe in balance. One must pay one's tariff, mustn't one? Each of us is entitled to just so much contentment in exchange for a measured amount of sorrow."

Erica sighed. "I suppose. I just wish . . ."

"Wishing is generally a most inefficient use of energies.

You would do better to order your priorities and work to see them realized."

She saluted. "Yes, sir."

His eyes narrowed. "Of course, it is not my place to direct you. Please forgive my presumptuous remark."

"No, it's all right. That was good advice. I'll try to figure out how to follow it."

A slender, sharp-featured blonde woman in a white coat wheeled Theresa out on the terrace. "There, Miss Bricklin. I'll bet you're ready for some lunch." She turned to Hemphill and spoke in a thickly accented voice. "Sir, your wife has been as cooperative as she can be. But, as I told you originally, her aphasia is quite severe. She has lost the ability to understand or express herself verbally. There has been no change, no improvement. And I don't expect to see any unless you are willing to allow me to introduce some alternative system—sign language, a symbol or picture board, some gestures, something. She cannot learn to speak again but she might be able to communicate in some other way. There's a chance at least."

"I hardly think such a discussion should be held in Tessa's presence, Miss Bochmann."

"I'm sorry. I don't think she understands a word I'm saying. But if she does, she has a right to know. I can understand your preference for speech, but if she can't, she can't."

"That is your opinion, Miss Bochmann, nothing more." His lips were drawn in a tight, bloodless line. "Have you considered that it might be your professional skill that is lacking and not Theresa's potential for recovery?"

"Mr. Hemphill, you have been through every speech therapist at the hospital and nearly every one in private practice in the area. If you feel you have overlooked someone, I cannot stop you from going on with this. But I have to tell you it's a waste of time and money."

"You needn't tell me a thing, Miss Bochmann. Kindly send a bill for your services and see yourself out." His chest heaved visibly with his efforts at control. "Tessa, would you like a nice salad for lunch? I believe Mrs. Ohringer found fresh endive and arugula at the market."

"Aphasia? Is that the name for Theresa's speech problem?" Erica kept her tone soft and even.

"That's what certain dullards choose to call it, a designation of convenience, I assure you. On occasion, following a stroke, there is a permanent loss of language function. The term, unfortunately, has been perverted in Tessa's case, used as an excuse for professional incompetence and laziness." He jerked the wheelchair until she was facing him and spoke in a low growl. "Tessa, I am most sorely displeased with your performance. We have discussed this time and time again. I expect you to cooperate with these rehabilitation people, dreadful though they may be. Otherwise, you cannot expect to make satisfactory progress."

"Hukkah gannnn." Theresa's face paled and tightened. Her good arm flew up to protect her face.

"No, Tessa. No! No excuses! I do not believe you're doing your best. In fact, you have demonstrated a tendency to be resistant. That shall not be tolerated. Do you understand? Do you?" He squeezed her arm until lemon circles spread from his fingertips.

Her eyes bulged in terror. "Ghaa . . . agh."

The color rose in his face and his lips were drawn in an angry scowl. "Babble, babble, babble. Enough! Quite enough! Do you understand me? Do you?"

Erica held her breath as he tipped the chair at a precarious angle and Theresa gasped in fright. Then, quickly as it came, the tirade passed and Goody settled back, clasped his hands, and smiled benignly. "You see? She understands. You understand everything, my darling. Don't you? You mustn't keep on with this foolish resistance, Tessa. Remember, I promised you a long cruise just as soon as you recover your speech. The Mediterranean, I think. A long, lovely, relaxing cruise."

Erica found her voice. Her mouth was dry as chalk. "You expect so much of her, Goody. Maybe it's too much."

He patted her hand. "Nonsense, my dear. Who has more to give than the great Theresa Bricklin?"

Erica's chest thumped in fury. The man was . . . No, Erica. No point allowing an overactive imagination to carry her beyond the bounds of reason. Hemphill was volatile, nothing more. Her future, the baby's future depended on this book and these people. Sometimes things were the way they were supposed to be. And sometimes you managed to live with things the way they were.

CHAPTER

7

Erica sat in the waiting room, next to a whimsical soft sculpture of an enormously pregnant woman peering in eternal accusation at a skinny little man with rimless glasses and an oversized briefcase. The room had soaring ceilings capped by skylights. Lush hanging plants and chairs upholstered in soft celery green and sunny yellow set an almost tropical mood. She half expected a barefoot native to appear bearing tall tropical brews in carved coconuts. Nice place, relaxing. If only she could slip the noose of anxiety off her neck.

Knowing no one else in town, she had asked at the hospital for a recommendation and made the next available appointment with Dr. John Wellings, Chief of Obstetrics. The sooner this was settled, the sooner she could get back to living.

While she waited, she filled out the medical history on a lucite clipboard in her lap and tried without success to read an article on spring fashion. No reason to be so nervous, she told herself. After all, she had thought it out rationally. Yes, the idea of being a mother was appealing. And, yes, this was probably her only chance. But babies should have two loving, accepting, enthusiastic parents. Babies should be wanted and planned. After an entire night of heated debate with herself, she knew abortion was the only sane possibility. Raising a child was a lifetime commitment, not something to be entered into on a whim of fate and feeling. Still she looked with envy at a young couple seated across the room. Daddy read to a squirming toddler while Mom smiled in approval, her hands folded over the swell of the next family addition.

"Miss Phillips . . ."

Erica followed a uniformed nurse down a short corridor to an office door.

"Doctor John was called out on an emergency," she said as she turned the knob. "You'll be seeing Doctor James."

In a rush of annoyance, Erica was tempted to leave. "Why wasn't I told?"

"Sorry, you're right. If you'd rather wait for my father, that's perfectly fine." A young man with an infectious grin and deep blue eyes stood and extended a hand toward her. "I'm Jim Wellings, Miss . . . Miss Phillips." He checked her chart and turned to the nurse. "Connie, you tell Rosalie she is not to spring me on any more innocent, unsuspecting patients. I'm very sorry, Miss Phillips. How about a cup of coffee before you go?" He gestured her to sit beside his desk. "How do you take it?"

She sat grudgingly. "Black. You're so young."

"I know. It's a problem I've had for years. But I'm sure I'll work it out in time. You're not exactly old yourself." He consulted her chart again. "In fact, I'm . . . twenty-seven days older."

She smiled. "That makes me feel *much* better."

"Good, that's what doctors are for."

"I suppose it doesn't matter who I see. I just didn't like the way it was handled. I should have been told."

"You're absolutely right." His gaze was too intense, unsettling. "Now, what can I do for you?"

She lowered her eyes and fiddled with her purse. "I'm . . . pregnant. I . . . want an abortion."

"What month?"

"Third."

"All right. Let's have a look."

In the examining room, she donned a disposable robe and sat on the paper-wrapped vinyl table. When young Dr. Wellings entered, his manner was deliberately crisp and businesslike. He examined her, his face set in a thoughtful frown. "Does that hurt? That? All right, Miss Phillips. You get dressed and I'll see you back in my office."

She found him behind his desk, scribbling something on a manila folder. "How soon can it be done?"

"The abortion is no problem. I can arrange it early in the week if you like. But, I have to tell you I doubt you'll be able to have other pregnancies. I'm sure you've been told before, you're a classic candidate for infertility. Tipped uterus. History of endometriosis. You know this pregnancy is something of a miracle considering . . ."

"It's a miracle of bad timing."

"The father? Is he in agreement?"

"He agreed about the bad timing," she said dully. "That's all."

"Then you're sure this is what you want? I would hate to think you'll have regrets . . ."

She blinked away the tears. "I have no choice. Regrets have nothing to do with it."

"Regrets have everything to do with it," he said gently. "And you do have a choice . . . several choices in fact. You can have the baby and keep it, or give it up for adoption. There are plenty of people who would give anything to be parents . . ."

"I could never give my baby away . . . never."

"Do yourself a favor, Miss Phillips. Think about it. A few days one way or the other won't make much difference now."

His gentle sincerity was disarming. "I don't see what's going to happen in a few days to change my mind."

"Probably nothing if you're sure. But I get the feeling you still have some reservations. I don't mean to push you in either direction but you can afford to give yourself a little more time. I'll tell you what. I'll schedule you for early next week. Then, if you change your mind, I can simply cancel. If you decide to go through with it, we haven't lost any time at all."

She wiped her eyes and shrugged. "I'm sure it won't make a difference. But, all right. I'll give you a call on Thursday and let you know."

"Here's my home number. If anything comes up . . . any questions or whatever. You can call."

"I'm sure I won't need to bother you at home." She rose to leave. "May I ask why you're being so nice?"

A slow grin spread over his face. "Beats me, Miss Phillips. But it's a good question. A very good question."

He was so open, appealing. My luck, she thought. Someone like Jim Wellings would have been an excellent antidote for Brian Bregman syndrome under other circumstances. Add that to the list, Erica. A baby would put an end to the casual, hopeful flirtation, possibly forever. "I'll speak to you Thursday, Dr. Wellings."

"Or before."

His voice was a caress. She could still feel the soothing effects as she shut the door behind her. In another life, this conversation might have ended differently. Would she ever return to a normal existence where there were stories without surprise endings?

She felt an odd sense of relief at the postponed decision. Was she sure about the abortion? Was she sure about anything? Maybe it was just the pregnancy that left her off center, unbalanced. Or maybe Bramble Farm, that odd little universe, was taking its toll, making it hard for her to think. In a way, she felt herself floating on invisible currents, drawn toward a conclusion that had nothing to do with her will or actions. Regrets or choices. Perhaps there were too many of both. Or perhaps there were none at all.

CHAPTER

8

When she returned to Bramble Farm, there was a forest-green Jaguar in the drive. Flumacher greeted her at the door, his face etched with worry. He rolled his eyes in admonition and held a gnarled finger to his pursed lips. Erica found Hemphill and Theresa in the living room. A middle-aged couple, weighted with fruity colognes and garish jewelry, were perched opposite the Hemphills on the edge of matching Regency chairs. The air was bristling with tension and hostility.

Goody seemed pleased by her intrusion. "Erica, my dear," he gushed. "There you are. My regrets for missing you at lunchtime. I trust your excursion was successful?"

"Fine, yes."

"Allow me to introduce Tessa's nephew, Mark Bloomway, and his latest wife, Sharon. Mark, Sharon, this is Miss Erica Phillips, a talented young editor from Prescott Press who has graciously consented to come and assist us with Tessa's papers."

"For a price," Bloomway muttered.

Hemphill issued a dramatic sigh. "You are the rudest man. Certainly, Erica is being compensated for her efforts. Some people actually do work for their money, my dear fellow. Odd though that may seem to you."

"Look who's talking, old Goody Gold Digger himself. You have no right to piss away Aunt Terry's money like this."

"Quite the contrary, my dear nephew. I have every right: legal, moral, ethical and conjugal to see to Tessa's well-being. I am not, as you so crudely put it, 'pissing away' her money in any event. I am utilizing our combined financial resources to facilitate your aunt's well-being and see to her recovery from this debilitating affliction."

"Pig shit on that! You are pissing away her money, pure and simple. Look at her, hanging on by a thread. She needs a fancy estate like I need a second asshole."

"It seems you are quite well equipped in that department, my dear fellow."

Erica suppressed a giggle. She couldn't help but take Hemphill's side in this gun battle. Mark Bloomway hardly looked at Theresa. He was too busy minding his possible inheritance.

Sharon Bloomway added her nasal whine. "We're not trying to be difficult. Mark and I just feel it's a waste, Goody. Aunt Terry doesn't even look like herself anymore with her face all twisted up like that. To tell the truth, I wouldn't have recognized her in a million years if I didn't know what happened. You should have seen her at our wedding. A real looker, even at her age. And full of the dickens. A real fun lady. Now she doesn't even know which end is up, poor thing. You can see that. Look at her, all soft and foggy. What's the point?"

"Sharon, my dear. You are full of surprises, truly a woman of rare talents. I had no idea of your expertise in neurology."

She blushed and tapped an oversized cigarette from a gold-toned case. Then she touched the tip with the tall flame from a matching lighter and filled the air with a cloud of smoke. "Look, we're not trying to tell you your business. It's just . . ."

"I'm delighted to hear that, my dear. For a moment, I thought that was precisely what you were attempting to tell me."

"Can it, Sharon," Bloomway said. "I'm not gonna play kissy face with that money-grubbing creep. I'm warning you, Hemphill. You quit playing the big spender or I'll haul your ass into court."

"Aaangh argakh!"

They all turned to Theresa, who had stiffened and risen nearly out of her chair. Her face was a mottled scarlet and a thin line of spittle ran from the corner of her mouth. "Amugguh!"

"Now that you have succeeded in upsetting Tessa, I will ask you to leave my house! Out!" Hemphill's teeth were clenched, his voice a volley of buckshot.

"You'll hear from my lawyer, you sticky-fingered toad. I swear it," Bloomway said. "We'll let the courts decide whether you should be pissing away Aunt Terry's fortune like this. We'll see."

"You leave this instant or I shall summon the authorities!" Hemphill shrieked.

"Jeez, Goody," Bloomway crooned. "Now you've gone and got me scared to death. He's a real big bully, Shar. I'm shivering in my boots."

"Come on, honey," Sharon said. "Let's all calm down now. We're all family after all."

"You see yourselves out," Goody rasped. "I have to attend to dear Tessa now. There now, darling. Mustn't allow these repulsive creatures to upset you."

"Ughuk . . . kuk . . . shit!" Theresa's eyes bulged with effort. She rapped the arm of her chair like someone calling a meeting to order.

Hemphill stood beside her and stroked her wrinkled forehead. "There, there. Don't concern yourself with that boorish lout and his painted trollop. Ssh, darling. There, that's better. Revolting sloth. Tessa has not seen her nephew in years. Suddenly in the face of a difficult illness, he wishes to be close family again. He hovers like a ravenous vulture, waiting for my darling's demise so he can avail himself of the fruits of her lifelong labors, the fruits of her brilliance! Disgusting troll. Ssh, my darling. Ssh . . ."

Theresa seemed to uncoil. The crooked twigs of her fingers opened in slow motion like the budding of some petrified flower. "You have such a wonderful way with her, Goody," Erica said.

"Nonsense, my dear. I do no more than any spouse would do in like circumstances. If our positions were reversed, Tessa would drown me with love and sympathies, wouldn't you, darling?"

"Ehekkuh!" She smacked her lips and tapped her fingers against the armrest in gentle rhythm.

"That's my darling. There, there." His fingers traced lazy circles on her shoulder. "Not to worry, Tessa. Justice will be served. Soon, very soon this will all be over."

"With your help, Goody," Erica said.

"Yes, dear, and yours."

Erica averted her eyes. The future kept moving and shifting. Jim Wellings' words would not leave her alone. Why did he dredge up all that business about regrets? Choices? She had made peace with the notion of childlessness years ago when the first of several doctors predicted her infertility. There were worse fates, far worse. In fact, she knew the darker side only too well. She could still picture her father coming home after Meg was born. She could still see him standing at the entrance to the kitchen, head bowed, shoulders slumped with the world's weight, a shocked, sheepish smile on his face. She remembered running in with her brothers to hear the news. "Boy or girl?" They clamored in gleeful staccato. "Boy or girl?"

Without looking up, he shrugged an apology. "A girl," he whispered. "But your mother . . ."

Her mother dead. The death of her childish trust and innocence. It was so hard to see past the cold void in their lives, so impossible to assuage the pangs of guilt and uselessness. She tried to make it right. But helping with Meg, Jeff and Michael was hard work, responsibility, endless demands, fights. Not at all a storybook proposition. Why, then, did she feel this unbearable ache about the chance to have

a baby of her own, a sweet, squirmy, warm, toothless, boneless little baby? Her baby.

Goody clapped his hands together in childish delight. "I
have a wonderful idea. Why don't we have dinner out? How
would you like that, darling? We haven't had a night out in
weeks."

Theresa clicked her tongue.

"Fine, then. It's all settled. I shall make a reservation at
the Inn. I know you'll enjoy it, Erica, marvellous food, delightful ambiance, impeccable service."

"That would be nice." It was the perfect time for a distraction. "Very nice."

The Silver Birch Inn was a short ride from Bramble
Farm. Erica sat between Goody and Theresa in the back
seat of the Bentley, staring past the flaming cloud of Theresa's
hair at the rambling properties along the way. "I can't
imagine what it must be like to grow up on a place like that,
so far away from neighbors. It must be lonely."

"The lack of constant playmates can be advantageous, actually," Hemphill mused. "One learns the value of inner
resource and the knack of self-amusement."

"I suppose families get closer when they're so isolated
from the world."

Hemphill cleared his throat. "That depends on the family, my dear. As you witnessed earlier, some family members are not the sort that inspire intimacy. Family can be
fate's naughtiest imposition."

"I miss mine," Erica said. "My sister is in Boston. One
brother lives in California. The other constantly travels."
Talking about them, Erica felt a sudden pang of loneliness.
"We hardly see each other anymore. What about you? Do
you have family?"

"I have Tessa. Don't I, darling? Tessa is my family, my
life. Before Tessa, there was no one."

"I'm sorry."

"Don't be, my dear. Surfeit survives. Deprivation
thrives."

Erica laughed in appreciation. "I bet you are never at a loss for words, Goody."

"I try never to be at a loss for anything, my dear. Preparedness is peace."

A cloud passed over her expression. "That depends," she said, "on what you're prepared to do."

What if she followed her instincts? How big a mistake could it possibly be? She could close her arms and feel the warm weight of an infant in her arms. She could press her cheek against the night air and feel the silky velvet of an infant's cheek. Regrets and choices and chances.

One chance. How could she fail to take advantage of her single chance? A thrill of fear rushed through her as she realized she had no choice at all.

CHAPTER

9

The chauffeur retrieved Theresa's wheelchair from the trunk and helped her from the car. Erica followed as Goody maneuvered the chair over the uneven flagstone path to a garden greenhouse where cocktails were served. Surrounded by lush palms and hanging ferns, they sat on wicker chairs with flowered cushions and ordered drinks.

"I'll have a dry martini and my wife would like a Manhattan on the rocks." Hemphill turned to Theresa. "You'd like a double, wouldn't you, darling? Make that a double."

"Yes, Mr. Hemphill."

"Do you come here often?" Erica said. "It's lovely."

Hemphill took Theresa's withered hand in his and stroked her like a wounded bird. "We try to get out as much as we can. Sometimes, Tessa is simply too weary from the demands of her therapeutic routines. But you are such a good sport about it most of the time, aren't you, darling? On occasion she does have her little lapse, a moment of resistance or laziness. Then I suppose that is understandable."

When the drinks arrived, he held the amber liquid to Theresa's lips and she sipped noisily. Then, he took his handkerchief and dabbed at the tinted spittle on her chin. "Is it adequate, darling? I don't believe that's the usual man at the bar . . . It's fine? Good."

Erica sipped at a lime-tinged Perrier. She forced herself

to look at Theresa and talk to her. Without thinking, she tended to turn away, disturbed by the odd twist of the woman's mouth; the vacant, weary eyes; the wasted arm and leg dangling from her body like mannequin parts. "I've read what we have of the new manuscript, Miss Bricklin. It's brilliant, a brilliant idea. So different."

He smiled broadly. "See, darling. I knew she'd love it. I must tell you, Erica. I think this is Tessa's finest effort, the culmination of a brilliant career."

"If the ending is anywhere near as powerful as the parts I've read, I would tend to agree with you. I can't imagine how she resolves the story." She wanted to say, I can't wait to see the rest, to see this project through to a happy ending. But she knew she might have to give up that possibility. Goody's response to her pregnancy might be moral indignation, revulsion. At best, he might want no part of the tangled mess of her life. Why should he get involved? Erica steeled herself to expect the worst.

"I'm certain we'll find it, won't we, darling?" He nodded at Theresa. "In the meantime, Erica, you continue with your work on the sections we already have. Mr. Underwood assured me you are the most thorough of editors. I imagine such painstaking efforts will take quite some time."

Her heart was pounding as she crossed an invisible bridge. "That's true and . . . and I don't know if I can continue with the project, Goody. Something has come up."

Goody pouted like an injured child. "But, my dear. We are counting on you. Can't whatever it is wait a few months? Tessa has her heart set on your staying."

"No, it can't wait a few months. I'm . . . I'm going to have a baby, Goody. I can't impose on you two. I can't ask you to keep me on under the circumstances." She held her breath, waiting for his reaction.

"A baby. I see." He sipped his martini. A trio of skewered olives tapped against his milky cheek. Replacing the glass on the table, he smoothed the cloth and brushed at an invisible crumb for several seconds before looking up at Erica. "I see no reason why that should make a difference. Do you, darling? Quite the contrary. This would seem the perfect setting for you to await your confinement. We will see to your needs. And the work is not strenuous. You must stay with us, Erica. I insist on it. *We* insist. Don't we, Tessa? There, it's all settled." He lifted his glass and cleared his throat. "To life's beginnings."

Erica clinked his glass with hers. She felt giddy with relief. "To choices and regrets."

"My dear," he smiled benevolently. "You are beginning to sound like me."

Hemphill made dinner a celebration. Without consulting the menu, he ordered wild duck, roast pheasant, and venison with wild rice and Roquefort-stuffed snap peas. He selected a bottle of expensive Bordeaux and poured a tiny trace for Erica. "A woman with child must be so scrupulous about what she consumes, my dear."

"Yes, Mom."

For the first time in days, Erica allowed herself to drift, heedless of the past or future. Goody was right. This was the perfect setting. She would have her work, solitude, distance from fish eyes and acid tongues. Nothing to consider but fine prose and the baby. Her baby. Sweet miracle of terrible timing. Her throat burned with mixed pain and pleasure. "Thank you."

"Our pleasure, my dear. We are looking forward to the next several months." He lifted his glass again. "To creations and masterpieces."

"To Miss Bricklin," Erica said. "May she have all that she deserves."

Hemphill nodded in brisk assent. "May justice, that vain, elusive lady, serve us all with grace and generosity, my dear."

"Amen." Still holding back the tides of emotion, she excused herself to go to the ladies' room. There would be years to rectify the error of unfortunate timing, years to write over a few small smudges on her life's plan.

A waitress nodded at her as she passed. "They're really something, those two. You know, when I first saw them I thought it was kinda weird. I mean, an old, sick woman like that, can't talk or anything. I have her picture on an old book of hers and you'd never believe it was the same person with her face all twisted up and everything. But he really gets off on her, doesn't he?"

"He cares about her a great deal, yes."

The waitress looked past Erica, a dreamy expression clouding her eyes. "You know I read in one of those advice columns that marrying a much older woman means a guy is trying to make up for something that got screwed up in his childhood. That guy must've had one helluva childhood."

In the bathroom, Erica splashed water on her burning cheeks. Now it was done, spoken. Real. She knew it was the right decision, the only one she could make. Still, she was troubled by a sense of powerlessness. For all her agonizing and planning, it seemed that matters beyond her control were pulling her along toward some unknown place and circumstance. And now she could only hope it was a place she cared to be.

CHAPTER

10

Back at Bramble Farm, Erica left Goody and Theresa in the parlor and went to the study. She sat beside the desk for several minutes, staring at the numberless dial on the antique phone.

He answered on the second ring. "Doctor Wellings? This is Erica Phillips. I was in to see you this morning."

"Correction, you were in to see my father. You settled for me because of my irresistible charm."

"I'm in a good mood, Doctor. Don't make me nauseous."

He laughed. "All right, I'll be properly humble. What can I do for you, Miss Phillips?"

"Erica."

"What can I do for you, Erica?"

"I've decided to cancel our . . . appointment."

"You're sure?"

"Yes, I'm sure."

"Okay then. I'll take care of it."

"You sound like you think I've made the wrong decision."

"Did anyone ever tell you you're not an easy person?"

Erica smiled. "I just wanted you to know . . . so you can cancel."

"I will, first thing in the morning. And you call and make an appointment for your next checkup. Four weeks, okay?"

"Four weeks."

There was a long pause on the line. "You can tell Connie, if you'd rather see my father. I'll understand."

"You would not."

Again he laughed, a light, pleasant sound like the clink of crystal. "I may be wrong about you, Erica, but something tells me you may be dangerous."

"One never knows, doctor."

Whistling, she walked back into the living room where Goody and Theresa sat sipping at huge heated snifters of brandy. "Milk for you, my dear? I'm told calcium is most important."

"No, no thanks. I'm pretty tired. I think I'll go upstairs. Thanks for the dinner. For everything."

"Our pleasure. Tessa and I do so enjoy the company of young people. I'm afraid we've stayed too much to ourselves since the illness. But soon, all will be well. Bramble Farm will resume her place in the social spotlight. The air will ring with youthful enthusiasm and the jubilant melody of celebration. We shall rejoice in the rites of justice. Very soon. Tessa, darling. Show Erica how you can say, 'Goodnight.' "

Her entire body tensed with effort and her face reddened. "Angaak . . . aak!"

"Slowly, darling. Good . . . night!" His lips traced an elaborate arc. "There now, you try."

She took a long, labored breath and stretched her mouth to a gaping chasm. "Reguk . . . bmmmm." Then she began to bubble like a playful infant.

"No, Tessa!" Hemphill barked. "We will have none of that. Stop it, I said. Stop it this instant!"

Erica recoiled from the sudden lash of his fury. "It's so hard for her," she said softly.

Hemphill turned on her. "It's hard on us all, Erica. This sort of behavior will not, I repeat, will not be tolerated. Tessa, you cease that juvenile display this instant! Cease or you will regret it!"

Theresa pursed her lips and lapsed into a dreamy silence.

Hemphill walked over and sat beside her. He traced small circles on her back and spoke in hushed melody. "That's better, darling. That's my good girl. You know how I detest having to be cross with you. Ssh, now. Dear, sweet, Tessa." He pressed her head against his shoulder and looked up at Erica. "That is the most difficult part of all, my dear. Tessa's physicians have warned me that certain regressive behaviors are to be expected. They must be firmly managed or she may simply lapse into an infantile state. Her balance is quite fragile, I fear. How it hurts me to have to speak to her in such a manner, a woman of such grace and dignity." His voice wavered.

Erica felt his anguish. "You're only doing what's best for her, Goody. If that's what she needs to get better, you have no choice. You just have to remember that."

"Yes, my dear. Your understanding makes me feel immeasurably better. I'm sure it's quite providential that you agreed to come and stay here with us."

"Things happen the way they're supposed to, the way they're meant to be," Erica mused. "That was my mother's favorite expression."

"Quite true. Though sometimes, we must prod them along in their proper course."

Impossible man. His tempers shifted with the force and whimsy of a storm. No wonder she felt so unsettled. Erica kept telling herself there was ample reason for her anxiety: Hemphill's moods, the pregnancy, the uncertainty of the future. Her worries were real, logical. Only a fool would feel completely comfortable given the real risks involved in any pregnancy, the uncertainty that went with any commitment to a new life.

A restful night's sleep would help, especially after last night's emotional struggles. She left Goody with Theresa and walked toward the Fallen Angel room. In the dim, uneven light, deep shadows stretched before her like warning arms urging her back and away. A clock ticked its solemn message and chimed the hour in plaintive apology. Then, for an instant, Bramble Farm was deathly still. Erica's pulse quickened in response. Anyone would worry, she assured herself again.

Suddenly, the strains of a Bach concerto swelled and flowed toward her from the ancient console Victrola in the living room. She could hear Goody humming along in a tremulous tenor and the insistent whine of Theresa's chair as he wheeled her across the room.

She entered the Fallen Angel room and slid the bolt closed. "Get lost, Hillary," she said to the emptiness. "The last thing I need tonight is a tragic, little ghost." Think happy thoughts, Erica.

She sat at the writing table, planning to send a long, chatty letter to her sister, Meg. "Dear Mugs," she began. "Nothing much to report."

Very funny, Erica. Nothing she could say in a letter was more like it. Disgusted with her own limitations, she crumpled the paper, tossed it in the wastebasket, and slipped into Hillary's womblike bed. Overhead, the canopy swayed, driven by a current of unease. Downstairs, the clock chimed again and fell silent. The music slowed to a dissonant end.

CHAPTER
11

Erica sat at the burled walnut desk in the study, working through the manuscript for what seemed the thousandth time. A mug of coffee cooled beside the thick stack of pages, reflecting her puzzled frown on its oily surface. As she read, she doodled on a yellow legal pad, endless variations on a question mark. Question marks with pleated skirts and curly wigs, professorial question marks with spectacles and pipes, question mark lovers wrapped in ardent embrace, a daredevil question mark in a crash helmet revving his souped-up Ferrari.

Bricklin's main character was a maddening enigma. The Grey Lady refused to reveal everything while revealing so much of herself that Erica was made to care about the rest. All very artful and infuriating. Again she read:

> My burden is not that of the oppressor. If I am held, then it is somehow by my own will. For if I am held by the will of another, then I lose my volition—which is everything, and pass to a state of grim nonexistence.
>
> So I am. Locked here in this bleak cell of obligation. The story must be told. And I alone possess the dark knowledge and must offer my strangled voice to truth and warning.
>
> Stories untold swim in a vacuum that swells to infin-

ity. Their power is limitless, their sense unchallenged. In the telling, evil is reduced to mortal terms: clever phrases, slick bracelets of thought, odd little characters puffed beyond themselves in a pale parody of the human form. In the telling we shake our heads at evil, chuckle at its clumsiness, smile sadly at its misguided victims. In the telling, evil becomes a naked mockery and we giggle like children at its foolish pomposity.

There is a woman I know, a woman long dead, who comes to my table and asks for weak tea and peasant bread with apple jelly. While we sit, flirting and posturing as women will, she asks me if I have finished her tale. She cannot rest until it is done. I know that but am powerless to cross beyond the fiery bounds of her truth.

We eat in strained silence, her dry black eyes accepting my guilty excuses with the even patience of long suffering. She knows the pitiful limits of my humanity. And I ache from her forgiveness.

After she goes, a colorless bird comes to take her crumbs. His beak is cracked, his feathers dangling from the bony desert of his carcass. As he pecks, the remains pass through him and fill the air with a gritty mist.

Disappointed, he peers at me through tears of bitter knowledge. Silently I beg his understanding but he shakes his woeful head and flies beyond my reach. So much is there, in that crypt of lost dreams and fallen idols. So much I yearn for and regret.

The lamp is lit by a beneficent stranger, the darkness swept away. A slim sword is set in my fingers but I am too weak to grasp and it falls to nothing. Nearby, there is salvation. The power of a thousand legs and the sinew of a brave and brilliant army to carry me off but I am immobile. One step would be a thousand. My power is consumed by the woeful quest for survival.

Evil outdistances me. And the story lies buried in a tomb of futility where I must unearth it by painful degrees.

Disgusted with herself, Erica put the manuscript aside and tore her doodles to satisfying bits. Maybe she was in over her head. Theresa Bricklin's genius deserved more than her meager blue pencil. All she felt qualified to do was a little professional sleuthing, a mental exercise for her but hardly just service to the manuscript.

Question: What did the reference to the dead woman's story mean? A holocaust victim? A Salem witch? A human sacrifice to the lust of man? And the bird? A vulture feeding on the dead woman? A bearer of mortal harm during the Black Death?

Erica's head started to ache with the impossibility of her task. Theresa Bricklin deserved better, needed more.

Maybe she should go to Goody and admit defeat. The manuscript was getting the better of her. She was experienced, yes. But maybe her skills were not enough for this work. Maybe he should find someone else.

She could almost hear Mel's voice. Now, Erica. You are running scared. That's all. A book is paper and ink combined with enough sweat to hold it together and enough air to fly it on. That's the whole business. Don't be intimidated by names and reputations. Most of them will go out of print long before you do.

All right, Erica. Mel's right. You are as competent and hard working as anyone. Don't throw it away. This book, this opportunity meant too much.

She retrieved the yellow pad and started yet another letter to Meg. If she got away for a little while, breathed real air and saw real outside people with real lives, she would feel better.

Buoyed by the thought, she managed to write a page of breezy nonsense without once hinting at the pregnancy or the way fate's fingers seemed to be closing around her throat.

Even as she considered giving up the manuscript, she knew she could not. This book was her future, her baby's future. The episode with Brian left her more convinced than ever that dependence was the shortest possible route to self-annihilation. An odd quirk of circumstance had delivered her to this place and given her this particular key to security. She had to see it through. No matter what.

"Dear Mugs," she wrote. "It occurs to me that I haven't seen you since Sherman took Atlanta (or is it since Fulton took the fish market?). In any event, I think it's time we got together. I can always tell when it's been too long. My nose itches like a fighter in need of a bout and I am filled to the top of my head with the sort of foolishness one can only unload on blood relatives.

"So, Miss Important Lady. Do you think you might break away from your moving and shaking to spend a couple of days with an aged sibling? I think it's the kind of thing you can deduct from your taxes."

Satisfied with the tone, light and not at all desperate, Erica folded the paper and sealed it in an envelope. No reason to burden Meg with her baseless anxieties. All she needed was a few days away to clear her head and get back on her emotional feet.

She tapped the manuscript into a neat pile and left the study. The outgoing mail sat in a square silver dish in the foyer. She placed Meg's letter on top and went out into a dim, humid afternoon.

Halfway down the walk, she changed her mind and went back for her letter. Her mail was her business. Snoopy Mrs. Ohringer didn't have to know. And Goody knew too much about everything already. He was the omniscient master of the palace. All-knowing, all-seeing. All over.

She folded the envelope and slid it into the deep pocket of her shapeless jumper. If Goody should make one of his frequent surprise appearances, Erica was in no mood to answer any questions. She could imagine his words: There you are, my dear. Mailing a letter, are you? It is so important to reach beyond the bounds of our limited existence. And who, may I ask, is the intended recipient of your clever communication? Your enviable epistle? Your magnificent missive?

Wait until she told old Meggy Muggins about Goodwin Hemphill. Then she knew something would be lost in the translation. Goody was the sort one had to see to believe. At least, they would have a good laugh.

She tapped her pocket in satisfaction. Even here it was possible to keep some things private. See, Erica. No one is watching. No one is looking over your shoulder.

Despite herself, she turned quickly to catch some invisible observer in the act. She kept reassuring herself it was the pregnancy, her body chemistry temporarily out of order. Still, she could not shake the feeling that prying eyes followed her.

At night she bolted the door to Hillary's room and lowered the opaque shades against the black world. But the feeling persisted. Eyes watching her as she bathed and dressed and slipped under the cool comforter. Ears tuned to her thunderous heartbeats and the piteous whimpers from her horrible dreams. Paranoia, she thought, must be contagious.

The mailbox was set in the stone post at the base of the rutted drive. She slipped Meg's letter inside and raised the small red metal flag to signal the postman. Seeing Meg would help put the world back in order. Her sister had always been an island of sanity in her loony sea of existence.

Turning, she walked back toward the house. Dense thickets of brambles seemed to close in on her and she crossed her arms for protection.

The path was narrowing, shutting out the light. Spines reached toward her, stabbing at her bare calves and forearms, poised to rip at her eyes.

Panic crept up her legs and turned them to frozen stumps. Her head was caught in a violent tremor. Blood roared in her temples, making it hard to see, to breathe.

Stop it, Erica. Get a hold of yourself. The brambles undulated in and out of focus. One step. Two.

Shivering violently, she managed to continue. Another step. Another. Her breath came in short, hot gasps. Burning coals in her chest. Hot stabs of terror.

There was an end. She moved toward it, one step at a time, groping for the hazy light. Slowly, carefully, she worked her way out, past the spiny nightmare and found herself on the warm brick circle of the drive.

She forced herself to breathe, slow steady breaths. Each measured and planned until she felt the coils of panic begin to recede. She was untied, bit by bit from the prison of her own terror. A blessed rush of relief followed and she rubbed at the sore, bruised places on her arms, surprised to find them unmarked. No blood, no mean gashes in her flesh. The whole thing was nothing but a hideous waking nightmare, the product of her own ghoulish imagination. Foolish, Erica. So foolish. Relieved weariness overwhelmed her.

Back inside, she tried to make sense of what had happened. A panic attack. But those were for other people. She had read about such episodes with detached curiosity.

Why, Erica? Was it just the pregnancy? Or was she sensing a real aura of malevolence? Crazy, Erica. You are just allowing yourself to climb right up on that great diving board in the sky and jump off the deep end.

Seeing Meg would make the difference. A few days away and everything would be different, better.

It had to be.

CHAPTER

12

What had she expected? Jim was no magician who could wave his wand and make her apprehensions disappear. She had spent half the night staring at the ceiling, waiting for his office to open. When the receptionist managed an immediate appointment, Erica felt a flood of relief. After yesterday, and then a night of feverish anxiety, she needed some immediate reassurance. She could not wait for her meeting with Meg, not if she were to keep her sanity. And Jim Wellings seemed her only possible source of comfort.

But the conversation was going nowhere. Erica was struggling to maintain her composure, to face Jim across his cluttered desk as a calm, rational patient with valid concerns. She fought the urge to crumple and beg him to hold her like a frightened child. His words were so soft, measured. "Everything's just fine, Erica. Honestly, I'd tell you if I saw anything wrong."

Naturally he was trying to reassure her. Wasn't that part of his job? "I'm not a hypochondriac. In fact, I'm never sick. Please believe me. Something's not right. I can feel it."

He sighed but not without compassion. "I think . . . please don't take it the wrong way. But I think you're just reacting to the whole thing with your mother. And that's perfectly understandable . . ."

"My mother has nothing to do with it," she bristled. "And

I don't need you to play psychiatrist. If you refuse to take
me seriously, I'll just go elsewhere, get another opinion. I
have no intention of risking the baby's health . . . or mine."

"All right," he soothed. "I understand. Would you feel
better if we ran some tests? To make sure? There's never
any harm in being cautious."

She felt the anxiety ease a bit. "No. There's no harm in
that at all. That's all I had in mind."

"I'll have Connie schedule an ultrasound. Nothing to it
really. At this stage, we should be able to get a decent picture of the fetus and your pelvic structure. We can make
sure everything is going smoothly."

"Good. Fine. That's all I want to know." She was perched
like a homing bird on the edge of the chair opposite his
desk. Now she leaned back and released her death grip on
the arm rests.

Jim folded his hands and assumed the voice of reason.
"I hope so. I can understand your concerns about placenta
previa. And I won't kid you. You may have a predisposition
to the problem. The fact that your mother had it does in-
crease your chances slightly but we can handle it. You know
the incidence of death in childbirth is almost nonexistent
nowadays. It's way down even since your mother . . ."

"I told you this has nothing to do with my mother. Nothing at all."

"Okay, okay. I'm not saying it does. I just want you to
know about how safe childbirth is today. Practically the only
problems happen when the woman has had no prenatal care
at all. Or when there's no medical help at the delivery."

She frowned. "Are you trying to tell me there is no risk?
Are you saying it's impossible that something could go
wrong?"

"No . . . I'm not saying that. You wouldn't believe me if I
did. But the odds are one in a million against it."

"That's comforting for everybody but that poor millionth
person."

Jim locked her in a deep, meaningful look. "Believe me,

that's not going to be you. Besides, it's my job to do all necessary worrying. You don't have to bother with that at all."

"That's easy for you to say."

He closed her chart and placed it atop the pile on his desk. "No, it isn't." Hands folded like a penitent, he stared into her eyes. "Look, I'm sure you're fine. I'm trained to look for potential problems, trouble spots. If I saw anything out of the ordinary, anything at all, I'd always check it out immediately. But I also understand your anxiety. Most women worry at some point during a pregnancy. About the baby, themselves. It's natural. Especially in your case . . ."

"I am not a special case, Jim. And I am not a nut case. I've been having some troubling symptoms and I want them checked out. It's as simple as that." She liked the way she sounded, controlled, rational. Jim didn't need to know she lay awake at night, heart thumping like the tail of a demented beaver, mind racing from one hideous possibility to the next.

He peeked at her chart again and scribbled something on a pad. "I'm also going to prescribe a glucose tolerance test. You have been gaining quickly. It's probably nothing but we'll check to be absolutely sure. You fast for twelve hours, go to the lab, and they'll ask you to drink some pure sugar solution. Then, they'll take blood and urine every half hour for five hours to see how your body is handling sugar. Pregnancy can sometimes affect that."

Erica made a face. "Sounds like fun."

"It isn't. And you don't have to do it. This is on the side of super cautious. I told you . . ."

"I'll do it." She rose to leave. "I'm not crazy. I wish I could make you understand."

"Relax. You'll get the test done and you'll feel better. That'll be the end of it."

"Sure. I know it will." Her smile faded as she shut the door behind her. The pregnancy was troubling enough without these other symptoms. Every time she saw Jim

Wellings, she felt like a foolish adolescent with sweaty palms and a mouthful of cotton balls. Every time she looked into the deep, honest blue of his eyes, she felt a magnetic tug at her most vulnerable places.

This was no time for childish yearnings. Anyway, despite the long looks and occasional flashes of electric current between them, Jim Wellings could not possibly have any real interest in her, not under the circumstances. He was simply expressing professional concern. Anything more would be ridiculous to expect.

Anyway, romance was the last thing she needed at the moment. All she wanted from Jim Wellings was good medical care coupled with a little support and understanding. If only he could make her feel better, surer of things. But something told her the tests would not resolve the concerns rumbling in her gut. Only time could do that.

Watching Erica leave, Jim felt a familiar sinking sensation. He waited a few seconds and crossed the hall to his father's office. "You busy?"

"Nothing that can't wait. Come in."

John Wellings was a softer, thicker version of his son. His blue eyes were flecked with grey and weary, his hair thinned and topped with a puff of white like a dollop of whipped cream. He regarded his son with a look of pure affection and stifled a yawn. "I'm getting too old for all-night delivery sessions, my son. Before long I'm going to bow out of the obstetrical end and leave it all in your capable hands."

"Not so capable yet, old pal. In fact, I'm here to pick your experienced mind about a patient of mine—a disturbing patient."

Doctor John folded his weathered hands on his desk. "I'm all ears."

"Patient has a history of endometriosis, tipped uterus, scarring in the Fallopian tubes . . ."

"Infertility cases can be very frustrating."

Jim held up a hand. "Let me finish. Patient happens to

be pregnant. Surprise! Anyway, her mother died delivering her fourth child. Placenta previa following an unfortunate accident. From what I understand, the accident may or may not have contributed to the premature separation of the placenta but my patient has some understandable concerns about her own delivery."

"For starters, I'd have the husband in, Jim. Talking it out with everyone present seems to help, drives away the demons if you know what I mean."

Jim frowned. "Good idea, only impossible in this case. There is no husband."

Doctor John's frown matched his son's. "Hmmm. May I ask why this young lady decided to go ahead with the pregnancy . . . given the risks?"

"She had mixed feelings at first. But knowing how slim her chances are for future pregnancies, she decided to go through with it. I think . . ." He lowered his eyes. "I think I had something to do with discouraging an abortion . . . but now . . ."

"Now, nothing. What's done is done. The uterus feels normal?"

"Yes. Nothing unusual."

"No bleeding? Pain?"

"Nothing," Jim said. "Just some worries on her part. And mine. I admit to caring about this particular patient more than the textbooks say I should."

Doctor John scratched his head. "Unmarried and pregnant. Sounds like a lot to take on, my son."

"Don't start playing parent with me, Dad. I just came to seek some professional advice."

"No, you didn't. You came for a pat on the head when what you probably need is a good kick in the butt."

"Just tell me this story is going to have a happy ending. That's all."

Doctor John stood and placed a hand on his son's shoulder. "There are no guarantees, Jimmy my boy. You know that. All I can tell you is what you already know. You'll have to deliver at the first sign of a problem. Maybe a caesarean. So keep a close eye on your young lady."

"That will be my pleasure. Thanks."

Back in his own office, Jim slumped in his desk chair and tried to sweep his head clear of Erica Phillips. Her dark mood had rubbed off on him, left him open to all the insidious doubts he had been pushing out of his mind since he first met her. It took every ounce of his will to keep from racing after her and wrapping her in the warm circle of his protection. But he knew there was no real, foolproof protection.

The world was so full of grim possibilities.

CHAPTER

13

Erica stared through the filmy train window trying to forget her parting battle with Goody. She had planned to avoid any unpleasantness by leaving him a note, saying she was called away suddenly on a family emergency. But just as she was finishing breakfast, he appeared at the entrance to the dining room, his face contorted with anger, as if he somehow already knew about her plans.

"So formally dressed so early, my dear. Are you planning an excursion of some sort?"

Her luck. Goody was always locked in his studio at this time. "I . . . I have to go into New York for a couple of days. A family emergency. I left you a note, Goody. I didn't want to disturb you at work." The lie seemed to hover in the air like a nasty insect.

"Indeed. A family emergency? You should have come to me at once. I assure you any such difficulty can be managed without your inconvenience. We retain a prominent attorney in Manhattan, an excellent accountant. We have direct access to the finest medical facilities and practitioners. Whatever the problem, we shall be delighted to apply the full force of our resources to its immediate resolution. No need for you to make such an arduous journey in your condition. I will not entertain such a notion."

"Thanks for the offer, Goody, but I'm afraid this is something I have to take care of myself. I'll only be a couple of days."

His color deepened and his voice was strained. "That is quite unnecessary, my dear. Come now. I have only your best interests in mind. You mustn't be stubborn."

Erica yielded to a flash of anger. "I don't intend to debate with you, Goody. I'm sorry if you don't approve, but I am going. I am not your prisoner and you do not have the right to tell me where and when I can go!"

Startled by her response, Goody seemed to argue with himself for a few minutes, his mouth working in a nervous flutter. Then he set his face in a forced conciliatory grin and tapped his fingers together. "I see it's all settled then, my dear. Certainly you are free to attend your personal affairs in whatever manner you choose. If I gave you an erroneous impression, please accept my humblest apologies. I simply wished to spare you unnecessary labors. Please be assured Tessa and I wish you a successful journey and anxiously anticipate your return."

Leaving, Erica felt doubly satisfied. For once she had won a round with Goody.

Despite the boost from her minor victory and her eagerness to see her family, the train ride seemed endless. For several weeks, she had struggled with exhaustion, discomfort, a sense of being a reluctant stranger in her own body. She was all right, Jim kept assuring her. Everything had checked out and there was no reason to worry.

Convinced or not, she was glad she could make the trip. Seeing her brothers and sister would be a pleasant, necessary distraction. This reunion was coming at a perfect time. Meg arranged it after getting Erica's letter. It couldn't have worked out better, Meg assured her. Everyone just happened to be in town and available. Finally, a stroke of good fortune, Erica thought. Getting together was rarely so easy since their lives had pulled in such separate directions.

Having completed a doctorate in psychobiology—whatever that was—Jeff was working as a researcher and

Associate Professor at Stanford. Erica had worried about Jeffy the Giant Brain, a precocious child, speaking in sentences by the time he was a year old. Too rational, too serious and purposeful, she thought. Nothing childish about him. Jeff could no sooner giggle or engage in wild boyish mischief than fly without a plane. But he fooled her as they all did. He was a solid, three-dimensional man with a full-blown capacity for love and intimacy.

Michael's passion for photography had burgeoned into a successful career. As a little boy, he drove everyone crazy with his obsessive attachment to a Kodak Instamatic. He wore it all the time, hanging around his neck like a religious medal. At any moment, little Mikey was liable to pop out from behind a chair or under a table and immortalize your sublime moment of clumsiness or ugliness for all eternity. Instead of worrying that it was a sign of insecurity, Erica might have predicted that passion would lead to his current prominence as a free-lance photojournalist. His series in *Life* on the idle rich won him a Pulitzer. What pride Erica felt on seeing little Mikey's picture on the front page of the *Times*. And how incredible it seemed that, somehow, with all his endless travel, he managed to meet and marry a bright, delightful woman and father two priceless little boys.

Then there was Meg. Sweet, quiet little Meggy Muggins. Mouth corked by a chubby thumb. Eyes wide with wonder and apprehension. Meg was such a passive, lethargic little girl that it seemed she might never get around to growing up. When she was six years old, she still called Erica "Wicka" and wet the bed. The perennial baby of the family. Who would have imagined Meg, of all people, would turn into an attractive, dynamic lawyer who found her niche in politics? Local at first, then quickly up through the ranks to become a congressperson from Massachusetts, offices in Washngton and Boston, a growing collection of fawning followers. Rumor had it that Meg was being groomed for bigger and better things. Imagine, Senator Meg Phillips. President Meggy Muggins Phillips. What would that make her? First Big Sister?

Big certainly said it all. Erica shifted uncomfortably in her seat. Her body was bloated beyond recognition and she felt so ungainly even the most routine movements took conscious thought and planning.

She tried not to consider how the clan might react to the pregnancy. For some reason, she could not bring herself to tell them long distance. Since moving to Bramble Farm, she had spoken to everyone but Michael at least once. He was off doing a feature on African elephants. But she had not been able to find the right words. The last time, she had had a long, chatty, expensive conversation with Meg including a number of perfect openings: talk about lovers, her split with Brian, the ticking of their respective biological clocks. Several times, Erica opened her mouth, ready to say, "I'm pregnant, Meg" or "Guess what Meggy Muggins? Big sister is going to have a . . ." but the words stuck in her throat.

She glanced down at the broad swell of her belly, Wicka the whale. They certainly were in for a surprise. An enormous surprise. More than once, Erica had tried to imagine their reactions. Not that she was hoping for much: perfect, immediate understanding; acceptance; delight; support; a chorus of "Oh, Erica, how wonderful!" (Two-part harmony would do.)

In truth, she needed their approval more than she cared to admit, even to herself. Her decision to have the baby, leaving New York and her normal life, moving into Bramble Farm, all were done in an odd vacuum. If she were to be honest with herself, she didn't want anyone she knew, trusted and respected to challenge the wisdom of what she was doing. Not that being honest with herself would change anything.

The train chugged asthmatically through a soot-black tunnel and into the lower level of Grand Central Station. With the constipated squeal of the pneumatic brakes, Erica felt a chill of apprehension. The real world could be so difficult.

She made her way through the dense knot of people and climbed the station stairs, panting with the effort. The air was thick with humidity and the acrid poison of diesel fumes. By the time she reached the cavernous waiting room, beads of sweat stood out on her forehead and her pink sundress (courtesy Omar the tentmaker) was sticking to her back. She was always so warm now she couldn't face more sensible fall clothing no matter what the calendar and thermometer told her. Her feet were swollen and painful despite her purchase of shoes two sizes larger than usual, soft and formless as old slippers. Nervously, she clutched her purse and fiddled with the mood ring stuck on the puffed sausage of her index finger. Maybe they would be too shocked by her appearance to burden her with their unbearable sanity.

Jeff had made reservations. They were all staying overnight at the St. Moritz and Erica's instructions were to check in and meet in Jeff's room.

She walked out through the Pan Am Building and stood at the curb, her hand outstretched like Miss Liberty. Midday traffic was slow and cranky. By the time a sullen driver in a Checker cab stopped in front of her, Erica's hair was drenched with perspiration and she felt the first warning prickles of an incipient swoon. "Hang on, girl," she said.

"Whaddya say, lady? Where to?"

As the cab crawled through the clot of traffic, the driver puffed at a thick cigar and leaned heavily on his horn. Dizziness crept up Erica's legs, numbing them, and her head seemed to float above her distended body. By the time they arrived at the hotel on Central Park South, the city had dimmed to a soft, gentle haze. The cabbie turned to collect his fare. "That'll be three-eighty, Miss. Oh shit, lady. You look like a friggin' ghost. Don'cha go gettin' sick on me. That's all I need. Lissen, lady. Do your passing out someplace else wouldya? I'm a busy guy. I gotta family to feed."

Somehow, she managed to stumble out and into the hotel lobby. Warm, so warm. And the lights were too bright, as if someone had set fire to the ceiling. Her eyes refused to focus and she held on to a marble pillar for support. A few minutes to cool off, collect herself.

"Wicka? Is that you? What in hell have you done to yourself?"

Grateful, she slipped into the strong circle of Mikey's hug. "This is not something you do to yourself, little brother."

He stood back and squinted for better focus. "Pregnant! You're pregnant."

She laughed at the shocked droop of his face. "I always knew you had a keen eye. Who but a photographer would have figured that out?"

"You didn't tell me. Anyone. You didn't say a word." Michael was incredulous. "I don't understand."

"Why don't we go upstairs and I'll explain it to everyone at once. I don't know if I have the strength for more than one long story this afternoon."

Jeff had reserved two adjoining suites. Meg and Jeff were in one of the twin sitting rooms, sipping glasses of Jeff's favorite Beaujolais. When Erica walked in with Michael, Jeff choked on a mouthful and spat a crimson spray over himself and the furniture. "My God!"

Meg stared dumbfounded. Her head lolled from side to side in gentle, demented protest.

Michael sat with a plop in the armchair. "Surprise! We're all going to be an aunt and uncle. Don't worry, Wick. They'll recover in a week or two. Are you all right? You look . . ."

"I'm fine," Erica said. "I know. I look . . . what would Dad say? A bit peaked."

"I was going to say you look like the Goodyear blimp in drag."

"Exactly," Jeff said.

Meg started to giggle a bit hysterically. "It's not like you, Wick. It's like . . . you and you and you . . ."

"Very funny. All right. You three go ahead and make fun of a mother-to-be. Be as cruel and insensitive as you like. Far be it from me to spoil your fun. That's why I came, in fact. I've had no one to pick on me."

Meg bit her lip. "I'm sorry. It's just such a . . . shock, a surprise. Jesus, you didn't say a word. I call you and we talk about the weather, work, the state of the union, the price of stone-washed denim, for Chrissakes. And you neglect to mention the little fact of your pregnancy. I suppose it slipped your mind, little thing like that."

"Don't be angry. I . . . I don't know why I didn't tell you. The last few months have been so . . . strange, so foreign. It's as if someone else has been pulling the strings and things simply happen. I have to believe they're happening the way they're supposed to, that it's meant to be, that it's all going to turn out right." She bit her lip. Family had that way of reducing you to gelatin."

Meg gave her an awkward hug. "I'm sure it will, Wick. You've always been able to handle yourself. Look how much you took on when you were just a kid yourself . . ."

"Thanks, little sister. That's exactly what I need, two teaspoons of encouragement every four hours."

"Tablespoons," Jeff said. "Of course you'll be fine. Everything will. And Uncle Jeff will be available for routine or emergency service . . ."

"Ditto Uncle Mikey. I'll even throw in a free snapshot of the little tyke every so often. You're going to be a terrific mother. No question about it."

Erica flopped heavily into the armchair. It squealed in protest, touching off a flood of relieved laughter. "Soon they're going to assign me my own zip code," Erica said.

"I think," Michael managed between gasps, "I think we'd better get the Army Corps of Engineers to take a look at your infrastructure . . ."

Love, laughter, the trading of insults. This was the stuff of which families were made. Maybe it was a mistake to pull away, to leave them out of what her life had become.

Or maybe it had to be.

Michael seemed to read her mind. "How can we help, Wick? What can we do?"

"Nothing really. Just be there, knowing that is all the help

I need. Actually, this job came along at the perfect time. I'll
stay at Bramble Farm for a few more months . . . I'll need
that much time to finish editing this manuscript. Then, I'll
figure out something."

"Come to Boston," Meg said. "I'd love to have you close
by. You and the . . . baby. God, that sounds strange. I can
help you find a place, a job, whatever. You know your little
sister is a big influential deal now, Wicka."

"Go suck your thumb," Jeff said.

Michael frowned. "Did you say 'Bramble Farm'?"

"Yes, that's where I'm staying. Theresa Bricklin bought
the place with her new husband. They're spending a fortune
to fix it up. I understand it was really something."

"Funny," Michael said. "That one's not familiar. I
thought I knew every estate in Greenwich after that piece
on the uppercrust. Do you know who they bought it from?"

"No. Goody may have mentioned a name but I don't
think so. He just said the former owners let the place go to
seed and it was sold in a tax auction. I guess it wasn't in any
shape for a photo layout when you did your shoot."

"Maybe not but it's an interesting angle. I could see a
before-and-after piece on this Bramble place. Nothing fasci-
nates people more than how other people spend their
money. That and the Bricklin angle. If I remember cor-
rectly, she was quite the femme fatale."

Jeff's brain seemed to click audibly. "Wasn't she in a
Newsweek feature a couple of years ago? 'A Way With More
Than Words' I think the piece was called. They showed the
whole rogues' gallery of former lovers and husbands. I don't
know how she had the time or energy left to do any
writing."

"I love it," Michael said. "Can you get the owners to give
me permission for a shoot, Erica? Tell them what a tasteful
job I do. And tell them what a terrific guy I am."

She frowned. "I doubt it, Mike. I really do. Goody Hemphill has quite a privacy fetish. Anyway, he's not the easiest
soul to get along with, to say the least. The last thing I need

is to have him think I come equipped with a snoopy brother."

"But you do, Wick. That's the fact. And you know how curiosity can get the better of me. The shoot is liable to happen whether he okays it or not."

"Don't you dare!" Erica knew he was perfectly capable of doing just what he threatened. "Please promise me you won't do anything like that. Please."

Michael disappeared behind the black face of his Nikon. "Don't you worry, my dear. You know you can trust your little brother to use excellent judgment. Smile, Wick. Say 'cheese.' "

"Fuck you, Michael."

"Beautiful."

She would let the matter drop. Michael wouldn't be foolish enough to show up at Bramble Farm without permission. He was an adventurer but he had his fair share of sense.

Anyway, this visit was too precious to waste on foolish arguments. Erica had not felt this calm and normal since she first arrived at Bramble Farm. For two more days she would think of nothing but fun and family. She would put the book, Theresa Bricklin, Goody's moods and tempers and the Bramble Farm bogey man out of her weary mind.

Dwelling on all of it changed nothing. She had to go back and finish editing the manuscript and, though the thought started the chill terror creeping up her legs, she had to go back. So much was at stake.

"You all right, Wicka?" Michael said. "You look sort of pale all of a sudden."

"I'm fine, Michael." These were her foolish worries. And the future was too precious to spend running from fears of her own invention. She placed a protective hand on the solid puff of her middle.

The baby kicked. And was still.

CHAPTER

14

Bramble Farm was undergoing a long, labored metamorphosis. Plans from the landscape architect were taped along the oak-panelled den walls and bit by bit, the ground crews were converting the paper dream to reality. A single old artisan, working with tinsnips and a spool of plastic-coated wire, had nearly completed the topiary garden, fastening long ribbons of ivy to the wire armatures. A pair of proud elephants trumpeted toward a majestic fountain and a verdant eagle gazed skyward, its wings spread, poised for flight. The nude wire frame of a blinking owl awaited its leafy cloak and a proud Arabian stallion was frozen in midstride, its plush mane trailing on the wind. The work was slow, painstaking. Goody insisted on perfection. And perfection could not be rushed.

His spirits seemed to improve with the estate's condition. There was a perceptible spring in his lopsided gait and the corner seams of his mouth were drawn upward by invisible thread. Though he still clasped his hands when he spoke, it now seemed to be a gesture of delight, a child's joyful clapping, and not the tense prayerful clutching of a desperate man.

"Tessa is recuperating, my dear. The land is beginning to raise its head in pride, revelling in its return to glory. The sky hums in grand harmony. My heart is truly full." He turned in a slow, deliberate circle. "I hope you will forgive an old man his poetic maundering. I find myself quite over-whelmed with good fortune."

"No apologies necessary. I can't imagine a better way to feel. To be honest, I'm a little overwhelmed myself." With a sardonic smile, she patted the grand swell of her midsection, wondering for the hundredth time how this little being who had slipped in so effortlessly would ever manage to get back out.

He cleared his throat to ease the embarrassment. "Quite natural, my dear. Quite, I'm sure. The marvels of nature . . ."

Erica rearranged her bulk. Time seemed to drag on her. Three months left. She wondered how she would ever manage three more months. Lately, everything seemed a mountain of effort. There was no comfortable way to sit, to stand, no position for a restful sleep. And the dreams . . . She tried to contain her irritability. Condition or no condition, she was still an employee, a guest in this house.

"Nothing new?" Her catch phrase for news of the manuscript.

Something flickered across his expression. "No . . . not as yet. But I feel somehow closer, more confident than ever that the remaining chapters will be found in short order. We mustn't be impatient, my dear. Great works are priced dearly in the currency of time, but well worth the extravagance."

"What am I ever going to do without your philosophies, Goody?"

He stopped short. "I trust you are not considering a departure, Erica. We expect you to stay on after the infant's arrival. Bramble Farm is coming alive, rising from the ashes of malignant neglect to assume its proper place in the community's regard. Youth and vitality are essential components, my dear. Surely, you can see that!" His arm rose by degrees like a creaky drawbridge until his finger pointed at the sun.

"That's sweet of you to offer. But I can't stay here after the baby is born. My sister has been looking for a place for us in Boston. We'll go there for a few months, settle in. Then I can look for a job . . ."

"No! I won't hear of it." He pulled back and lowered his voice. "I mean, you must stay with us. We have plenty of space. Your child will have every advantage. You must promise to stay until the manuscript is completed. Please, Erica. Your debt of loyalty must be that substantial. I am certain Theresa's improvement is directly related to her interest in this manuscript."

"The manuscript has nothing to do with this, Goody. It's nearly finished. There might be two more chapters, maybe three. I'm not the issue here. When you find the rest of it, I'll be glad to finish. You can send it to me."

His voice was a low growl. "This book will not leave this property until it is completed. Completed! Anything less would be unthinkable."

"There's no point in discussing it now. You haven't found the rest. Maybe you never will . . . I was hoping to finish the book, of course. But I never imagined it would take this long. How can I stay on with a newborn infant?"

"You can. You must. So much depends on you. Don't you see?" He slumped in his chair and began to weep. Great gulps of anguish shook his body and broke in muted bursts against his cupped hands. His wig shifted slightly off-center.

Watching him, Erica felt an awkward stab of pity. Her stake in the manuscript was as substantial as his, maybe more so. But the thought of having her infant in this place . . .

"Let me think about it. Please. I'll do my best."

The sobs gradually abated. "We are counting on you, my dear. You have no idea how much we are counting on you, how essential you are."

Flumacher wheeled Theresa onto the terrace. She was perched at an odd angle in her chair. Listing to starboard, Erica thought.

"There's my darling. Isn't it a divine afternoon, Tessa? Perfect sky, perfect."

The old woman took a deep, hopeful breath and pushed the words with the weight of her head and chest. "Sinkugh . . . mmmm."

"Yes, dear. Clearing up indeed. Just the slightest wisp of cloud. What is the name for them—cumulus, is it? Cirrus? I always confuse the two. You see, Erica? My darling is much better, much easier to interpret, don't you think?"

Erica stared into the murky pool of Theresa's expression. "She looks well."

"My dear one is working so hard. I'm so proud of you, Tessa, so very proud of your efforts." He leaned down to kiss her powdered cheek and his wig slipped further off-center until it hung rakishly off to one side like an artist's beret, revealing patches of flaxen stubble. "Soon, my love. Soon you will be well."

The slack half of Theresa's face was drawn in a muscled grimace. "Kibbup. Slenurup . . . Fuck."

He smoothed the flaming mass of her hair, slowly, methodically. "Soon, it will all be made right. The mighty appetite of justice satiated at last, at long last."

"Arigh. Mmmupuh!" Theresa stiffened and fisted her good hand.

"I hope so," Erica said. "For Miss Bricklin's sake."

He flashed a peculiar look. "Each a vain beginning. Each a worthy end," he muttered.

"Interesting quote. I can't seem to place it . . ."

He waved her away. "You needn't try, my dear. I am quite capable of original thought now and then."

"I'm sure you are, Goody. I didn't mean . . ."

"Your excellent intentions can make one weary, exceedingly weary, Erica. Be so kind as to assume my capabilities and failed intentions will cease to be at issue." His lip curled in an angry sneer.

Erica bit back an urge to apologize. What had she done? She was sick of Goody's hairtrigger tempers, sick of having to tiptoe around his endless sensitivities. If only she could leave Bramble Farm. If only getting out of a trap was as easy as it was to enter. But the manuscript was so close to finished. How could she walk away? If only the rest could be found now. Before it was too late.

CHAPTER
15

Erica changed her dress for the fourth time and scowled again at her image in Hillary's framed mirror. From the side, she resembled a sloop in full sail. She could imagine herself at the restaurant, tacking toward the ladies' room. Head on, there was a garish expanse of teal-blue fabric, from which two pale scrawny, freckled arms and one fatigue-ridden face emerged. Deep circles ringed her eyes, her cheeks sunk in dark hollows. "Not a pretty picture, Erica. Not pretty at all." Almost out of choices, she looked in disgust at the heap of discarded dresses on the bed and returned to the closet for her green shirtwaist. Shirtwaist indeed, she thought. No shirt. No waist. Still, green was a perfect complement for the present state of her complexion, best described as a cross between sickly pallor and lying-in-state.

No big deal, Erica, she told herself. Why are you so worried about looking nice for Jim Wellings anyway? What's the difference? Just pretend you are off to the Macy's Thanksgiving Day parade. You could be one of the giant balloons.

Mrs. Ohringer's nasal whine crackled over the intercom. "Your young man is here, Miss Phillips. He wants to know are you ready?"

"In a minute." Bless the woman. She could always be

counted on to say precisely the wrong thing. *Your* young man, indeed. Jim Wellings was certainly not hers, though the possessive did have a certain appeal. He was simply being nice to her, friendly. She supposed he had a bad case of Mother Hen syndrome. Or he had his eye on some particular merit badge. She could imagine how he saw her predicament: poor Erica, unmarried, alone, pregnant, neurotic, built like a beached whale, plagued by a series of troubling symptoms. Sure, everything seemed to work out well. But as soon as one problem was resolved, another cropped up to take its place. She shuddered remembering the glucose tolerance test. The lab vampires sucking vial after vial of blood from her reluctant veins. "So sorry, Miss Phillips, but I'll have to try again. Your veins roll, you know. So hard to get at." As if it weren't enough that the test left her with sickly blue bruises all over her arms, she had to suffer the torment of waiting several days for the results. Negative, Jim's nurse assured. In medicine, even good news was presented in dismal terms.

And it didn't stop there. The latest scare was a round of premature contractions. She awoke one night and felt as if her abdomen had been inserted in a giant electric juicer. Horatio aching to greet the world. Erica had taken to calling the baby Horatio. Boy or girl, whatever, Horatio was better than "it." According to Jim, the pains were probably nothing, Braxton-Hicks contractions, he thought. But he tended to think with that worried expression on his face, his forehead crinkled, his eyes in that particular squint that made you think he was searching for some hidden solution to the problem.

She would ask for more tests. Just to make sure. No, she wasn't crazy. And she wasn't looking for trouble. She just wanted everything to turn out well. Who could fault her for that?

Jim was not unsympathetic. Nor could he be called uncaring. This was the eighth dinner in as many weeks. He usually called on some medical pretext. "I wanted to be sure

I told you to take two of the calcium tablets, Erica." "Yes, you told me." "Good, then. Oh, by the way, there's a new seafood place I've been meaning to try . . ."

Mother Hen syndrome. No doubt. Not that Erica minded. He was so genuine, so easy to be with. Nothing like Brian, she thought. There was none of the hype, the show biz energy, the stifling self-love. Jim would never sit across from her as Brian once did, mesmerized by his own reflection in the mirror behind her back.

"Your young man said to tell you not to hurry just because he happens to be starving to death and probably won't have enough energy left to drive to the restaurant, Miss Phillips. He says you can drive if he's unconscious by the time you get down here. So, not to hurry yourself."

She laughed. "Tell Doctor Wellings to leave his keys on the coffee table, just in case."

Jim had made reservations at The Gardens. They drove out onto the Post Road and through the Riverside Section into Old Greenwich. Past the manicured green with its ancient bandstand, they followed a long lazy winding street that led through the village to the Long Island Sound. The restaurant was at the foot of the street, tucked behind a busy marina. Enormous yachts were moored along the jetty. Several hearty sailors braved the autumn chill to take cocktails on their polished decks.

Jim and Erica sat side-by-side on a tapestried banquette at a window table overlooking the Sound. The table was set with a dusty pink cloth and a single spiky orchid in a crystal vase. A candle flickered in some unseen current. Erica was hypnotized by the view. A symphony of apartment lights played on the black gloss of the water. The sky had dimmed to grey flannel and a few intrepid stars twinkled between the billowing clouds. "How do you find such wonderful places, Jim? It's like a movie setting—so peaceful, lovely."

He sipped his wine and followed her gaze out the window. "It's not the place, Erica. Can't you see that? It's us."

She turned away and hoped the restaurant's dim light

would mask her flush. "Dr. Jekyll and Mrs. Wide, interesting pair we are indeed."

He put a hand over hers. "I'm serious, Erica. There's something special going on between us. I've felt it since you first came into my office."

An odd pulse was thumping in her head, making it hard to think to breathe. A giant fist punched at her abdomen. "Jim . . . I—"

"Ssh. Don't say anything unless you're going to tell me you feel it too. I've been trying to get up the nerve to tell you this for months. I care about you, Erica. A lot. I don't know what to call it but it feels serious."

Her mouth was blotting paper. "That makes no sense, Jim. Look at me. I'm like a giant balloon. And what about the baby?" As if on cue, she felt a flutter kick followed by another punch of pain.

"I like balloons and babies. It's perfect."

"It's not that simple. Nothing's that simple."

He pressed her trembling fingers to his lips. "If you feel the way I do, the rest will work out, Erica. That's the question here, the only question."

For some reason, she felt like crying. The pregnant crazies strike again, trial by hormone. She couldn't absorb the things Jim was saying, couldn't sort through her own fears and feelings. "I . . . I don't have easy answers, Jim. There's just too much going on, too much to consider. Now is just the wrong time."

"You say that like a condemned prisoner. I'm not going to rush you into anything." He fused her eyes with his. Deep honest blue eyes, eyes you could get lost in. "I'm not in a rush. You think about it. I'll be here."

Her belly knotted again, so tightly she could hardly breathe, then just as abruptly, relaxed. "I hope so, Jim. I think I may be in labor."

His expression darkened, then turned crisp and controlled. "Eleven weeks to go? Probably a false alarm but no point taking chances." He motioned for the check and guided her out of the restaurant. She relaxed in the firm grip of his authority, dismissing the fear that held her with frigid fingers. Too early. Way too early. The end could not be like this. Come on, Horatio. This isn't the time to play games, not after all this time, after all we've been through together.

On the way to the hospital, a dreadful scene kept playing in her mind. A pink, chubby baby swimming in a crystal pool. Streams of tiny bubbles rising gaily to the surface. Feathers of fine blonde curl framing the round, toothless face. A pleasure gurgle, a baby laugh. Erica reaching out, her fingers straining, aching. Then the cold. And the darkness. Sudden solid darkness. Her hand stopped. Dead. Useless.

Jim held her hand as he drove, squeezed reassuringly when she whimpered. The sound rose from somewhere in her gut, some place she could not control. Part of her had been taken over by unseen forces of pain and fear. Several times, her belly rose in an iron mound, clenched like a giant furious fist, then collapsed in relieved exhaustion. "Will I lose it? Will the baby be . . . ."

"Don't worry. Just try to relax. Take deep breaths."

She tried to mimic the exaggerated rhythms of his breathing. The cords seemed to unwind for an instant, then panic gripped her again and she gasped for air. "Why now? What did I do wrong?"

"Nothing. You did nothing wrong at all. Everything is going to be all right. Please . . . try to relax." He placed his open palm on her abdomen and made slow, soothing circles. "Ssh."

The emergency entrance was a garish flame in the ebony sky. Jim pulled up under the canopy and helped her through the automatic doors and into the fluorescent glare of the lobby. He retrieved a wheelchair from behind the reception desk. "Just relax . . . relax." It was a chant, almost hypnotic. The warm weight of his hand was on hers. She tried to focus on that.

Time was behaving strangely, racing by as if pursued. The polished floor tiles seemed to undulate as the nurse wheeled her to a labor room. She shivered at the sight of the mechanical bed, its slatted sides raised like a giant crib. She was lifted and positioned, gowned and poked with needles. Firecrackers seared the dull surface of her brain. A round of crisp explosions. Then blackness crept over her like a shroud.

And she slept.

CHAPTER

16

She awoke to a fuzzy haze and the dull aftermath of drugged sleep. Without thinking, she felt for the taut mound of her abdomen and smiled when she found it intact. Horatio kicked her hand for emphasis. "Good little whatever you are. Some nerve you had scaring me like that."

"You're up. Welcome back, Sleeping Beauty." Jim was sitting on a chair at her side. He looked rumpled and weary.

"If that's your diagnosis, I'd like a second opinion." Her tongue was a soggy towel. "Thank you. You saved the baby."

"The labor hadn't gone anywhere, Erica. We used some medication." He nodded at the IV still dripping into her splinted arm. "I think you can go to full term if you take it easy."

Her eyes filled with tears. "I thought it was over. Finished."

"I suspect Horatio will be around to provide you with a full mother's share of aggravation. Don't you worry."

She turned away. "What do I have to do? Stay in bed?"

"Just for a couple of days. I'd like you to stay here so I can keep an eye on you. Then you can go back to Bramble Farm but I want you to be as lazy as possible."

"No pole vaulting? No trampoline? Come on, doctor. What am I going to do to keep busy?"

"I'm sure you'll think of something, Miss Phillips. I know pole vaulting is your life but . . ."

"I was planning to go to Boston next weekend. My sister, Meg, made some plans, some places she wants me to see."

"No travelling, Erica. You need to rest. And close medical supervision. Just in case. No travelling. It would be asking for trouble."

"When will I be able to move? I mean, I wouldn't be doing any of the actual work myself. I promise."

A flicker of pain crossed his expression. "I didn't know you'd be moving."

"I meant to tell you, Jim. Meg's been looking for an apartment for me. In Boston, I'll have my sister. She can help me out for a while. With the baby and all, it'll be easier if I'm near family."

He took her hand. "What about an adoptive family—like me?"

She turned to him. His eyes were charcoal-rimmed with weariness. "I can't think about that now. I just can't. It wouldn't be fair to either of us."

"I'm sorry. I know I promised not to pressure you." He pressed his lips to her forehead. "But I don't want you to leave. That wouldn't give us a chance."

"Is that why the ban on travel?"

"No." He looked hurt. "I would never do anything so underhanded." He smiled ruefully. "Maybe if I had been clever enough to think of it. But, no, it's a medical necessity, not a personal preference. Here, we can stay on top of things. Make sure you get the proper treatment if anything is necessary. The baby could survive at this point, technically, but the odds aren't good. I have to be honest with you."

"You don't have to be that honest." She bit her lip. "I'll do whatever you say."

"I wish you would."

She smiled at him. Her mouth felt dry and dull. A blunt hammer banged against her temple. "Maybe not everything.

I don't know. I don't want to confuse one feeling for another. I've already made more than my quota of mistakes."

"There's always room for one more risk."

"I don't know." Sleep was pushing her down against the pillow. "Thank you, Jim. Thanks for helping me and Horatio."

He watched her lids droop like a theatre curtain. The soft rhythms of sleep overtook her. "Not yet. Don't thank me yet."

When she first returned to Bramble Farm, Goody smothered her with care and attention. Erica was under strict orders to stay in bed until nine, when Mrs. Ohringer appeared with a breakfast tray. On Goody's instructions, Mrs. Oh was to spare Erica even the mildest exertion. She stayed to fold the morning paper to the section of Erica's choice, butter her toast, and pour her coffee from the ceramic pitcher.

"You lissen to Mr. Hemphill, you'd think pregnancy was some kinda disease or something. Imagine how he'd feel if he saw those peasant women who drop their babies in the field. When the time comes, just plop and back to work. No big deal when you let nature have its way. You know, when I had my Lynnie, I worked till the ninth month. Then I only stayed home to scrub and paint the spare room for the baby. Did the whole thing myself, even the ceiling . . . the ninth month. It was better, believe me. There was no one to wait on me, I'll tell you. Philly was working two shifts then. I didn't have time for problems."

"Goody's just concerned, I guess," Erica said. "He wants everything to turn out all right."

"Pain in the butt, if you ask me. Can't wait for him to get back to normal. Thank heavens for his precious studio. At least there he's out of the way, him and his precious paintings and his precious horses. Treats those dumb animals better than children he does. You know what he feeds them? Real people food. Steaks, lamb chops. Takes stuff from the table, he does. Doesn't know I see him. Hay ain't good

enough for those fancy nags, I suppose. Probably make
them sick with all that rich food. Then he'll be sorry."

Mrs. Oh's tongue often ran yards ahead of her brain.
Other times, there seemed to be no tongue-brain link whatsoever. The mouth just went on and on, like a leaky faucet.
Out of necessity, Erica had learned how to tune her down
until she was a picture without the sound. "He has his own
ideas about things. That's all," Erica said absently.

After breakfast, the woman finally left her in peace and
she got up to dress. There were just a few shapeless shifts
that still fit. She had planned to shop for more maternity
clothing before the latest scare. Not that it mattered. She
hardly went anywhere these days. In her enforced laziness,
she was the self-appointed inflatable ghost of Bramble
Farm.

At this point, the editing was tedious, painstaking work.
Erica used Theresa's extensive library to check the historical tidbits that set the novel. In her standard manner, she
kept voluminous notes to trace the course of events and in-
sure congruence and flow. Though the central character was
a woman alone in a nearly bare room, a rich riot of events
filtered through her perceptions. The spare setting was a
remarkable literary device. By contrast, the thunder of
thoughts and recollections was even more dramatic. Again
and again, the story captivated her and she read through it,
wanting to know the end, wanting the end to match the
promise of the beginning.

Extending the longest finger of my soul to the
wrenching, meager limits of its influence, I can touch
the blood-black edge of the horror. Horror reflected in
the face of innocence. Innocence scarred and left to its
mutant remains. All are caught, good and evil alike, in
the mindless claws of destruction. Caught with them, I
weep my foolish tears. His best amusement.

Tomorrow he will come and poise his anger in mortal threat over my failing energies. Then, only then will

I yield the words, starved to bone of heart and substance. The thought—nothing but blind, mad imagin-
ings. My offerings have come to this, rotted bits of
putrid flesh, slim revolting morsels of my final decay.
Never enough. Never enough to satisfy and send him
off to other, more lively appetites. I pray for the end. I
pray for the madness to seek its necessary annihilation.

Goody appeared in triumph one morning and handed
Erica another chapter. It was clean and crisp as a newly
minted bill. "Under my easel, Erica. Remarkable, don't you
think? I tipped the frame for better light and there it was,
wrapped in bright foil paper like a birthday gift. Astonishing
what lengths my darling went to in pursuit of security."

She flipped through the pages. "It has to be close to the
end, Goody. There can't be more than another chapter or
two. I can feel it."

"I have the same conviction, my dear. Truly exhilarating,
don't you think? Soon, the world will have a new work of
Theresa Bricklin's. Remarkable, is it not? Even as she recu-
perates, her genius is glowing with the health and vitality of
a growing child."

"Did you check everywhere in your studio? You've found
so much of the book there. Maybe there's more."

"Of course I have investigated thoroughly. I only missed
this one because it was secreted in so clever a fashion. I can
assure you there is nothing else I have overlooked. I imagine the remaining chapters are somewhere in the house. It
is the vastness of the hiding place that makes the treasure
so elusive, my dear. And patience so imperative."

"I'm afraid I'm not a very patient soul. Especially now."
She rubbed at the persistent ache in her lower back. "You
know, it's amazing that we've found the chapters nearly in
order."

He shook his head in firm agreement. "Isn't it intriguing
you should mention that! I have devoted quite a bit of
thought to that perplexity myself. And I can only speculate

that Tessa planned it that way. Somehow, she possessed prescient knowledge of my actions. And she hid the chapters in some preplanned order. A few were found out of sequence . . . but . . ."

"Maybe it's just dumb luck."

"I do not believe in luck, my dear. Luck is a fool's excuse that stands between the self and its best destiny. All things of value are by design."

Horatio's foot danced against a rib, then scurried across her abdomen. "Sometimes the design is hard to see."

"Blindness can often be cured by simply opening the eyes, my dear."

She clutched the latest pages against the sore swell of her bosom. "I think I'll get started on these right away, Goody. Please excuse me."

"Of course. I am ever so pleased to see the order of your priorities remains constant. The work, the book must come first, above everything."

Erica walked toward the study. Goody's gaze seemed to burn in her back. That mirrored stare, so distant and unyielding. Under her weight, the floor creaked in gentle protest. It was the sound, she thought, of shifting priorities.

CHAPTER

17

Erica was lost in her work when Mrs. Oh came to get her for the call. "Long distance," she said gravely. "Never like getting one of those calls where the operator says your name and all. Scares me, if you want to know. I always figure it has to be something real serious or who would spend the money for person to person. When I call my mother, you know, for Christmas, Mother's Day, or whatever, I wait till after eleven. You get thirty, forty percent off that way. We like to have a nice chat, catch up on things. Thirty percent makes a big difference, I'll tell you."

Mrs. Oh followed her down the hall, babbling nonstop. "Once my Cousin Bertie called me, must've been nine, ten in the morning. I knew right away something had to be real wrong. Bertie's always been tight as a clam, you know the type. When my Lynnie was born, Bertie took one of her Peter's old pram suits, dyed it pink and tried to pass if off as new. Did you ever hear of such nerve? I said to her, Bertie, you can't take it with you. Shrouds don't come with pockets, I told her. And there's no savings and loans in heaven or wherever they send the cheapskates . . ."

She took the call in the parlor.

"Erica?"

"Michael? Is that you? You sound a million miles away."

"Close. I'm in Zimbabwe."

"Come on. That's not a real place. At least, not a place anyone really goes."

"It's not exactly a hotbed of tourism. But I'm here. At least, that's what I'm told."

"All right. I believe you. But why are you calling? Is something wrong?"

"No . . . nothing. I mean, I just wanted to check in, see how you're doing."

"You called from the dark side of the moon to have a little chat? To check on my health? Do you expect me to believe that?"

He sounded sheepish. "I was hoping you would. Really, it's nothing. I was talking with L.C. Kipness last night. You remember L.C. He's the reporter who worked with me on the idle rich piece. Anyway, L.C. agrees that the place you're staying would be a terrific shoot. When I described it to him he was ready to hop on his elephant and ride right over. Did you, by any chance, ask for permission?"

"I told you, Mike. It's useless. Goody would never agree and the suggestion would probably make him furious. He's a privacy nut. Forget about it, will you?"

"I'll try."

"You don't sound convincing. Not convincing at all. Be reasonable, Michael. You will only succeed in making things uncomfortable for me."

"You know I wouldn't do anything like that. But the place intrigues me. I can't help it, Wicka. I was born curious and stubborn. L.C. can't remember a place named Bramble Farm either. Funny that neither of us would remember. He even checked through his notes for the *Life* piece. Nothing."

"Listen, Mikey. Your sleuth imitations are a pain in the ass. Big estates like Bramble Farm are a dime a dozen in Green Witch. Besides, I told you, the place was in no shape to pose for pictures when you were in the area."

"We still would have heard of it. Greenwich may have its share of estates but L.C. is thorough. They must have changed the name or something, which is funny in itself unless there was a reason . . ."

A sharp pulse was jabbing at her temples but she kept her voice even, offhanded. "Everything's a big mystery to you, Michael. If they changed the name, I'm sure it was for some really sordid reason like Goody or Theresa didn't like the original name. There's no big mystery here. Poor Theresa is old and feeble, suffering from the results of a bad stroke. And Goody is . . . well, Goody. Strange but harmless." Yes, strange was an understatement, but she was not about to pass along to Sherlock Phillips. He would use any excuse to appear on the scene with his shutter cocked.

"I don't know, Wicka. For some reason, I can't get the place out of my mind. It's just a feeling I have, a feeling that there's a story there. A terrific story. Besides, I don't like the way you sound. It's almost as if you're afraid of something."

"Mikey, I don't think that Zimbabwe place agrees with you. Why don't you wrap things up and come home?"

"Soon, Wicka. You take care."

"I'll try." Her bravado faltered as she hung up. Family was nice and all but she worried more than enough without their help. The calls were constant, relentless. Meg, Jeff, Michael, Michael's wife Kathy, Dad and Monika. Even Mel Underwood had escalated his calls from once a month to once, and then several, times a week. Yes, it was nice to have all that love and interest, but she couldn't help thinking they might all have some real reason to worry.

She was relying more and more on Jim's reassurances. He came to see her every few days after work. At first, she protested. "Doctors don't make house calls any more. Haven't you heard?"

"It's no big deal. I live right near here."

"Where?"

"Right up the road—twenty, thirty miles tops."

Despite herself, she always looked forward to Jim's visits, watched for the silver snub nose of his antique MG. She spent most days in the house, dividing her time between work and aimless worry. Her attention wandered and she had to force her eyes to stick to the words she was trying to read. Though she had vowed to postpone her feelings and confusion about Jim, it was not easy to do.

Anticipating his next visit, Erica was feeling more anxious than ever. But when Jim arrived, flushed with fresh air and reality, she felt better, saner. Goody grudgingly allowed them their privacy in the solarium and they took their now familiar places. Erica on the flowered chintz sofa, Jim perched opposite on the edge of the matching chaise.

He looked around at the cluttered shelves, the ancient faded photographs lining the walls. "Bramble Farm is such a funny place," he said finally.

"What do you mean?"

"I can't explain it exactly. It's as if the past is still here, not just in things and pictures, if you know what I mean. It's more a feeling." He shrugged.

"I think I understand," she said, trying to sound only mildly interested. "There is something unusual about Bramble Farm. I've felt it myself from time to time. Silly superstition, I guess."

"Maybe. Or an infestation of negative ions . . . or ghoulies and ghosties. I could imagine a vampire movie set right over there in the parlor. They wouldn't even have to change the furniture." He looked around and shook his head at the dingy upholstery, the odd puddles of shadow cast by dim and dying lights. With all the work and expense, Bramble Farm still had a long way to go. "You know if this place makes you uncomfortable, I can think of a nice young doctor who'd be willing to take you in." He took her hand in his and she gently disengaged herself.

"No pressure, Jim. Remember."

"Sometimes, I forget. I plead guilty." His eyes tugged at her. "You know, Erica, I thought it was a terrible mistake coming here. I thought I would suffocate working in Small-town, Connecticut. I was ready to tell my father to forget the whole arrangement, son or no son, I wasn't cut out for this. Then, I met you . . . Do you believe in fate?"

"Is that a trick question?"

"Probably." The way he had of staring into her eyes made her feel open, vulnerable. He stood and stepped away from her as if it were hard to do. Slowly, he scanned the rows of faded sepia photos in dainty tarnished silver frames. "Looks like Hemphill or Miss Bricklin had quite a collection of relatives."

She shrugged. "Actually, I don't think either of them has any family to speak of." As far as she knew, Mark and Sharon Bloomway were Theresa's only living relatives. And Goody said he had no one but Theresa.

"Then I guess all these belonged to the people who lived here before. Nice-looking. Funny to think of all these fresh-faced, athletic types growing old and dying."

"Pleasant thought," Erica said joining him at the row of portraits. A fashionable young matron in a prim nautical maternity blouse smiled back at her. Her hair was sculpted in a modified flapper haircut. "I prefer to wonder which ones went together and how they survived without microwaves and cable television. And then I wonder if my picture will ever hang in obscurity on some stranger's wall. Or whether anything will be left of me after . . ." She sat down again.

"Pleasant thought." He knelt beside her chair and laid his head in her lap like a little child. "Life is so unpredictable. I wonder if we really have any control at all."

"We probably have as much as we want," Erica said. "Sometimes it's easier to drift. At least . . . it's easier until you hit a rock."

The door squeaked open and Flumacher tipped his craggy face into the room. He wheeled Theresa in front of him and he held a note covered with Goody's dramatic scrawl.

Erica read it aloud. "It says, 'Tessa wishes to spend some time in the solarium. I trust you two will not mind her charming company.'" Erica nodded at Flumacher, who seemed to cower behind the chair. "It's all right. We're glad to have her with us." Smiling, she turned to Jim. "Goody must think we need a chaperone. And I suspect he may be right."

"Hello, Miss Bricklin. It's nice to see you."

"Ingill . . . aagh . . . upp!" She strained so her entire body stiffened and her face flushed crimson.

"It's okay, Miss Bricklin. You relax. How are you feeling today?"

"She can't answer you."

"I just wanted to see if there's anything . . . any response. These conditions aren't black and white. There may be some automatic speech left. Some way for her to communicate."

"Arup . . . shit!" She smacked her lips.

"Goody believes she's getting better. You should hear him, interpreting, trying to figure out what she's saying. It makes me want to cry."

Jim stood and walked closer to Theresa. "Miss Bricklin, can you say, one . . . two . . . three?"

She stared at his mouth and pursed her lips. "Pedjurik . . . sikup."

"Can you sing, 'Happy birthday to . . .'"

Theresa released a loud, disgusted sigh, like a balloon spewing air. And belched for emphasis.

Jim shrugged. "I'm not the expert, mind you. But I don't see much potential for communication. Why don't I talk it over with one of the neurologists at the hospital? Maybe there's something that can be done, even now."

"I hope it's not too late," Erica said. "Such talent shouldn't be silenced. It's a crime."

"I hope it's not too late also. For a lot of things."

The baby kicked a reminder. If only, Erica thought. But there was no going back. No doing things over in a different way. She pulled her eyes away from Jim and looked at Theresa. How must she feel about her dreadful condition? What was worse than being locked inside the iron gates of a paralyzed mind? Thinking of Theresa's plight, Erica chided herself on railing against her own petty predicaments. She peered into the clouded eyes, the light of genius dimmed to a pitiful flicker. Then, staring beyond the defeat and frustration, she could see something else. A look of desperation, Erica thought. And fear.

CHAPTER

18

Erica sat in the plump leather desk chair, staring at the manuscript, wishing she could somehow creep beneath the words. She kept going over the process Mel taught her when she started at Prescott. "For the best authors, the work must be approached like an archaeological dig. Every grain, every layer is lifted, examined. The digging is slow and methodical so that no minor treasure is destroyed the way it might be if you used a bulldozer. Never take short-cuts, Erica. That's the trap a good editor can fall into."

At that point in the lecture, Mel's thick fingers plucked a felt-tipped pen from the metal cylinder on his desk and he began doodling. To Erica's amazement, he structured a de-tailed map, roads and rivers with tributaries fine as insect legs, plateaus and mountain ranges rising in majestic minia-ture. The form of an imaginary world took shape on the white blotter lining his desktop. In finale, he drew a con-vincing anatomical model of a brain, complete with striated grey matter. "This is the author, the significant part of the author anyway. You have to learn how to get at this, see if there's any current flowing or if the thing is dead. It can be, you know. The battery just runs dry after a while. Happens more often than you'd imagine."

Then, he travelled the length of the map in a crisp red line. At the other end, he drew the hind end of a horse.

"And this is my portrait of the average editor." He looked up at Erica, his dachshund eyes sober and earnest. "I don't expect you to be anything near average."

Grinning, she remembered the scene. Mel was the perfect teacher, as demanding of himself as he was of Erica. Demanding but gentle, respectful under the gruff exterior. He was the father she wished she had. Her own ran from unpleasantness and confrontation. The motto of the Phillips house was "I don't care to discuss it." "Good morning" could be too unpleasant for Dad.

"Not that you're much better, girlie," she told herself aloud. Her voice echoed eerily in the cavernous study. She was no amateur when it came to avoidance. The whole situation with Jim was a perfect example. Inaction. Why couldn't she bring herself to end it? To tell him it wasn't right for either of them? Logically, she needed time to adjust to motherhood, single motherhood. She was in no position to make a sane commitment to Jim or anyone. The baby was enough, more than enough for her to deal with for a while. Yes, he was warm and open and appealing. Yes, she enjoyed his company, found herself reacting to his touch, his presence, matching his adolescent yearnings with some pretty powerful ones of her own. But she was not inclined to trust her own feelings. Look where that trick had gotten her.

Horatio cuffed her in protest. "Ssh, don't take it personally. I'm glad about you . . . I think."

She forced her attention back to the manuscript. Perfect editing wasn't the only thing at stake here. Goody kept reminding her to check for clues on locating the final chapters. "The information is in the prose, my dear. That was Tessa's procedure."

Try as she did, she could not find a hint. No location clues. Nothing to indicate a point of search. Frustrating. The closest she got was a prickling sense of uneasiness, some vague incongruity she could not pinpoint. She read the manuscript again and again hoping it would come to her.

The young man stands before me, guilt drenching his form like the sweat of exertion. "So, old woman. Get on with it. Your threats are jokes without humor and I am getting tired. Sick and tired of them. And you."

I try to reach him with words or desperate gropings but that was never possible. He flits away from the gentle quilt of love like a rootless insect, driven by inner need. In the face of love he is too warm and prone to suffocation. Too oppressed by the seeking hands of connection. A serpentine boy. Not human in any real sense.

At times, when there is strength to be frittered on such a luxury as prayer, I implore the fates to deliver me from his indelicate grasp. And I am sent on a journey past light and substance for a deceptive moment. But the evil is the only real element in my life. And the only chance for escape is the flight of words. The story is unravelled bit by bit in the unyielding fabric of words. I am nearing the end.

Can I do something of value? Can I move the next victim to run before time completes its bloody mischief? If words can work that magic, then all is not lost.

She was interrupted by Goody's butterfly knock.

"Erica, my dear. You are laboring far too long and hard. I insist you join Tessa and myself for lunch. I have asked Flumacher to serve us in the parlor beside a roaring fire. A special indulgence, quite cozy and restful you'll find."

Rising with difficulty, Erica winced at the persistent pain in her back. "I accept your insistence, Goody. I wasn't getting anywhere this morning."

"Now, now, my dear. One mustn't be impatient. I trust completely in the ultimate triumph of your worthy efforts."

They walked in awkward synchrony, Erica's waddle tuned to Goody's labored gait. "It's so difficult without the rest of the manuscript. I still think . . ." She hesitated, knowing she was about to jump head first into familiar quicksand. "I still think we should conduct a search, a systematic search."

His body stiffened and taut strings pulled at his face. Erica could imagine him without his omnipresent sunglasses, eyes flashing fury. "I am quite aware of your feelings on this subject, Erica. You have not reserved your opinions. However, I must remain adamant. I will not have my things invaded, my privacy reduced to rubble. I will not permit strange hands and eyes to rape and pillage! Do you understand?"

She sighed. Fool, you knew you wouldn't get anywhere. Old argument, old conclusion. "We could do it together, Goody. Just you and me, a room at a time." For some reason, she could not give it up.

"You are a lovely child, Erica, but I fear your stubborn nature will serve you ill." His voice was a rubber band, stretched to the point of rupture. "I am afraid I must include you when I speak of strange hands. I don't wish to offend, but you are new to my life, relatively speaking. The history imbued in my possessions spans centuries, generations. My ancestors! The very core of my being! I will not hear another word on the subject, is that clear?" Again, he assumed the pose of a ranting professor, finger raised skyward, the universe his witness.

"All right. I'm sorry. It's just so frustrating. I only have a little time left, Goody. So little time."

"The infant will not change a thing, Erica. You'll see. You will have the remainder of the manuscript in time, in due time."

Due time, good pun. Horatio seemed to be doing intermediate gymnastics as she walked. Limbs flailing against her insides like a windmill. "I hope so."

The parlor lights were dimmed and Goody motioned Erica to sit beside Theresa on the flowered Victorian loveseat. Her wheelchair was folded and tucked in the corner. "Hello, Miss Bricklin. How are you feeling?" The heavy

drapes were drawn, shutting out the daylight. And eager
flames licked the blackened side walls of the fireplace. Erica
half expected someone to pull out the roasting marshmal-
lows and start telling ghost stories. They ate in near silence.
"This is pleasant, Goody. You were right."

The firelight danced in the reflective circles of his eye-
glasses. "I'm delighted you find it so. We did so hope to find
the perfect setting. Shall we tell her, Tessa?" His lips pursed
in a gleeful smile. "Tessa and I have arranged a bit of a
surprise for you, my dear. Would you like to see it?"

She shook her head, not sure at all.

"Good, then. Come, Tessa." He opened her chair and
placed it beside the love seat. He tugged and strained
against Theresa's impassive form until she slid over to the
wheelchair.

Erica raced to keep up with them as he pushed Theresa
through the maze of dim corridors, bumped her rudely up
the intruding stairs, and stopped finally in front of a room at
the end of Erica's corridor. A pale yellow porcelain plaque,
lettered in fine italic, proclaimed this the "Child of Eternity" room.

Goody flashed a mischievous smile, took hold of the ornate brass doorhandle, and flung the door open with a dramatic flourish.

The breath caught in Erica's throat. The Child of Eternity. She remembered the story well. A child born to impov-
erished migrant workers during a severe storm. The infant's
first wail lost in a murderous clap of thunder. At the depths
of the workers' despair this child is born—a tragic, un-
wanted child.

The family mourns. How will they feed the baby? How
will they survive? The infant suckles at his mother's parched
breast as the storm destroys their wagon, kills their animals.
With nature's final fit of destruction they are left in total
desolation and hopelessness.

Then, the owner of the enormous property they are working rides by. His wife has had several miscarriages, includ-

ing one just a few days before. She seems on the verge of insanity and he will pay dearly for a child. The infant is sold to him and installed in a great house in the most opulent nursery imaginable. A nursery like the one Goody had decorated. Erica's flesh was crawling.

"It's . . . it's—"

"I know, my dear. It's quite overwhelming. I'm so pleased you find it so. We went to great lengths, didn't we, Tessa? But then, any child of yours is worthy of such extravagance."

Erica couldn't respond. He looked so pleased with himself. Didn't he know? No, he couldn't. It was all a stupid mistake.

"The crib was crafted by an artisan in Chicago. That is genuine mother-of-pearl, my dear. And the comforter was hand-tatted in Brazil. No expense was spared, I assure you."

"I can imagine," she managed. It had to be a stupid mistake. For some reason, Goody didn't know, hadn't read the book.

"You see, Tessa. You see! I knew she'd be overwhelmed. Virtually speechless, aren't you, Erica? Tessa was concerned you might wish to pick the baby's things yourself but I assured her a person of your obvious literary tastes would welcome such a tribute. The *Child of Eternity*. Such a marvelous work."

"You . . . you read it?"

"Certainly, my dear. I have naturally read all of dear Tessa's books again and again. Your infant will surely be as gifted and grand."

Erica shivered and hugged herself to still the tremor. It was all a terrible, foolish mistake.

She could not consider the alternatives.

CHAPTER
19

At odd moments, Bramble Farm lapsed into a blessed state of tranquility; a napping infant on a stormy afternoon; a breath of cool relief from a virulent heatwave. There was that particular stillness this morning played against the soft rhythms of routine. Mrs. Oh's dance of spray, polish, sweep, and mumble; Flumacher's slow, aimless pacing; Chopin's piano nocturnes played on some brilliant piano over Goody's Victrola. Erica's self-imposed assignment was to catch up on the world events that had slipped further and further away in recent weeks, leaving her to float in a sea of self-absorption. She sank into the cushioned comfort of a glove-leather easy chair and leafed through a huge pile of accumulated newspapers and magazines, her eyes drawn to the ads for infant furnishings and pictures of lithe, lovely models whose bodies had all those miraculous valleys and bones. Bones were one of those things you took for granted until they were reduced to a poignant memory. Looking down at the rolling swells of her body, she wondered if her bones would ever find their way back to the surface.

When the doorbell rang, she wished Flumacher would simply ignore it and go on about his mindless patrol. The balance was too right to disturb; the peace hung on too slight a foundation. Instead, he made his way across the marble foyer, opened the door and allowed the light and trouble to enter.

The visitor was a tiny, stooped, ageless man in a dark flannel suit that hung on his bony frame like a drape. He held a folded document in his outstretched hand. "Goodwin Hemphill?"

Flumacher shook his head and pointed in Goody's direction. The man walked to the parlor in abbreviated rodent steps. "Mr. Hemphill? For you." He held out the papers. His hand was trembling with a palsy of fright.

Before Hemphill's brow reached its pinnacle, the visitor had retreated, backing quickly down the long foyer and out to his battered Buick like a film run in reverse.

"Bad news?" Erica said.

Hemphill held the document toward her. "I am too distressed to read it myself, Erica. Would you be so kind?"

She took the papers with reluctance, remembering the ancient tradition of shooting the messenger who came bearing ill tidings. "It says . . . if you don't mind me skipping all the wherefores and parties-of-the-first-parts, it's a petition for guardianship. Mark Bloomway wants to be put in charge of Theresa's person and property. There's going to be a hearing at the probate court to decide who would act in her best interests."

Goody gasped in disbelief and began muttering under his breath. "Absurd! Vile, vicious little creature! I could never understand how a lovely woman like my darling Tessa might be related to such a revolting sloth. That dreadful cur. He has gone too far this time, Erica. Entirely too far!"

"I'm sure the whole thing can be worked out, Goody. Try not to be too upset."

Hemphill took the document from Erica, crumpled it in a furious fist and tossed it on the cocktail table. "That pusillanimous creature intends to harass me with all manner of foolish legal maneuver. Vicious blood-sucking toad!"

Erica suppressed a nervous giggle. Goody's rage was building, thickening the air. "I'm sure your lawyer can handle it."

"Thus far, it has been foolish little annoyances, vain challenges to my obvious rights. Now he seems intent on parading our family differences in public. Can you imagine such audacity? He wants his coarse fingers implanted in Tessa's financial affairs. Audacious twit. Avaricious mongrel. Vile, vicious . . ."

"Take it easy, Goody. I know it's a nuisance. But you don't need to make yourself sick over it. The court will surely recognize what Bloomway is trying to do. They'll rule in your favor and that will be the end of it."

Hemphill paced the parlor floor, his leather soles slapping unevenly at the polished boards. "That cur will not have his way. I will not be dragged through a humiliating string of futile procedures! I will not have my personal enterprise dissected and scrutinized by overbearing bureaucrats!"

Erica dropped her tone to a chant of gentle reason. "Why don't you speak to your lawyer? I'm sure this can all be taken care of without a lot of fuss."

"I will not be forced to participate in this churlish charade! This is beyond all human limits!" He crossed to the antique wall phone and dialed. As Erica watched, a thick curtain of control dropped over his expression. By the time Bloomway answered, Goody's voice was smooth as cream. "Mark? Goodwin Hemphill here . . . Yes, I was duly served, as it is said . . . As you might imagine, I was rather dismayed by such an action . . . I can assure you that your aunt's affairs are being managed with every consideration for her present and future well-being . . . Yes, I see . . . Groundless, I assure you, Mark . . . If only you had discussed it with me first . . . We are family, after all. And small disagreements aside, there is certainly no need to pursue this matter through tedious, expensive legal channels. In fact, I was hoping you might be available to discuss this on a personal level. Why don't you bring your dear wife to dinner and we shall endeavor to find a mutually satisfactory solution . . ."

Goody held the phone away from his ear and Erica heard

snatches of Bloomway's diatribe, shouted loudly enough to
be audible where she stood.

"Sonavabitch . . . I'll see your ass in court . . . I got nothing to say to you, you goddamn golddigger. We got nothing
to discuss, buddy. Nothing . . ."

Goody's fingers tightened to claws on the ebony throat of
the receiver. Finally, he cradled the instrument and turned
back to the room. "Shall we have a spot of sherry before
dinner, Erica? I'm certain a small indulgence every so often
would be acceptable."

"Sure. I guess so." His feigned control was even more
unsettling than the open fits of fury. "Is everything . . ."

"Sherry for you, Tessa dear?" He poured from the cut-
crystal decanter on the Regency sideboard, his hand
trembling.

Erica bit back her wisdoms and curiosities. This was one
of those subjects better left alone.

Hemphill drank greedily, filling his glass again and again
until the knots of rage began to ease. His voice fell back to
a normal pitch and the pulsing cords in his neck receded.
He slumped in the armchair. "My latest work is proceeding
quite smoothly, Erica. Before long, I shall be able to move
ahead with broader plans." His speech was getting fuzzy,
his head lolling slightly off center.

"That's wonderful. You know, I'd be delighted to see your
painting . . . when you're ready, that is." She seemed always
to be walking on tiptoe around the minefield of his temper.

"Yes, my dear. Of course. You have been most patient. All
things in time, in due course." He yawned expansively.
"And your work? How is that progressing? I have been in
contact with your Mr. Underwood. He assures me that
Prescott Press would be most interested in publishing the
manuscript when you have completed your editing."

"I'm sure they'd do a wonderful job with it. You couldn't
find a better publishing house." Erica's loyalty to Prescott
was firm as ever. For an instant, she could picture herself
back behind her desk, back in the real world where she

could find her way without groping through a maze of dark secrets. Maybe some day. "I'm sure you'll be delighted with what they do. And I'll be happy to work with Mel, or whoever he assigns."

"His plans for this work are rather ambitious. He speaks of a hundred thousand first printing, a seven-figure paperback sale, serializations in several major publications, main book club selections, a sizable promotion effort, of course. He has had a number of exceptional offers based on nothing more than the rumor of the book's existence. And I assure you your efforts will be suitably rewarded in the financial realm. Tessa and I intend to provide you with a percentage of the proceeds."

"You don't have to do anything like that," Erica said. Without permission, her brain was busy calculating the enormity of the offer.

"Don't be a foolish child, Erica. You will need a cushion of monetary support to care for your infant. And your loyalty must be suitably repaid. We will not have it any other way."

Erica looked at Theresa in her wheelchair, the blank expression, the awkward tilt of her head. "It only matters . . . *if* we find the rest of the manuscript."

"When, my dear. Not 'if.' We are approaching the grand conclusion of our respective efforts. Rest assured. I know it as a certainty." He stretched and shook his head as if to clear it. Then he rose and stood beside Theresa, petting the crimson cloud of her hair. "How we shall rejoice when justice is done, my darling. Final justice."

Erica shivered. Her anxieties were building like a child's block house, level on level of black suspicions. The nursery, Hemphill, the shrill night sounds, Bramble Farm itself were tightening around her throat, suffocating her. She hadn't made it official yet, but she had decided to go to Boston after all. She would leave right after the baby was born. Jim, Theresa, the manuscript, all of that aside, she needed her own space and distance. A few private conversations with Meg convinced her even further. This was not the right time for outside commitments.

"And your health, my dear? The grand event is what? Five weeks off?"

"Six."

"Six weeks. Six weeks might be a snap of fate's fingers or the long, slow crafting of a shift in nature's course. Fascinating."

"If only we could find more of the manuscript, Goody. I feel like someone put me on hold and the Muzak is giving me a headache."

"In this case, Erica, the end will surely justify the enduring."

"Yes, I hope so."

"You have my assurance, my firmest assurance."

Erica shook her head without conviction. For some reason, Hemphill's "firmest" assurances were not much comfort. "Things will turn out the way they're supposed to, the way they're meant to be."

"Yes, they will at long last."

A poison menace had seeped into his tone. And she wondered once again what had filled him with so much simmering anger. Hemphill was such an odd mass of contradictions.

She did not want to be around if he were ever pushed too far.

CHAPTER

20

Goody's brief absence seemed to tip Bramble Farm off center. In such a circumscribed world, the smallest change in normal routine was unsettling, even his overnight excursion to New York to "tend to some rather pressing affairs."

Erica had kept her curiosities in check. And Goody volunteered nothing beyond vague explanations. "Something I must see to personally though I do so hate to leave Tessa and venture into the crowds and filth of that wretched plague of urban unrest. Still," he sighed, "obligations beckon that simply cannot be ignored."

She watched him leave, dressed in a drab grey pinstriped suit, a stiff white shirt and a rep tie in the place of his customary ascot. An undersized straw boater made him look Chaplinesque.

As he placed his plaid suitcase in the Bentley's rear seat, she tried to imagine him doing business in New York, joining the hordes of numb, self-concerned jostlers on the street, making his way through the clots of pedestrian traffic and darting across the streets where terrified tourists and numb cabbies played their real-life version of bumper cars. Beyond his occasional evenings out and local shopping forays, Erica had never known Goody to go anywhere. He spoke at length about his former life as a well-travelled importer, but none of that ever struck Erica as real or relevant.

Goody Hemphill belonged at Bramble Farm, limping along its bowered paths, painting his mysterious masterworks in the tack room, prodding and overseeing and venting his baseless tempers.

She had dinner in the dining room with Theresa. They sat opposite each other at the gleaming banquet table, separated by a delicate arrangement of spiky pink cymbidium orchids and an ornate silver candelabra. Erica conducted a nervous monologue to fill the silence while Theresa made clumsy attempts to feed herself.

"So, as I was saying, I keep thinking about the Grey Lady, as you call her, and why she doesn't just pick up and leave that room. You don't make her an actual prisoner, no real bonds or chains or anything like that. And the door may or may not be locked but one would think she'd do something. Bang on the walls, scream, do something to try to escape. Instead, she sits there, eats what she's given, which, by the way, seems like pretty fancy fare for a prisoner. And, she struggles with herself over some undefined obligations.

"I keep thinking that if it were me, I'd do something, bang at the walls until my hands were raw, scream until my voice quit. What would make someone just sit and take it? Just do the work she is required to do and put up with such a dreadful situation? It seems to go against the basic human drive for survival. There has to be a reason, an explanation. If only you could tell me . . ."

Erica chewed slowly on a piece of grilled chicken. "Let's suppose the Grey Lady is an actual prisoner. And let's suppose she's being held by something far more subtle than ropes. So she's in the room because she cannot leave. If she does, what? Maybe the room is wired to explode. No, that's not Theresa Bricklin's style. What . . . Will you please tell me?"

Theresa was chewing a mouthful of nothing. Erica reached across the table and held a heaping mound of creamed potatoes to the crinkled lips. Without thinking, she opened her mouth in encouragement, closed and chewed

along with the old woman. "Maybe the Grey Lady is cata-
tonic. Now, that would be more in the Bricklin manner. A
prisoner of her own sick mind. Interesting. Suppose she was
hauled to this cell or room or whatever by a sadistic guard
at the mental hospital. She's stuck in this awful mental
prison, the most helpless of slaves, unable to do anything to
save herself. God, Miss Bricklin, you have a fiendish imagination."

Watching the twisted face, the vacant expression, it was
difficult to believe a vital mind had ever operated beneath
the froth of red hair. Erica fed her a large bite of chicken.
"I have an idea, Miss Bricklin. You eat up and after dinner
you and I are going on little treasure hunt."

Crazy. Even as the idea surfaced, she knew it was crazy.
But it was worth a try. No harm would be done. With Goody
gone, this was the perfect opportunity, possibly the only
chance she would have. Maybe, just maybe, Theresa remembered where the manuscript was hidden. What had
Jim said? These things aren't black or white. Some function
might remain. In Theresa's case, why couldn't it be that particular memory?

"It'll be our little secret. Just a little harmless secret."

The idea lifted Erica's spirits. A harmless little search.
Think how pleased Goody would be if she found the remaining chapters. He wouldn't be angry about her snooping
then. At the thought of his discovery, a fist of fear punched
her in the stomach. Silly, he wouldn't be angry if she found
the chapters. He'd be delighted. Anyway, if the search was
fruitless, he would never even know about it. How could
he?

She dawdled over coffee until Mrs. Oh was finished with
the dishes and stood in the doorway wiping her thick, pink
hands on the skirt of her apron. "If you're all set, I'll take
Miss Bricklin up and get on home. Philly's playing poker
with the boys tonight and I promised myself a long, hot
soak. My back's been acting up again. I get these spasms,
you know. Feels like I'm being wrung out like a wet towel.

Or like somebody's kicking me with those football shoes on. Real pain in the ass, I'll tell you."

"You go on home, Mrs. Oh. I'll take Miss Bricklin up later. She can keep me company."

"You sure? She weighs a ton, you know. More than she looks for sure. Dead weight, you know. Like a sack of potatoes. Don't want you hurting yourself. Mr. Hemphill would have my head for sure."

"I'll manage. Don't worry."

"Whatever you say, honey. You're a big girl." Covering her mouth, she giggled. "Big girl, get it?"

"Yes, Mrs. Oh. I get it. Very funny."

She waited impatiently for the door to slam, the retreating clump of Mrs. Ohringer's feet on the stone walk, the steady drone of her voice as she continued her relentless monologue for the shadows. ". . . Another day another dollar, Lorraine. Wonder if Lynnie put up the meat loaf like I told her. Girl'd forget her head if it wasn't screwed on. I could always do with a grilled cheese, I suppose. And a little of the boob tube. Wonder what's on tonight. Never a thing to watch, I swear it . . ." The sounds grew fainter as she disappeared down the drive.

Theresa's plate was nearly empty. Erica wiped the traces of food from the corners of the old woman's mouth. "Ready, Miss Bricklin? Good. Let's see what we can find." She wheeled the chair out of the dining room and stopped in the center of the foyer. "Now you show me where to go." Erica stared into the murky eyes. A flicker, a sign. Please. "How about the parlor? Those corner cabinets would be a perfect hiding place, all those tempting little drawers and cubbies." No sign, not a blink. "All right. We'll start there."

She pulled open drawer after drawer. Nothing. Coasters, stacks of embroidered linen napkins, a humidor packed with stale tobacco, a pair of rimless spectacles, pens and pencils in an orderly row.

The living room was next. She rummaged through drawers and cabinets that held nothing more exciting than ancient board games: Parcheesi, Chinese Checkers, Go to the Head of the Class. There were decks of gilt-edged playing cards, tins and boxes of dinner mints and filled chocolates. What, she thought, was Goody so secretive about? His taste for cream centers?

Weary. Frustrated. She knelt with difficulty in front of Theresa's chair and looked directly into the cob-webbed eyes. "Please. If you know something, please tell me."

A flutter, nothing more. At first, Erica thought it was her imagination, the strength of wishes. "Miss Bricklin?"

Again, the flutter. An eyebrow raised and lowered. Nothing monumental, Erica told herself. Probably a meaningless tic. "Are you . . . are you trying to tell me something?"

She held her breath and watched. There it was. Effort. The set of concentration and the eyebrow tugged upward. A tiny lift at first. Then a triumphant arc and the slack half of Theresa's face registered a satisfied smile. Erica's heart thumped like a dog's tail. She spoke with care, afraid to frighten the miracle away. "Miss Bricklin. If you understand, lift once."

The brow arched. Firmly this time. And drooped back in place. "Can you help me find the rest of the manuscript? Do you remember where you put it?" She held her breath. Please!

Nothing.

"Please try. It's so important. You have to try!" She winced at the childish whine in her voice.

Theresa seemed to recoil. "Angukuh . . . picka."

"Ssh . . . I'm sorry. Let's take it easy. All right? If you know where the manuscript is, raise your eyebrow."

Again nothing. "All right. Let's try something else . . . A code. How would that be? One lift means yes, two means no. Got that?"

Slowly, the brow lifted. Erica smiled and shook her head. "Yes, yes! That's it. Now. Where should I look next? The music room?" Nothing. "The library?" Almost imperceptible at first. Patience, Erica. Yes, the arch was forming. There it was.

She wheeled Theresa to the library and scanned the endless rows of possibilities. A dull feeling of helplessness crept over her. Every book was a potential hiding place, the desk, the closets that lined the rear wall. So many places to look. Too many. Begin, she ordered herself. Somewhere. Anywhere.

She began plodding through the packed shelves, a volume at a time. Knowing nothing of Goody's reading tastes, she was working without a clue. If a book were the hiding place, it would be one that Goody was likely to read. But she had no idea which one of the vast number that might be. In truth, she had never seen Goody read anything. What might he like? Mystery, adventure, biography? Impossible, unpredictable man.

"Please, Miss Bricklin. Give me a hint, will you. I could be at this all night." All year.

The old woman had drifted off to sleep, her head bobbling on a frail shoulder, her breathing labored. Even at rest, her arm was stuck in flag-pledging position and half her face registered surprise. Erica shook her gently. "Miss Bricklin, Theresa . . . wake up."

One dim eye peeked from under a wrinkled lid, then drooped shut again. "Wake up. Please." But it was useless. The grip of sleep was stronger than Erica's will. "Shit, as you would say, Miss Bricklin. Anguk, shit."

She left Theresa snoring in light rhythm and returned to her search, extracting each volume in turn from its place, shaking it to dislodge any hidden snips of information, skimming quickly through the pages. Theresa, it seemed, was in the habit of scribbling messages to herself in the margins as she did her research. Erica rubbed the fatigue from her eyes as she skimmed the notes in the author's firm hand. Fascinating reading for another time, she thought. The woman's brilliant mind laid bare in scribbled snippets of thought. But nothing about missing chapters. Hiding places. Not a clue.

Numb with weariness, Erica forced herself to continue. So many books. So many possible hiding places.

Her back was throbbing and her shoes pinched her swollen feet. She carried another stack of books to the desk and sank gratefully into the cool leather chair. Propping her feet on the edge of the polished wood desk, she leafed through the volumes in turn. One was an ancient family album full of smiling strangers. Mr. and Mrs. Perfect and little Priscilla Perfect. Mrs. Perfect in the advanced stages of a perfect pregnancy, oozing health and righteousness. A virgin birth no doubt.

Several times Erica paused to shake off the fog of exhaustion closing in on her. Dreams danced at the edge of her mind. Driving with Jim in his convertible. A soft summer breeze ruffling her hair like an affectionate parent. His firm fingers woven into hers. His warmth spreading through her, filling her.

"Stop it, Erica!" she rebuked herself aloud, startling herself back to attention. "Wake up!"

The bottom volume caught her eye. It was a thick tome with yellowed pages, entitled *Fundamentals of Obstetrical Practice*. The bindings were crackling dry with disuse and several pages came loose as she scanned the index. Cold prickles of dread crept up her arms as she flipped to the right section. This wasn't wise, she knew, but she had never been burdened by an excess of wisdom. Twenty years of blind denial had not diminished her morbid curiosity.

There was an entire chapter on placenta previa. She read greedily, her mind ice clear with horror. And the words were twisted into a vivid scene by her imagination. All more alive than reality. She could hear the cries of pain. The wrenching, stabbing pain. And the blood. Sweet, sticky rivers of warm crimson, pulsing from her mother's helpless body. The infant stuggling loose, caught, drowning.

Bile rose in Erica's throat as she read, powerless to tear herself from the sickening images. She could see the delivery room—the splattered blood on the cold white walls; the sharp antiseptic smell made her eyes water. The doctors' shocked faces pressed against the cold window of her mind, slackjawed behind the masks. Eyes clouded with fright and impotence.

Then the birth. She could see the doctors with their frozen metal tongs, pulling at the drowning infant. Wrenching her from the bloody horror, filling her tiny lungs with precious bits of air. The meek, little coughs. Tiny breaths of life. Hope.

And then turning back. Knowing it was too late. Watching the last pulses of life seep away in dense puddles of blood. Listening to her mother's pitiful cries for help, her wretched pleas for life. Then the gurgles of death. The choking. The dread, final silence.

Erica felt the wracking sobs rising from some deep, lost place in her gut. Rising and rising to break over her in violent waves of pain. On and on it went, lashing at her, tossing her with the power of years of stored fury and fear.

It was all her fault. She had always known the fault was hers. She was responsible for the so-called accident; the shocked, defeated look on her mother's face, the dreadful end to her own childhood.

And somehow, in the worst possible way, she would be made to pay.

CHAPTER

21

Goody found a wicker-wrapped bottle of cheap Chianti in the refrigerator and a thick glass tumbler on the rubber drying rack beside the sink. The kitchen was narrow, its faded yellow walls stained with oil splatters and smudged fingerprints. Scraggly plants were suspended from the ceiling by garish chains, and a motley array of dull pots and tarnished copper molds were nailed to the walls in no particular order. Cooking smells clung to the frilled curtains—stewed onions, cabbage, and tomatoes. Goody winced as the scents assaulted his pounding head.

The wine was sweet and heavy with tannin and preservatives. Tossing his head back, he took it down like medicine and chased away the aftertaste with a swig of lukewarm tap water. "Revolting swill," he spat. "Poisonous rot."

Still trembling, he groped through the cabinets, hoping to discover a decent whiskey or, better yet, a fine Cognac stored for some special occasion. He found nothing but cheap, glazed stoneware; packages of paper plates; tinny mismatched flatware; stiff plastic placemats; and a huge collection of sugar and condiment packets stolen, no doubt, from some vile dispensary of fast foods. When the final cabinet yielded nothing more promising than folded brown paper bags and cleaning supplies, he poured another tumblerful of wine and left the kitchen in disgust.

With no sense of haste or urgency, he walked around the apartment. From the tiny entrance hall with its miniscule closet, he strode through the main room. Furnished in an unfortunate blend of shabby brown corduroys and garish pink cut velvets, the place was reminiscent of the sleazy bordello Goody had once visited. He shook his head and shuddered, remembering.

Young, frightfully innocent, sheltered from all but a few censored, literary accounts of worldly pleasures, he sought a proper place for his initiation to the wonders of the flesh.

After several solitary evenings at a local tavern, he made the acquaintance of a rather coarse, burly young man with the unlikely name of Rip. During their brief ensuing discussion, Rip somehow gleaned Goody's predicament and recommended him to one "Madame Charlotte's," a large pearl grey Victorian mansion near the center of town.

"You want tail? Charlotte's got long, short, fat, you name it. And she's not a bad old broad herself. Keeps her girls clean, if you catch my meaning." Rip smiled broadly and winked a rheumy eye at Goody, who had only the vaguest notion of his companion's reference, though he intended to appear experienced and sophisticated at all costs.

With some trepidation, Goody secured the necessary funds from his savings, dressed with utmost care in a deep blue sport coat, grey flannel trousers and a woven blue sport shirt purchased for the occasion, and set out for Madame Charlotte's early the following evening. He was greeted at the door by a rotund woman with red circles for cheeks and dim eyes set in smudged black shadows like a raccoon's. She spoke through a thick wad of cherry-flavored gum as her eyes walked in lazy amusement down Goody's trembling body. "So, honey. What can we do for you today?"

Goody felt an ancient, almost forgotten stammer tightening around his throat. He took several careful breaths, as the stern, impatient therapist had taught him, before trying to speak. "I . . . I. A Mmm . . . Mr. Rip Mangese suggested I visit."

"You looking for love, honey? 'Cause you sure came to the right place." She gestured expansively. "Madame Charlotte's love palace, I call it. Everything a body could ever want. Not bad, huh? I inherited the house from a rich uncle. He thought it would be a great place to raise a bunch of kids. Imagine how he'd roll over if he saw what I was raising." She brushed her hand lightly over the fly front of his trousers and he recoiled in embarrassment.

She ushered him into the drawing room where several young women sat in varying states of undress. Goody tried to swallow back the terror as he searched in vain for a neutral place to fix his gaze. A heavy woman in a sheer, red negligee was smoking a long brown cigarette. A tall, cadaverous brunette clad in nothing but bikini pants and a push-up bra waggled a teasing finger at him.

Madame Charlotte laid a proprietary arm across his shoulders. "Take your pick, honey. You come early, you get the pick of the litter. We get twenty for a straight screw, everything else is a la carte. Ten for a blow job, fifteen extra for a head to tail. Like that. You got any kinks? We can accommodate most anything except rough stuff. Last week one of my best girls got a fat lip and a coupla broken ribs. Poor thing will be on injured reserve for a month or two. Cost us both a bundle. Can't have that."

Goody felt hot color rise in his cheeks. "I . . . I . . ."

"There now, honey. Take your time. Don't get excited."

"I . . . uh . . ." He struggled to breathe but a taut, choking screech escaped him instead. "I . . . ack . . ."

One of the girls started to giggle, a polite little snicker buried in the palm of her manicured hand. Madame Charlotte raised a finger in rebuke. "Now, Cissy, be nice. Don't make fun of our . . ." But the sentence dissolved in a fit of laughter that spread to the others. Hysterical laughter. Lunatic laughter. Thrown at him like thick lumps of stinking humiliation.

"Ssssstop it!" he screamed. But they only laughed harder. A circle of smeared hysterical faces. Like animals.

He raced out slamming his fury against the polished door. Raced until the breath burned his chest and the weak muscles in his bad leg tore in sharp, agonizing shreds. Raced until he came at last to the cottage where he could shut out the world and rest in the comforting litter of his own life.

Now he shook off the memory and surveyed the meager contents of the apartment. Lamps with dime store shades. Cheap Mediterranean furniture in garish wood veneer. A stack of tattered magazines and potboilers with bent pages. In the dining alcove, the congealed remains of a Chinese take-out dinner spilled from paper cartons.

"Such a pity you two were not able to finish your elegant repast," he clucked. He sipped again at the wine. The warmth was beginning to penetrate the tense chill he always felt at such times. When the glass was empty, he filled it with the remaining Chianti. Then he crossed to the corduroy lounge and sat to admire his work.

The Bloomways might have been posing for a Norman Rockwell cover. Mark was sitting erect, his head settled against the soiled lace doily on the sofa cushion. His wife was beside him, one arm raised in an unfinished gesture of defense, the other resting lightly on her husband's knee. Though he saw them in dim silhouette, Goody could imagine the expressions. Mouths wide with idiotic grimaces of silent protest, eyes bulging in mock surprise from the shock and terror . . .

The Chianti was beginning to improve. "A breath of air, perhaps?" he mused. "The sediment settled? No matter. Not the ideal means to quench a proper thirst but better than nothing. One must make do."

He rose stiffly and crossed to the couple. "There now," he said lowering Sharon's stiffening hand and smoothing Mark's rumpled hair back from his furrowed brow. "I trust you enjoyed your cocktails as well, my dear niece and nephew."

Enjoying his little joke, Goody returned to his chair, crossed his legs and folded his hands. Their cocktails indeed. A gift of fine aged Scotch laced with cyanide. Those greedy boors had drunk their deadly fill with no prodding whatsoever. "How I shall enjoy reading the reports of your untimely demise. If only the police were more cunning. If only they were possessed with the vaguest hint of human intelligence the game would be a bracing challenge. As it is, I shall of need be content with what small amusement I am able to derive from their bumbling incompetence." He sighed and retrieved his glass from the dusty end table. "No doubt they will conclude this was a murder-suicide. The husband poisoned the wife, then himself. Or vice versa. Whatever those boorish oafs find more plausible and convenient. Throats bruised in the mild ensuing struggle. Case closed.

"It is frightful, when you consider it, that our safety and well-being rest in the hands of such unimaginative dolts. Don't you find it so, Mark? Sharon? Do you not shudder at our vulnerability in the face of such inadequate security?

"My dear Tessa does so enjoy feeling safe and protected. We have undertaken a rather ambitious security plan for Bramble Farm. Have I described it to you? No? An oversight to be sure. Then I know how you two dear people do worry over the smallest expenditure. Understandably, I am most reluctant to share our plans when they concern a financial outlay.

"No matter. What is important is that dear Tessa and I have that which we deem necessary to our own comforts. Surely you two can appreciate that posture. One has only to observe the care you have taken to structure your own surroundings." He chuckled again at his wit and patted the worn corduroy chair with a gloved hand. "Such elegance. Such impeccable taste. I am truly overwhelmed."

Mark's head slipped from the sofa back and hung at a precarious angle. Wearily Goody crossed to the couch again and propped the head back in place against the lace doily. "Now I would be most appreciative if you would maintain that position for just a few more moments until nature comes to your assistance. Rigor mortis shall soon arrive to ease the rigors of mortality." It was most critical for the couple to be in a pose that reflected the precise balance of despair and unity when the police discovered the bodies. Mark's head began to drift again and Goody punched a depression in the back of the sofa to hold him upright. "Always the bother, weren't you, my dear nephew?"

Goody stood back, squinted, and cocked his head like an artist studying a finished canvas. Satisfied, he slumped back in the easy chair. "So you see, Mark, I am rather in your debt after all. Were it not for your audacity and avarice, I might have borne the burden of your tiresome existence indefinitely. You were Tessa's kin, so to speak, her only living relative. I had no serious intention of depriving my darling of her sole link to a dubious posterity. You were a petty annoyance, at first. Prying as you did. Insinuating yourself in the private crevices of our existence. But we bear a great deal in the name of family, do we not?"

He drank again and felt a welcome numbness creep up his legs to replace the tension. "More than you can imagine, my dear nephew. More than you will ever have the misfortune to know."

Weariness was pressing him back against the dense cushions. He raised his legs onto the plump ottoman and closed his eyes. "Tessa, though Lord knows she has her faults, is angelic when compared to some. Tessa has her talent, her contribution to make. Tessa's gifts are negotiable in the currency of fame, fortune, power. She has the means to repay her debt to the right child of justice."

Goody was alert now. Anger had set him on the edge of his chair. "Far, far more than can be said for either of you. What gifts have you? The gift of intrusion? Of vulgarity? Of coarseness and rudeness?" Goody lifted his arms overhead like a zealous evangelist and raised his gaze to the cracked ceiling. "I commend these vulgar souls to you, oh glorious judge of all undertakings. Oh righteous guardian of the balance of destiny. May they suffer the eternal torment of your omnipotent wrath!"

He settled back again, his rage spent. "Now then. I have fulfilled my noble purpose. Justice is satisfied, her voracious appetite quelled for the moment. In death, you finally meet your fit destiny. Nothing to nothingness. Trash to trash."

His eyes drifted closed again. "A noble cause, nobly dispatched." Then, he remembered the final obligation. The last moment was always the same. He extracted the tiny automatic camera from his breast pocket, cocked the shutter and immortalized his dear ones on film. Later, he would develop the images himself, enlarge them to near lifesize, a fitting addition to his memorial. Shutting his eyes against the flash, he took several more pictures to be certain. Failed opportunities lay like hazardous shards of broken glass to tear at the human spirit.

Finished, he put the camera away, refreshed himself with a splash of cool water from the sink, and felt for the proper placement of his wig. He detested the pale stubble, all that remained of his hair after years of forced shaving. Another indignity to repay.

"So my dear niece and nephew. I must bid you farewell. In just a short while, the shops will close and I do so wish to return with gifts for the dear members of my little household. Some small tokens to commemorate this grand event. A tribute to the complete success of my noble undertaking. I trust you will not suffer for my departure. I trust you shall not suffer earthly discomforts ever again. You may thank me for that, dear ones."

Crossing the room, Goody straightened his tie and retrieved his straw boater from the hat rack. He pressed the center of the door knob to set the lock and let himself out of the apartment. The hall was deserted and he hummed a gay tune as he pressed a gloved finger on the elevator button.

Things were going rather well.

CHAPTER

22

Erica had fallen asleep beside Theresa's chair on the parlor lounge. Stiff and sore, she rubbed her eyes against the stubborn fog of fatigue and ran her tongue over the grainy surfaces of her teeth. "You okay, Miss Bricklin?" She felt more than a little guilty for allowing the old woman to sleep sitting up, bent and cramped. Gently, she massaged the stiffness from Theresa's joints and stretched her limbs the way she had seen Goody do it, with slow insistence.

"Garg . . . bennip," Theresa whimpered. "Arugh . . . iguk."

"Am I hurting you? Oh, Miss Bricklin, I'm so sorry. I don't know what got into me with all that craziness last night." Her mother's death. No, she wouldn't think about that any more. Better to keep those horrors locked away and forgotten. Nothing could be changed, nothing done a different way. She could only look ahead. Hope for the best.

She hauled herself up and helped Theresa into the bathroom to wash. Mrs. Ohringer was not in the kitchen yet. Ten to eight. Mrs. Oh would appear at eight sharp. Erica put the copper kettle on for tea.

"I'm sorry. Really I am. I don't know what got into me, dragging you around like that, badgering you. I just wanted to find the rest of the manuscript. There's so little time left. Do you understand?"

"Emm . . . emmup." The eyebrow shot up. Firm. No hesitation now. The old woman allowed a twisted smirk.

"That's still with us. Good. We can communicate, can't we? You understand that I was foolish, tearing through things like that? I didn't mean to let you spend the night in the chair. Does anything hurt?"

Slowly, Theresa uncurled the fingers of her good hand and pointed at her knee. "Muck shhish . . . kip."

"You want me to rub it? There, is that better?"

The brow arched in answer.

Erica was still massaging the limp knee when Mrs. Ohringer's key clacked in the back door.

"Morning, you two. Early birds today, both of you. Brr . . . chilly out, a little foggy still. Supposed to be a gorgeous day, gorgeous they said on the news. What do they know anyway? Want to know the weather? Ask me. When my back acts up—cold. When it's my neck—rain. Sure as you're standing there. Those weather men don't know nothin'. I always tell my Philly they're guessing, that's all. But he sits and listens like it's the gospel. They say rain, Philly takes his umbrella. Sunny and warm, he dresses like he's going to the beach. Last year he got himself a helluva cold listening. Could've gotten pneumonia or worse, hacking and wheezing he was. Ran a fever and all. But does he change his ways? Heaven forbid. He's a peach, my Philly. But stubborn, God bless him. A regular mule. Gorgeous, hah! Want some breakfast? An egg? A little bran maybe? Keeps the old pipes chugging."

"Nothing for me yet, thanks. I'm not quite awake."

"Had a rough night? Gets that way. I remember when I was pregnant with my Lynnie. Got so I couldn't find a place to put myself. Couldn't breathe so good lying down. All that belly gets in the way, don't it? You tried a little hot milk before bed? Used to give me gas but it was worth it. I'd go right out." She snapped her fingers. "Like the dead."

Erica wondered if the woman talked in her sleep. "Mrs. Oh, tell me. Do you know anything about the people who lived here before the Hemphills?"

"Those rich ones. The whatchamacallits?" She shrugged. "Whatever. No, not much. Only what Mr. Hemphill told me. Bunch of no-good miseries, they were. Worst kind of people from what he said. I didn't know much about Greenwich before I came to work for the Hemphills. Used to keep house for a real nice family in Great Neck. Had a place in the Kings Point section, real fancy, but the Gillespies were down to earth, money or no. Two nice little girls they had. They were just crazy about me, especially that little one, Ashley. Anyway, they got transferred to Indianapolis, Indian No Place, they called it, and the agency found me this job. An offer I couldn't refuse, Philly said, you know, with the apartment and all."

"Apartment?" Erica felt her eyes widen.

"Yeah, didn't you know? Mr. Hemphill gives us free rent in that little place near the front gate. Not a palace, mind you. In fact, when we moved in it was some kinda mess. Must've been a bachelor living there or something. Junk all over the place. Like nobody really gave it a good cleaning for years, you know? You woulda thought it was home to a bunch of pigs to look at the kitchen and bathroom." She rolled her eyes. "Woulda thought it could never be cleaned so real people would want it. But we fixed it up. Used some good old elbow grease. Plain soap. A lot of ammonia. Nothing like ammonia for cleaning. Even smells clean."

"I didn't know you got the apartment as part of the job."

"Sure. That's why we came to Greenwich. Philly's been a little down on his luck, you know. Had a real good job at this auto plant, was even in line for a promotion but the place had some reverses and they laid off most everyone. Bad luck is all. Now he can relax about the rent, at least. And Lynnie gets to go to a real nice school, real nice. Kids are a little too fancy for my blood but I guess it don't hurt her to see how the other half lives."

Erica sipped at the steaming tea. "That's unusual, I guess. Getting free rent like that."

"Philly said it was a fat, fucking miracle. Excuse my

French. Bit of good luck for sure. And we could use it, I'll tell you. Things haven't been easy."

"I wonder why Goody didn't just hire someone local. I mean, if he didn't want you living here in the house?"

"Do me a favor, will you, Miss Phillips? I don't even like to think about it. For some reason, he doesn't like hiring local folks. Has funny thoughts about hiring altogether if you ask me. Has just me and poor old Flumacher full-time. Place like this, you'd think he'd have a whole crew living in, gardener, chauffeur, stable boys, couple of maids, you know. Not him. Night comes. Everyone goes home but you. Work needs doing, he has to hire a service. Doesn't even own that fancy car, you know. Has it brought around from the agency when he wants it. Costs him more the way he does it for sure. But I'm not talking. Truth is, he could rent our place for a nice fat price—four, five hundred a month, I bet. Maybe even more. They get some fancy rents in Greenwich. Crazy. Philly and I keep our fingers crossed, hoping it won't occur to him."

"I won't say a word, I promise. I was just wondering . . ."

"Some things it don't pay to wonder about. You just get yourself in trouble."

A chill passed through her. "You're right, Mrs. Oh. You can't imagine how right you are."

Goody returned after lunch in a jolly mood, face set in a satisfied smirk, arms laden with gift-wrapped boxes. "There I was, strolling along Madison Avenue after my appointment, passing all these divine shops. And I started to imagine all the people who have birthdays today, anniversaries, weddings, engagements, new babies. It seemed only fitting that we celebrate."

Erica enjoyed his rare attack of silliness. "Only fitting."

He began distributing the gifts. An antique scarab brooch for Theresa with a matching bracelet and earrings. A flowered challis scarf for Mrs. Ohringer. Fur-lined leather gloves for Flumacher. For Erica, there were several maternity dresses, some stern, some fussy—culled, it seemed, from a former era. "Thank you. They're so . . . different," she managed.

"You like them! I'm so pleased. You must run right up this instant and put one on, my dear. Dear sweet Mummy Erica. We want everything to be fresh and perfect for you and your precious infant, don't we?"

"I'll change later, Goody. Before dinner."

"Now, my dear. I must insist. Who is more important than the dear mummy-to-be? We must keep you looking and feeling perfect."

He was not to be denied. "Sure, okay. I guess I have been less than glamorous these last few weeks."

A dark cloud crossed his expression. "The time is approaching, dear Mummy. The moment of birth when the very promise of life is at its fullest. Such grand drama must be properly played."

Erica went to her room cradling the oversized dress box, furious with herself and Hemphill. No one had the right to order her dressed up in velvet and Victorian frill like an overblown bisque doll. She should have stood up to Goody, told him she would rather choose her own clothing, her own everything.

Soon, she consoled herself. Soon she would be in Boston with Horatio. No point in arguing with Goody now. She could put up with his nonsense for the little time she had left. So little time, a few weeks.

Staring at her image in the mirror, Erica felt an odd sense of foreboding. Something about the dress? No, that made no sense. What could be ominous about a dress? Still, looking at herself, she thought how strange it was for Goody to care so vehemently about her appearance. "Grand drama must be carefully orchestrated and properly played," she murmured, aping his dramatic voice. "You'd think he had some personal stake in this baby," she thought. And the very idea made her shiver.

Now come on, Erica, she rebuked herself. Don't get carried away. The dress was no worse than ridiculous. No reason to search under every rock for dark intentions. To match the mood of the outfit, she shook her hair out around her shoulders and tied the cameo on a thin black velvet ribbon to hang around her neck. If she was to look foolish, she intended to do it right.

Back downstairs, Goody bubbled his approval. "Lovely, my dear. Only . . ." He ordered her to sit on the loveseat and began shaping her hair with his pasty fingers, pressing it against her scalp and holding it in place until it forgot its former freedom.

He pressed and shaped and held, his face taut with concentration. "You might consider a shorter style, Mummy dear. With the infant and all, there won't be nearly as much time for grooming such long tresses."

"I'll manage." She allowed a trace of annoyance to creep into her tone. Next, he'd be telling her how to breathe. "If you'll excuse me. I'm going to finish up in the study."

As she stood, he leaned close and scrutinized her like a curious child. "Lovely, simply lovely, Erica." He peered into her face and she caught her reflection in the mirrored lenses of his sunglasses. The fear in her eyes was unmistakable. Stop, she told herself. Nothing to be afraid of, nothing.

"Thanks, Goody. I'll be going now."

"By all means. Do whatever you must."

Erica flashed a sympathetic smile at Theresa and left the two of them together. Do whatever you must. That was advice she intended to follow.

CHAPTER

23

Jim took one look at Erica and bit his lip to keep from laughing. "Let me guess," he said. "Rebecca of Sunnybrook Farm? No, wait a minute. One of the sisters from *Little Women*, right?"

"Don't make fun. Please, Jim. This is not funny." She spoke in a harsh whisper. All afternoon, she had waited for him to arrive. Her rock. A home base in the great state of sanity. Goody was acting even stranger than usual, even more intense and unreasonable. Erica had decided not to tell him anything about Theresa's code. By the time Jim's car pulled into the driveway, she was frantic to talk sense with a person capable of speaking that language.

His expression settled in a worried frown. "What's wrong, Erica? What happened?"

She told him everything. "Nothing's really wrong, I guess," she said at last. "Goody's just acting so weird. And I feel so . . . disconnected, so overwhelmed." Tears of relief streaked her face.

He kissed the wet spots on her cheeks. "Look, you've been through a lot of difficult experiences, Erica. The pregnancy, the premature labor, living with strangers, fighting me off . . ."

"Please, be serious."

"I am being serious. Really. Let's sort it out. Okay? Goody is acting a little weird. Is that startling for Goody?"

"No," Erica sniffled. "I guess weird is pretty normal for him."

"Right. And the eyebrow thing. It may or may not mean much. There are ways to find that out without aggravating Hemphill. Right?"

"I don't think . . ."

He held up a hand. "Whatever. It's not a bad thing. Right?"

"What about the 'Child of Eternity' room?"

Jim paused. "You're reading a lot into that, Erica. Maybe he thinks all Theresa's characters deserve to be immortalized."

"Not that one," she shuddered. "Not that hideous . . ."

"All right, take it easy. Let's say he . . . he didn't really read the book at all."

"But he said he did. Why would he lie about it? That kind of thing is easy enough to check."

"Check, then. Satisfy yourself."

"I don't think I want to know for sure, Jim." She stood and walked to the window. "I'm beginning to feel like a prisoner in this house. I wish I could get away. Right now. Today."

"You can. Come stay with me."

"No. That's not the answer. Goody won't let the manuscript leave the house until it's finished. It's my chance, the baby's chance. I have to stay and hope we find the rest before it's too late."

He stared into her eyes. "You don't have to. There are other ways."

She felt the pull, the undertow of feeling. "No. Not now, Jim. There are no other ways for me right now."

He pressed her hand between his. "I'll give you all the space you need. Whatever you want."

"I don't even know what I want. That's the problem. It's just not the right time."

He shrugged in defeat and thrust his hands in his pockets. "How can I help, then? You tell me."

"I don't know. I feel so . . . so confused." The faucet of tears started again. "Look at me, dressed like a baby, crying like a baby. It's a good thing I'm having this child. I'll have someone at my own maturity level to play with."

Jim offered a hug and a handkerchief. "I have an idea. A constructive idea. Why don't we concentrate on Miss Bricklin's speech. At least that's something positive, something with a purpose."

"Good, yes." She blew her nose noisily. "What did you have in mind?"

"The neurologist, Dr. Magida. Let him take a look at her. He's had a lot of experience with stroke victims. Maybe he'll have some suggestions."

Frowning, Erica shook her head. "No way. Goody would never allow it. He has his particular specialists. Foley in Chicago. McAndrews in D.C. 'Only the field's finest for dear Tessa,' " she mimicked.

"Then I'll talk to him, describe what she's doing with the eyebrow thing. Maybe he doesn't have to see her. Magida's good and he's worked with plenty of aphasics."

"How about hysterics?" Erica smiled.

Jim's kiss was deep and searching. She felt an unwelcome surge of arousal, her insides turning to melted butter. Horatio kicked a field goal in retribution. "I think I have the perfect cure," he murmured.

Goody cleared his throat dramatically. "So sorry to disturb you two. Tessa and I were hoping you might join us for a brandy. It seems we have true cause to celebrate . . . perhaps several causes."

He led them to the parlor and made a great fuss over the seating arrangement. Theresa next to Jim on the sofa. Erica perched awkwardly on the delicate Victorian corner chair. Goody facing all of them like a lecturing professor. "I wanted all of you here to share the delightful news." He pursed his lips and paused for effect. "I have found another chapter! Imagine, Erica. I returned from my journey in, as you know, the brightest of tempers. As you might imagine, such a surge of emotion can take its toll. After tea this afternoon, I felt quite worn from it all and I lay down for a brief rest in the studio, something I used to do with some regularity but stopped because napping seemed to interfere with my night's repose. And there it was! Right under the cushion of the settee! A blessed lump under my weary head! Quite incredible good fortune, don't you think?"

A flicker of concern crossed Erica's face. Jim's nod was reassuring. "I . . . I'm anxious to read it."

"Wonderful, my dear. And I am most anxious to have your reaction. I frankly can't wait for the moment you tell me the work is complete. Our collective efforts consummated at long last. That will be the end of an arduous period of anxious anticipations and the dawning of the era of just reward."

"I'm ready for that," Erica said. "I think we all are." She cast a meaningful smile in Theresa's direction. "You too, aren't you, Miss Bricklin?"

Erica masked her reaction as the old woman raised her eyebrow. The movement was distinct now, definite. The brow raised to a triumphant arch, lowered again. Then, as she watched, the brow raised again. Two arches. Erica was not mistaken.

Theresa was saying no.

CHAPTER

24

Forcing her scattered attention to the book, Erica reread the latest chapter Goody had found. The story was still stuck in disturbing limbo, the Grey Lady struggling to rid herself of the burden of knowledge that would somehow keep an evil force from multiplying. Enough, Erica felt like screaming. Theresa Bricklin knew better than to dangle the reader by the thumbnails for such an interminable time. In her previous works, the pacing was flawless.

But now.

He returns and regards me with dull, empty eyes. His soul is yet unformed and I imagine a putrid hole in the surface of his being. So many have been sucked into that rotten void. So many sacrificed. But evil's appetite is greedy and relentless.

So many. Two trusting, beautiful children. Two proud mothers with aching wombs and breasts laden with love and succor. Two who stood by in naked innocence, victims of capricious circumstance. Two who laughed at darkness and were swallowed. One who erected a lie and climbed the vine of falsehood to his own destruction. Others unknown and lost to all future or nobler purpose. Lost to all purpose for eternity.

This morning, I knew it was morning by the scent of

it on his clothing, he came and forced my hand to grasp
the sword. "Hurry," he ordered as if speed could be
summoned in such matters. "Time is running out.
Time is of the essence."

And when he left, I considered a fitting end. My own
end. But I cannot, will not, allow this evil to remain
unchallenged and unchronicled. My debt to humanity
cannot be paid by cowardice or retreat.

Power thunders in my hearing and beckons me to its
heady succor. If only I could mount that final possibility and be carried free. If only freedom were a mighty
steed whose thick flanks and pounding hooves might
carry me to a lost serenity.

Erica's head throbbed with the words. The more she
read, the less satisfied she felt. Much as she wanted to trust
the Bricklin genius, spiders of doubt crept over her.

Jim knocked lightly and opened the study door. "Busy?"

She rubbed the fog from her eyes. "Busy running around
in useless little circles. You came at the perfect time." Perfect. To think she had almost refused his offer to come by
again today and check on her. Dumb Erica.

"Glad to hear that. I wouldn't want to interrupt your
work."

"Work? Is that what you call it? It feels more like banging
my head against the wall, Jim. It's such a relief to stop."

He smoothed the hair back from her forehead. "I had a
talk with that neurologist, Dr. Magida, today. I told him all
about Miss Bricklin."

"And? What did he think? Is there any hope?"

Jim sat beside her and took her hand. "Naturally, he said
it was hard to tell without actually seeing her. But I described the eyebrow raising and he thought that was an encouraging sign. In fact, he has had patients with similar
histories who learned to use eyebrows, nods, whatever, after
several years without any meaningful communication."

Erica brightened. "Then we shouldn't give up?"

"No, not at all. Magida told me about one patient he had from the Laurel Hills Convalescent Center who was ten years post-CVA. Ten years after her stroke and she had no way to communicate at all, just meaningless grunts and gestures.

"One day, the patients were taken to a local church for an amateur performance and one of the custodians took a fancy to this lady. He started coming around to see her, once or twice a week at first. Then nearly every day. Magida said this guy would sit and talk and talk and the old lady really seemed to tune in. They had some kind of private code going between them. I guess it's the old love conquers all trick. The old lady's name was Bertha Boyargin, Magida said. Perfect name for a lady wrestler, don't you think? In this corner . . . Dirty Bertie Boyargin.

"Anyway, after a while this guy petitioned for custody and took the old lady to live with him. He wanted to marry her but the court wouldn't allow it, said she wasn't competent. Can you imagine? Poor old woman had nothing. No family, no money. Nothing. Guy was no bargain, according to Magida. But he cared about her."

The story touched Erica. "So the moral is . . . never give up."

"Where there's life there's hope. Magida's words. Guy's a real original. He said you should try to give her something more than the eyebrow code. Maybe a word board. All she has to do is learn to point at a picture."

"That's what the speech therapist wanted to try," Erica said. "Goody wouldn't hear of it."

"I told Magida there might be a problem with the husband but he said you don't have to make a big deal about it. If you can just put something together and work with her for a few minutes a day, you can see if such a device would be helpful. I'm sure you can find a few minutes when Goody isn't around to object. That's probably all she can take anyway. Magida warned me that fatigue is a big problem in these cases. You don't want to wear her out. And you'll have to be patient. From what Magida told me, these things take time."

Erica frowned. "I'll give it a try. Unfortunately, I don't have much time for patience. Just a few more weeks."

"Doesn't hurt to try," Jim said. "If you get anywhere, maybe Hemphill will be willing to keep up with it. I don't see how he can refuse if he sees some success. At least you'll be giving Miss Bricklin a chance."

"As long as Goody doesn't find out . . ." A terrifying image flashed in her mind. "The last thing I want to do is cross him. He's . . ."

"He's what? You said he was just a garden variety weirdo, Erica. If you have real worries about him . . ." Jim was studying her, looking for hidden messages.

She managed a twisted grin, rubbed her hands together, and lapsed into a creditable Dracula voice. "Didn't I tell you, Doctor? I think he has come to us from Transylvania. At night, his claws grow and his face gets hairier and hairier and he develops this terrible thirst for blood. He takes it on the rocks . . . with a twist."

"Cute, Erica. Very cute. Listen, I mean it. If this guy is making you uneasy, you don't have to stay at Bramble Farm. I happen to have an extra bedroom, a pullout couch, and at least three spare feet on my own mattress. Very comfortable. Orthopedic, extra firm. Excellent for the aches and pains of advanced pregnancy."

She nodded in approval. "I'm glad to hear that. If you ever get pregnant, you're all set."

Jim pouted. "I can't get through to you, can I?"

"You can. But I try not to let you. Not now."

"Later then?" His pout yielded to a hopeful grin.

"Maybe." She winced in discomfort. "Let's get out of here, Jim. I could use some real air for a change."

He drove out of Bramble Farm and out along River Road. The night was ink black and still, the road deserted. They drove in silence past the dim shadows of distant mansions. Jewel boxes that held the solitary lives of the privileged and protected.

Erica settled back against the plump contours of her seat. She would have been content to drive on indefinitely, as far away from Bramble Farm as any road might lead them. If not for Theresa and the manuscript, she knew she would not go back at all. She needed to be off in her own life, attending to her own moods and tempers.

"Come home with me, Erica. Let me take care of you," Jim said at last. His voice was a gentle plea. Tempting.

"I don't need to be taken care of, Jim. I'm a grown-up."

"Then you come and take care of me. I need it. Grown-up or not."

"I'm afraid my mommy services are all booked up for the time being. I'm . . . I'm sorry."

He shrugged. "Then I'll just have to settle for the waiting list."

She looked over at him, the chiselled features, the deep honest eyes. Something about him compelled her like a lifeline dangling near a terrified swimmer. "I don't know why you hang around, Jim. You could certainly get better treatment elsewhere. You deserve better."

"Do me a favor, will you? Shut up."

On the drive back to Bramble Farm, she felt the dread creeping back to displace the momentary sense of calm. She didn't want to go back. That was the plain truth. She wanted to be as far away as possible from the fickle pendulum of Goody's moods, the urgency of the book, the desperation in Theresa's eye, the frightened neighing of the horses, the relentless hammering and fixing. All of it!

Several times, she bit back the urge to tell Jim to turn around, to take her to his place after all, any place but Bramble Farm.

"Jim, if I need you. Can I . . . ?"

"Any time."

He pressed his hand over hers as they drove. She had been lucky in so many ways. Why couldn't she focus on that? As they approached the scarred, narrow drive leading to Bramble Farm, she tensed in spite of her good intentions.

No more, cried a frightened little voice inside her head. No more!

With every shred of her resolve, she kept from begging Jim to stop, to turn around. Come on, Erica. Get a hold of yourself. Remember you're a grown-up. There are no bogey men, no evil spirits lurking in the shadows.

He was on the drive, moving closer and closer to the house. Seeking branches clawed the sides of the MG. Jim's car slowed to a reluctant crawl.

CHAPTER

25

She was not surprised by the pain. For days, she had waited for it, steeled herself against its inevitable appearance. It was exactly as she had imagined, a sharp rip. The fabric of her insides tearing like an old sheet.

In the blackness of her room, Erica took a mental step away from it, tried to visualize the pain as a mischievous little boy, carving his messages on a school desk. No real harm in the carving. A little change but no real harm.

The printed words danced across her mind. ". . . The condition may be heralded by the onset of premature contractions in the second or third trimester. The physician should be alerted to the subsequent presence of discomfort, especially in the lower-right quadrant. Particular attention should be paid to the primiparous patient and the patient with a familial history of the disorder."

Primiparous. That was her. Pregnant for the first time. And she certainly had the familial history. Her mother. Her dead mother. Now there was the discomfort, the pain.

She tried to fight off the terror, to wait for a decent hour to call Jim. After all, there was no emergency here. No emergency, she kept telling herself.

The pain again. How fast would it happen? Was it all done in a minute? Or did it take days, weeks, the way it did with her mother? The rip starts and deepens, widens until there is a gaping void only the blood can fill . . . the sickly sweet scarlet rivers of splashing blood.

"Jim . . . Jim, I'm sorry to call so late. I hope I didn't wake you." She tried to keep her voice even, sane. Someone was beating a rug in her chest.

"What is it, Erica? What's wrong?"

"Probably nothing. Probably just something I ate . . . I have this . . . pain, Jim."

She described it to him. A sharp pain. Lower-right quadrant. And she was at risk, she reminded him, for placenta previa. "I do have the family history, Jim. And, there was that bout of premature contractions."

"You've been reading medical books," he chided. "Haven't you?"

"I don't see what that has to do with anything. What if I have? I'm entitled to get the best information, aren't I? As an intelligent medical consumer, it's my right to have all the facts about my care and condition."

"You do, Erica. I'm not arguing with that. In fact, I think you should have all the facts. But you're not going to get them from the particular source you consulted. *Gravely's Complete Manual of Obstetrics*, right?"

"How did you know?"

"My father had a copy. When I was a kid, I used to sneak it off his shelf and look at the pictures. By the time I finished my adolescence, I practically knew the whole book by heart. It's a good book, Erica. Only one problem with it."

"What's that?"

"It was written in 1853."

She hung up feeling relieved and foolish. One day, she would laugh about all this. One day, she would be far enough away to turn all her fears and fantasies into parlor stories. Erica Phillips, master of the bizarre and improbable.

She tiptoed back to her room, trying to ignore the dense shadows lurking in the hallways like predatory beasts. Was her imagination the only fault? Or was there something about this house, this place with all its moods and secrets? Soon, she thought, none of this would matter. All she had to do was last a few more weeks and she would be free of Bramble Farm. Free and safe.

CHAPTER

26

Erica had the latest chapter nearly memorized but still the Grey Lady refused to yield her secrets. The conclusion was close at hand. No more than another chapter or two and she would be done with this whole maddening process.

The editing was tedious, routine checking and rechecking, broken only by Goody's enthusiasm, and by Mel's. His calls were tinged with a definite air of professional hysteria. Without a single page in circulation, without the rumor of a plot line, the paperback houses were already engaged in a frantic, cutthroat auction for the rights. Nine movie companies had called Mel with informal, but dizzying, offers for the screen rights. And, enormous, unparalleled numbers were being tossed about in *Publisher's Weekly*, which joined the lively media speculation about the nature and fate of Bricklin's latest, and most likely last, work.

"You are sitting on a gold mine, my dear Erica," Mel had said in his last call. "Editing this book will put you in the spotlight. After this, I suspect you can write your own ticket. Wait a minute, forget I said that."

"I don't think you have to worry, Mel. Right now, ticket-writing is way at the bottom of my list."

He sighed heavily. "Not for long, my dear. I've already heard from all three of the networks. They want you for feature interviews. We're not talking three-minute book-

hype pieces here, Miss Phillips. We're talking a major seg-
ment on 'Sixty Minutes.' The woman behind the woman.
An insider's view of America's greatest woman novelist.
That sort of thing. Big time."

"Only if they have a wide-angle lens, Mel. I'm in no shape
to . . ."

"You will be. Before you know it, Erica. Geez, if I had
known what would come out of all this, I would have taken
this assignment myself."

"Tell you what—let's trade places."

Another theatrical sigh. "An empty offer at best. You are
far too intelligent a woman to trade fame and fortune for a
noisy two-bedroom apartment with a view of the city's
largest landfill and Jeannie's cuisine—nouvelle atrocious, I
call it."

Erica laughed. "You don't look like you're suffering from
malnutrition, Mel. Not by a long shot."

"The distended abdomen is a classic symptom, Erica. I'm
probably on my last legs. Lucky I have a little bag of Milky
Way bars in my first-aid kit. I don't think I'd last the day
otherwise."

She could picture his office: the clutter, the friendly disorder, the 'first-aid kit': scotch, Maalox, Excedrin Extra-
Strength, tavern nuts, candy bars. How she ached for a
return to such an earthy reality. "Maybe when things settle
down, I could come by and take some of those empty calo-
ries off your heavy hands."

"Yes. I told you. We want you back anytime. I'll even
have the doors enlarged to accommodate your head if it
swells too much from all the attention."

"Please, promise me, Mel. If I ever come back. No reno-
vations."

She was sure part of her unease came from living through
Bramble Farm's monumental facelift. Every day, there were
crews of workmen, clattering trucks, the distracting cacoph-
ony of power tools and pounding hammers, heavy equip-
ment and the loud banter of affable laborers. Her wandering

attentions were buffeted until her head ached with the effort to focus. She longed for quiet and solitude.

It seemed the restoration would never be done. Goody
was impossible to please, reaching for some standard of perfection beyond the mortal arm span. When there was a
brief, welcome respite from the construction and destruction noises, Erica could count on a loud encounter between
Goody and one of the myriad subcontractors. Today it was
the nervous little man in charge of the security systems,
Goody's obsession. As the argument escalated, the little
man's voice became sharper and sharper until Erica thought
his flitting tongue would simply snap off and take flight like
a wooden airplane.

"I don't know what you want, Mr. Hemphill. I don't think
you know what you want yourself. You told me electric, I
put in seventeen PB-27s. Here it is, right in the proposal.
Right above where you signed, see? PB-27s, our finest, top-
of-the-line electrics. Now you want ultrasound. You want
me to pull out the PB-27s and put in Reacta-15s. Tell me,
Mr. Hemphill. What am I supposed to do with seventeen
used PB-27s?"

"That, Mr. Tirozzi, is not my concern. For all I care, you
could use them as rectal suppositories." He waved dismis-
sively. "I am not concerned about the cost, I assure you.
Either find somewhere else on the property to install them,
or simply discard them. Security is of paramount impor-
tance here. I explained that to you at our preliminary meeting. And I mistakenly assumed you were a person of normal
intelligence."

"You know what a PB-27 costs, Hemphill? Six hundred
twenty-seven bucks plus installation. That's each one. You
got seventeen."

"I am truly blessed, aren't I, Mr. Tirozzi? Such bounty.
Pull them out . . . today!"

Erica avoided the aftershocks of these encounters. More
and more, she avoided Goody altogether, preferring to
spend her time with Theresa.

After Jim's meeting with the neurologist, Erica found the necessary supplies in the bookcases in the Fallen Angel room and set to work on a communication board. As she worked, she thought how fortunate it was that Hillary, the book's child heroine, had been such a privileged little girl. Everything she needed to construct the word board was there, in the room. She didn't have to ask Goody for anything. He did not have to know a thing about the project.

Pleading fatigue, she stole time in the evenings to work on the board. Her first task was preparing a list of life's most essential thoughts and words. There would be room for twenty-four at most. The print had to be large enough in case Theresa had suffered the typical age-related loss of vision. And Erica wanted to add pictures beside the words as extra clues. Without knowing how such a board generally looked, Erica planned to make the necessary adjustments as she went along. Any effort was worthwhile if there was a way to break Theresa's long enforced silence.

She began with the obvious words: Erica, Theresa, Goody, eat, drink, sad, happy, angry, tired . . . Feelings and needs, needs and feelings. Out, in, cold, hot, love, hate . . . Words should never have to be rationed.

Using the pots of colored ink from Hillary's maple desk, she wrote each word in bold block letters, each one in a separate square, each one with a picture or symbol beside it. Once, Mrs. Ohringer knocked to check on her and Erica hid the board beneath her bed.

"You okay, Miss Phillips? Mr. Hemphill asked me to look in before I go home. Worries about you like you was breakable or something, I swear it. Man doesn't understand people have been having babies since time started. Maybe before."

"You can tell him I'm perfectly fine. Just a little tired. That's all." Erica stretched and feigned a yawn to cover the guilty flush rising in her cheeks.

Mrs. Oh hesitated with a hand on the door as if she'd forgotten something. She looked around the room, checking. "So . . . you don't need me to get you anything before you turn in? My Lynnie always has a little something, you know, likes to have her little tummy satisfied before she goes night-night. Funny, been that way since she was little. Has to have a bite of something. A cracker or two, a little juice. Must find it a comfort, I guess. Even though she's a big-deal teenager now, thinks she knows everything. Still likes her bedtime snack. Some things never change. So, you want anything?"

"I'm fine, Mrs. Oh. Thanks anyway."

Still searching, Mrs. Ohringer gave Erica a pentrating look. "Good, then. You know when I was as far along as you, I had a devil of a time getting off to sleep. Couldn't lie on my belly. No way. My side, I'd feel like I was choking. On my back, I'd spend half the night counting those little holes in the ceiling. One night there'd be two thousand forty-eight; next night twenty-two hundred thirty-six. Damned ceiling kept playing tricks till I thought I was losing my mind. I was plain exhausted was all. Philly used to take a look at me in the morning and cluck like an old hen. 'Poor thing,' he'd say. 'I don't know how you women put up with all the bother.' Good thing we do, I told him. Or you wouldn't be here to worry, would you?"

"Good night, Mrs. Ohringer. I'll see you in the morning."

"Sure. Sleep tight. Don't let the bed bugs bite. I always say that for my . . ."

"Good night now."

Erica retrieved the board from under the bed. So many secrets. So much to hide. Her fears, feelings. All the doubt fluttering in her head like startled insects. Maybe Mrs. Oh was right for a change. Maybe weariness was the culprit. Enough of the word board for tonight. Enough of everything.

She walked to the window to lower her shade. Menacing clouds sat on the horizon like warring soldiers poised for battle. The vent fan roared for a startling instant. And a horse neighed in frightened protest.

Erica waited for the animal to calm. But the neighing grew more frantic, the horse's mad cries carrying through the still air like the terror screams of a child's nightmare. The cries stabbed at her head and she covered her ears in a vain attempt to shut them out.

Downstairs a door slammed and footsteps moved at a clumsy trot. Erica tuned Hillary's ancient box radio to the news and turned up the volume.

Things were not going well in the world.

CHAPTER

27

How many times had the questions stuck in her throat, blocked by her inexplicable fear of the truth? This was the perfect moment to douse some of her worries with cold water. She was alone with Goody in the parlor. Mrs. Ohringer had gone home and Flumacher was clearing the dinner dishes in the dining room. Theresa was already upstairs, suffering, as Goody put it, from "the weighty pangs of stubborn resistance."

"As with a child, my dear Mummy, Tessa's naughtiness must be countered with prompt, appropriate retributions. And, as a child might, Tessa detests isolation. Being sent to her room is an effective deterrent to repeated unsavory behaviors."

He referred to the storm of frustrated ranting that suddenly erupted in the middle of dinner. Theresa was chewing sloppily at a mouthful of vegetables. Erica was talking to Goody, only occasionally looking in Theresa's direction. Watching the old woman eat was not the most pleasant experience.

Suddenly, Theresa stiffened so she nearly fell out of her chair. Then, she slumped back in the seat, green and yellow mush dribbling stupidly down her chin. For a few seconds, she sat perfectly still. Dazed. Then, she began burbling and hiccupping and spewing obscene nonsense. "Reckup . . . fuck . . . fuck!"

"Now, Tessa. That's quite enough. Quite enough. I'll ask you to stop that this instant!" A vague flush rose in his chalky cheek and his fists clenched in a vain grasp against his failing control. "This instant!"

Erica camouflaged the fear that thumped at her chest. "Give her a minute, Goody, I'm sure she'll calm down."

"She most certainly will. I intend to see to that!" He stood beside the old woman and pressed his fingers into her slack forearm until the skin blanched white. "Such behavior will not be tolerated, Tessa. I have warned you!"

"Please, Goody . . ." Erica cringed at the magnitude of his fury. He could be moved in a spilt second from reasoned calm to murderous rage.

His voice was a taut rasp. "You will go to your room, Tessa. And you will remain there for the rest of the evening."

Erica bit back a giggle of relief. What had she expected? Bullwhips and cattle prods?

Her wild expectations were the whole problem. She had always been saddled with a hyperactive imagination. As a little girl, it was a monster in every closet, a trio of escaped convicts living in the attic, a dragon with a passion for green-eyed girls who had chosen Erica's, of all the worlds' beds, to hide under. She could remember her mother's un-failing patience during the nightly ritual. Each night at bed-time, they climbed the stairs together and Erica cowered in the hall until every closet was checked and rechecked, every drawer opened and examined, every inch of her bed frisked in case emaciated demons were somehow hiding be-neath the covers. Now it was Frankenstein Hemphill, the Bramble Farm Ripper. She owed it to him and herself to use the perfect opening he provided. "I've never been in Miss Bricklin's room," she lied. "Which book is it decorated for?"

In fact, Erica had gone to Theresa's room early that

morning to show her the finished word board. She was shocked by the spare, stark furnishings. The room was spartan, almost cell-like. An ancient ceiling fixture held a single bare bulb and a thin mattress was set in a metal frame reminiscent of summer camp. The walls were a dull white, the floor bare wood planks. There were no bookshelves, no pictures, nothing to indicate a personal presence.

He sighed heavily. "Unfortunately, I have not been able to have her room suitably refurbished as yet. Tessa's physicians have counseled me to keep her sleeping area as spare and free of distracting stimuli as possible. For months after the stroke, her slumber patterns were quite unsettled. There were nights she didn't rest for an instant. It does, however, disturb me to see her in such unattractive surroundings . . . One of those awful quandaries . . ."

Simple logic. All she had to do was ask. "Tell me, Goody. If you could redo her room, which book would you choose?"

"Hmmm. Not a simple matter, as you might imagine. My darling won so many prizes for *The Debtor*. But *Gryphon* was among her personal favorites . . . Difficult at best. I imagine I would have to arrange some manner of compromise, perhaps an amalgam of several books."

"It's such an interesting idea. Do you do the actual decorating yourself?"

"No, my dear. Certainly not. Interiors are hardly my forte. I engaged a very talented gentleman by the name of Latham Parks. His studios are right here in Greenwich. Of course, I would be proud to call the efforts my own, quite remarkable, don't you think?"

"Yes." She measured her words carefully. "Especially the 'Child of Eternity' room . . . Did you, did you tell the decorator which features of the nursery to reproduce or does he get artistic freedom in a case like that? As I remember, the nursery suite in the book had ten rooms."

"Ten, yes. I believe so. No, I don't confine Mr. Parks that way. I have complete faith in his creative judgment. Once I have told him which volume he is to draw from, I withdraw and allow him to work his magic. True artists must never be confined or constrained. Creation is best cultivated in the soil of freedom and discretion, don't you agree?"

"Oh yes, absolutely." Then maybe he didn't know. Her heart was pounding so hard she was afraid he could hear it. "You know, I read *Child of Eternity* so long ago, I can't remember the baby's name. What was it again?"

"Hmmm. Odd. I can't recall it myself at the moment. The numbing effects of the spirits on the memory, I fear." He tapped his glass and set his face in a benign grin of apology. "Then I fear time dims the mind's eye as well."

"Was it Gabriel? . . . Yes, I think that was it." She held her breath, hoping.

"Gabriel. Certainly, my dear. How fortunate you remembered. I should not have rested until I had the answer."

Erica smiled in relief. He hadn't read the book after all. The "child of eternity" was nameless through most of the book, nameless and devoid of soul or humanity. Erica shuddered at the mental image of the horrors that child had perpetrated against his innocent family, his neighbors, the village priest. Vicious mutilations. Murder for murder's sake. Blood lust so horrifying it extended the dark side of human possibility, Keeping the child nameless added to the terrifying image. No name, no connection to any recognizable moral structure. Only at the end of the book, before the last failed attempt on the child's life, did he take a name for himself. It was not the kind of name any reader would forget. "Call me what I am," the child had said. "Call me Death." "I'm glad to have the answer myself," Erica almost whispered.

Goody sipped at the large snifter, staring through his dark glasses at a vacant place on the wall. "I am most eager to have this manuscript done and delivered, my dear. It weighs quite heavily on my consciousness, I'm afraid. The burden of anticipation and vain concern can deform the courage after a time. I feel my resolve crumbling, my certainty falling to ash."

"I'm sure it will be done . . . soon. The Grey Lady is close to revealing everything, don't you think?"

"Ah yes. Secrets of an old woman. Quite a difficult subject to bring to life. But then my dear Tessa always preferred the spark of a challenge."

"What is your guess, Goody? Why is she in such a spot?"

"That," he shrugged. "Oh, I imagine the predicament is of her own making. These things tend to be, don't you think?"

"But . . ." Erica frowned. She was about a argue against the illogic of voluntary imprisonment in this case. Then, the obvious struck her. Goody knew nothing about this book either. He hadn't read the manuscript. The sunglasses, the vague tilt of his head, the simple, obvious truth. Goody hadn't read any of Theresa's books or anything else. Something was wrong with his eyes. She stared at him, wondering how much he could actually see. Well enough to get around without help, well enough to recognize people. But . . . "I suppose you're right, Goody. I never thought of it that way." Simple, logical explanations. The darkest mysteries fading to oblivion in the harsh light of the truth. How silly she had been. She couldn't wait to tell Jim. It would be worth listening to his I-told-you-so's. One final splinter to remove. "The people who lived here before . . ."

"Yes?"

"Do you know anything about the family? I mean, how many children? That sort of thing. It's odd to live in a place, walk where people walked before, eat where they ate, sleep where they slept, and not know anything about them."

He leaned toward Erica, inclined as if ready to pounce. "I told you all you need to know, my dear Mummy. Again, it seems you are a victim of your own destructive curiosities."

"I was just . . ."

He gestured her to silence. "If it will satisfy some unfortunate compulsion of yours, my dear, I will repeat the story, unsavory though it is." He paused and appeared to be ordering his thoughts with enormous care. "A family named

Garrett built Bramble Farm near the turn of the century. Their steel fortune had grown to the point where it seemed suitable to acquire several properties in the most desirable locations. Brandon Garrett, the patriarch, selected Greenwich on the advice of friends and purchased the estate through a business associate.

"As I understand it, Garrett commissioned the finest craftsmen and spared no expense in turning the property into a showplace. He imported the finest Italian tiles, marble fittings from a demolished French castle, shiploads of handhewn beams and stained glass windows. The finest architects were engaged and master craftsmen from all over the world were brought to Bramble to execute the plans. Garrett was a man of impeccable taste with a flawless eye for detail.

"Once the property was in order, Brandon's wife, Annabelle, a woman of impeccable breeding, rapidly distinguished herself as the ablest hostess. Before long, invitations to Bramble Farm were prized and all of New York and Connecticut's upper crust looked to Annabelle as a prime arbiter of social taste. Bramble Farm held its proper place in those days, it was a haven for artists and intellectuals; the captains of enterprise and creativity."

He cleared his throat and sipped his brandy. "When Brandon died, the property was left to his son, Drew, who married well and perpetuated the family's social statute with ease. Drew was a fine young man, a true Garrett, but after a few short years, he met a tragic death in a boating accident and the property passed to his son, Bertram."

Goody placed the snifter on the cocktail table and folded his hands. His voice dropped to an angry rasp. "Bertram was a small man with large appetites, totally lacking the critical attributes for successful management of stature, wealth and their concomitant social responsibility. Young, inexperienced, impossibly self-centered, he had no regard for position or form. He married a similarly afflicted young woman, shallow, egotistical, and proceeded to sire a spoiled, petulant little girl. When they were confronted with adversity, they simply turned away, behaved like the overindulged, insensitive creatures they were. I don't care to detail the various atrocities perpetrated by that dreadful pair. Suffice it to say nothing was of interest to them save their petty needs and selfish pleasures. They were spendthrifts, frittering their inheritance shamelessly, with no loyalty to form or tradition. Spoiled, selfish, vile creatures!" His voice had risen to a hysterical crescendo. "They deserved to be exiled in piteous disgrace, destitute of right and soul and future! They deserved to lose the birthright wrested from the right child of justice and placed in such vile, insensitive hands!"

Mouth cottony dry, Erica watched the tirade, the impassioned fury, too intense to feed on a stranger's moral pique. How did Goody know so much about the Garretts? What made him care so deeply? Erica was afraid to think about the logic of that.

As quickly as it began, the ranting subsided. The tension drained from Goody's body and he crumpled in the chair in a weary heap. He scratched his forehead as if searching for a lost memory and hummed a soothing tune Erica could not immediately place. After a few minutes, he turned to her, a sheepish smile on his lips. "Forgive my outburst, my dear Mummy. Tessa often said I suffered from the tendency to wrap others' transgressions in the weighty cloak of my own sense of justice. A flaw of character, I fear." He had the endearing look of a small boy caught in charming mischief. How could she be afraid of such a peculiar little man? What was there to fear?

"We all have our fair share of character flaws, Goody. That's for sure." Stupid Erica. Always looking for the dragon under the bed.

"I am most grateful for your forebearance, my dear."

If he could read her mind . . . Poking around was useless and destructive. There was nothing she could do to change things. The final pages of the manuscript would be found, as her mother liked to say, if it was meant to be. And there would be no more probing, nosy questions. Not even the one that sat on the tip of her tongue, aching to jump off. What became of the Garretts? She wanted to ask. Where are they now? With so much family money and prestige, some member of the family would surely have survived, re-surfaced. Idle curiosities. She wouldn't ask where they were, what had finally happened to them.

She was not at all sure she wanted to know.

CHAPTER
28

Waiting for the light to change, Erica reviewed the possibilities again. Jim was so mysterious on the phone, so unlike his usual open self. The last thing she needed was another mystery, another puzzle to add to the ones already chipping away at her sanity. Even the call was out of character. She never heard from him during office hours. Doctor James was all business from ten to six. Under ordinary circumstances, if he needed to tell her something during the day, he had his receptionist call. But this morning . . .

"It's no big deal, Erica. Just a piece of interesting news I thought you'd want to hear . . . No, I can't discuss it now. I'm running late . . . No, not even a hint."

The bank clock flashed eleven twenty-seven. Jim had asked her to come to his office at twelve but curiosity drove her to leave Bramble Farm early. She told the driver she had shopping to do and asked him to drop her at the corner of East Putnam and Greenwich Avenue.

A corpulent policeman, ruddy with the cold, stood on the corner. He directed traffic with the flailing motions of a symphony conductor and his breath came in soft, grey puffs. A Salvation Army Santa, whose own scruffy brown beard poked out from beneath the white cotton, caught her eye and winked. Looking down the avenue, she was put off by the milling crowd of frenetic holiday shoppers. Turning, her eye caught a store sign up East Putnam and she walked in that direction.

The shop window was draped in lavish lengths of woven silk. A pair of antique Rose Medallion lamps on matching Louis XIV end tables flanked a white plastic Christmas tree trimmed with red and green velvet bows. As she opened the door, the tinkle of brass bells announced her arrival.

A slight, bald man with a pinched expression emerged from the back room wiping his hands on a plaid cobbler apron. "Welcome, young lady. And how may I be of service?"

Erica extended a hand to meet the damp, limpid one he offered. "Are you Latham Parks, the decorator?"

"Designer, not decorator. A clear difference, you understand. Decorator smacks of an old woman placing lace doilies on the sofa to catch the hair oil. A fussy old woman setting out her family portraits on the piano and dusting her little collection of Hummel mugs and cheap figurines. Design relates to the total environment, the impact on mood, personal welfare, psychological health. The effects of color and tone, form and function, the complex interplay of the aesthetic and pragmatic are all weighed and measured, all carefully integrated in the total scheme. In the end, fine design has a profound, positive effect on quality of life. It has been established, you know, scientifically."

Erica shook her head in concession. "Yes, I see, Mr. Parks. I came about the work you did at Bramble Farm, the rooms you did there."

He took a feather duster from behind his inlaid mahogany desk and began to swipe like a matador at the piled bolts of fabric and books of sample swatches. "Incredible," he mumbled furiously. "Absolutely incredible. Are you suggesting that dreadful creature . . . But no. It could not be. To think he would have the audacity, the gall. To think he would consider making a recommendation after . . ." He fixed Erica with a murderous look. "I am sorry, madame. But if you have any connection with that terrible Hemphill person, I cannot consent to work with you."

"I didn't come about work, Mr. Parks, I just admired what you did at Bramble Farm. I wanted to tell you."

He waved her away. "Lovely gesture to be sure. I am flattered by your approval, Miss . . ."

"Phillips."

"Yes. I appreciate your comments but I would just as soon forget that particular commission."

Erica measured her words. "If it's any comfort to you, Mr. Parks, Mr. Hemphill has only the kindest things to say about you."

"Frankly, it is no comfort at all, madame. May I ask your connection to Mr. Hemphill? Are you a friend? A relative?"

"No. Nothing like that."

He pursed his lips. "No matter. If I may speak frankly, Miss Phillips. I have worked with difficult clients. In fact, I have worked with impossible clients but none has come close to your Mr. Hemphill. The man is nuts, wacko, crazy."

Erica bit her tongue, not wanting to prolong the tirade.

"Ask him about his precious secrets. Ask him about his secrets and hiding places. Ask him about the time he nearly chopped off my head for pulling down a few of his precious boards. You know that blocked-off corridor? I had the carpenter right there, mind you. All I wanted to do was see the back bathroom, to see if we could get by with the old plumbing or whether we had to go with an entire overhaul. I could have saved the man money, mind you. Have you any idea of the price of copper piping nowadays? Outrageous. And the restoration at Bramble Farm is costly enough by any stretch of the imagination. So I logically assumed any economies would be appreciated. But no. Hemphill comes in and finds the carpenter prying off a couple of boards . . . and he goes crazy. 'What right have you to insinuate your vile fingers in my personal affairs?' he says. 'Who gave you the right to delve in areas that are my private domain?' Christ, you'd think the man had dead bodies in there or something."

Erica had backed nearly to the door. "If you'll excuse me, Mr. Parks, I have to be going now."

Back on the street, she took a greedy breath of the chill air and berated herself for yet another foolish mission. Dead bodies indeed. Talk about crazy.

She quickly walked the two blocks to Jim's office. He was waiting behind his desk, eyes droopy with exhaustion. "Three deliveries last night. Please promise me you'll have this child during regular business hours, Erica. You're a considerate soul."

"I'll do my best, Jim. Now tell me your news. I'm dying to hear." She sank into the plump leather chair opposite him and put her swollen feet opposite his on the desk.

"It's no big deal, Erica. I told you."

"No big deal? Don't tell me you had me drag all the way down here and bite my nails for three hours for no big deal. You aren't that mean."

"All right. You be the judge. Last night, I happened to mention Bramble Farm to my father and when I described where it is, he said he thought he knew the woman who lived there before, a Mrs. Garrett. Seems he was covering for her regular doctor when she delivered, twins, he thinks."

"And?" Erica put her feet down and leaned forward.

Jim shrugged. "And nothing. I just thought you'd be interested."

"Come on," she urged. "That can't be all. You didn't keep me in suspense for that. I knew there was a family named Garrett living there before. Tell me something new."

"All right. I sort of figured you would want more so I asked my father how you could find out about the Garretts. He said there's a woman at the Historical Society named Eunice Bailey. According to Dad, if you sneeze in Greenwich, Eunice knows."

Erica smiled in satisfaction while Jim called and made arrangements for her to go right over to the Historical Society. "All set," he said. "It's just a few blocks away. On Mason. I hope you find out what you want to know, once and for all."

"Let's hope the Garretts did a lot of sneezing."

Erica left Jim's office and hurried back into the chill afternoon. She turned down a narrow cross street, a shortcut, Jim said, and passed the old brick elementary school on Marks Street. A group of little girls were jumping rope in the courtyard, their faces polished pink with cold and enthusiasm. A cat, perched atop the jungle gym, gazed at her in bored disinterest as she passed.

She walked quickly at first, anxious for . . . what? What would the town snoop have to tell her that she might really wish to know? This would likely be another of her maddening, fruitless detours. For every answer she found, there was a new question. She was beginning to think Goody was right. Her curiosities were useless, destructive.

She walked to the end of Marks and turned into the Lincoln Mews, a tiny street lined with quaint shops and small family restaurants. If she had any sense, she would forget this little excursion. She could spend a pleasant hour on the avenue, buying things she didn't need.

Then, who said she had any sense?

She turned again onto Mason and was buffeted by a sudden blast of frigid wind. A menacing cloud crossed the sun, casting the street in bleak shadow, and burdening the sky with the threat of a storm. Erica burrowed into the tall collar of her coat and thrust her hands into her pockets. She spotted the Historical Society in the distance and slowed her pace. An odd feeling told her she was crossing some critical boundary. And somehow she knew there was no going back.

CHAPTER

29

The Historical Society occupied a one-room Colonial schoolhouse at the corner of a preserved country green. Signing the guest book, Erica noted that no one had visited in several weeks but the old woman behind the desk seemed caught in a frenzy of purposeful activity, shuffling papers, flipping through the stacks of yellowed clippings, signing official-looking documents in a miniscule, fussy hand. She pursed her lips and held up a finger in Erica's direction. "Be right with you."

"Sure, I'll wait." Erica walked through the main room. It was littered with books and papers and smelled of moth balls. Sketches and faded sepia photographs traced the town's history.

"That's our downtown area in about 1838 or nine. See? Over there's the Town Hall. Not much bigger than this place it was. Housed the Town Council, the Hall of Records, the License Bureau, the Sheriff's office. The whole ball of wax. Man by the name of Eliphalet Dawkins was the major back then. He was great grandnephew of Bozrah Dawkins, one of the town founders. Conservative type Eliphalet was. Didn't want anyone riding a horse carriage on Sundays. Made it illegal for the local kids to cross the border to Stamford. Dawkins said the youngsters just went there for no

good. Thought Stamford was a regular Sodom and Go-
morrah."

Turning, Erica found Mrs. Bailey, a tiny stooped woman
with a spare silver top knot, pursed lips and sunken eyes.
She was squinting through rimless bifocals at the next picture in the series. "That's the old Bellville Inn. Used to get
all the arty-smarty folks in the summer. Painters and the lot.
Poets. Bawdy crowd they were from what I hear. Not that I
ever went near it myself. Place was shut down during prohi-
bition. Regular gin mill. Used to hear the laughing and sing-
ing all the way over to the church. Preacher should've shut
them down years earlier only he was right there with a pint
in his hand himself every chance he got. That was Mrs. Peli-
can's grandfather, you know. Big fancy society lady. She'd
just as soon everyone forget one of her people was a sot
minister. Pretty handy with the ladies too, if you want to
know."

The pictures traced the town's development from a small
cluster of pristine buildings to the sprawling maze of business and affluence it had become. "I'm interested in a particular property up north. Do you think you could help
me?"

"I can't, nobody can. Been doing this for forty-seven
years, you know. Hard to believe. I remember this town
when everyone knew everybody. Used to walk down the
street and never once see a stranger. Hi, Eunice, the folks
would say. How's mother's sciatica? Coming along, I'd say.
And Hattie? Did she have her baby yet? You know, it was a
friendly little town. We had any sense, we would've kept it
to ourselves. People went telling the world what a nice
place we had. Right away, it doesn't belong to us anymore.
You see over there? That was Peeble's Grocery. Did all my
marketing there in the old days. Made apple bran muffins
so good you'd think you died and went to heaven. My boy,
Albin, used to stop every morning on his way to school for
a muffin and a tin of milk. Real cream on top."

"This property is on Stone Hollow Road," Erica said.
"It's called Bramble Farm."

"You see over there, that little place in the background behind the tailor's? That's Caulkin's Mill. Pete Caulkins, the oldest boy, took quite a shine to me back in high school. There were seven boys, you know. One taller and stronger than the next. But Pete was the smartest of the lot, and handsome. Quite a catch, if you know what I mean." She winked. "Of course, I was already engaged to Malcolm at the time. We were sweethearts way back in the eighth grade. Malcolm. That's Mr. Bailey. Been dead twelve years now. Hard to believe . . ."

Erica's amusement was turning to impatience. "Bramble Farm. Do you know it, Mrs. Bailey? I have an appointment in a little while."

The old woman's face drooped to a pleated frown. "You youngsters today are always in a hurry. Rush, rush. No time to sit, chat, get to know one another. Pity it is. Real pity. Tell me, when's your due date? Had my Isabel right on Christmas Day. Think you'll go that long?"

"It's hard to say. Listen, I'd love to chat. I just don't have the time right now. Maybe another day."

A grin danced on Mrs. Bailey's lips. "First of the month we have our annual meeting. Elect officers. Plan our fund-raisers. The whole ball of wax. Maybe you'd like to come? Lizzie Siskin brings her brownies. Best brownies you ever tasted. And we have real egg nog, the kind'll warm your insides. Course you'd be welcome to bring the baby to meetings and all. The girls would be delighted. Nothing like a new baby."

"If I can. I'll see. Now, if you don't mind, I only have a few minutes . . ."

The bony hands were suddenly aflutter, the flowered dirndl skirt bustling about the scrawny bowed legs. "Sure, sure. I'm a busy woman myself, you know. Wasn't expecting you this morning at all. Planned to catch up on some paper work. Always gets the better of me, it does. But your friend said you're in the neighborhood so I'll see to your question. Next time you can call a day or two in advance for an appointment. All right? We're open ten to twelve, two to four-thirty weekdays. One to four Saturdays. Sundays we can open for special appointments if we get enough notice. You need me to write that down?"

"No. That's not necessary."

Mrs. Bailey rearranged the glasses on the wrinkled bridge of her nose and peered over a large ledger. "Stone Hollow Road you said? Way out there in God's country? What number Stone Hollow?"

"I don't know the number. The mail comes addressed to Bramble Farm."

"La-dee-da. Very fancy. Those north country folks think theirs don't smell, you know what I mean? Put on all those airs. Truth is every place has to have a number, fancy or no. Have to look it up in the land records. House is in whose name did you say?"

Erica frowned. "I'm not sure. Hemphill or Bricklin."

The old woman clucked and shook her head as she scanned the shelf for the proper volume. "Have to get after that Leanne. She comes Tuesdays. Thinks she owns the place. Never puts things back in their places, just shoves the books in any old place . . . Lazy girl. And a terrible temper to boot. You wouldn't believe how she talks to her mother. Shocking, I'll tell you. If she was my girl, I'd take her over my knee. Someone should've years ago. Wait. Here it is. Should be in here."

Slowly, she traced page after page of listings with a crooked finger. "Joe Pace. Quite a character he was. Liked to give you a little pat on the fanny when he thought no one was looking. Got himself in more trouble." She chuckled.

"Do you find anything for Bramble Farm? Or either of the names?"

"I'm looking, I'm looking. Don't see Bricklin or Hemp-hill. You near the Emorys? The Boltons?"

"Bolton sounds familiar."

"Wait. I got it. Bricklin it is. Theresa Bricklin. A hundred and sixty-four acres . . . Phew, that's worth a fat fortune today. They're getting seventy-five, eighty thousand an acre even closer to town."

"I want to know something about the history of the place."

Squinting, Mrs. Bailey read for several minutes, her tongue tasting the words. Finally, she looked up over her glasses. "Interesting indeed. It's the old Garrett place. Funny, I didn't think anyone was living out there since . . . but it takes all kinds, doesn't it? Some people got more nerve than you can imagine. Wouldn't catch me living there. Not me. I don't believe all that superstition bunk like black cats and ladders but I'm not one to take foolish chances, if you know what I mean. Can't see that it hurts to be a little careful. Can't hurt anything I can imagine.

"Hmm . . . funny. I haven't heard anything about the old place for years. Never called it Bramble Farm. That's for sure. Used to be called Four Winds officially but people had plenty of private names for it. Jinx house was one, I remember. And Mae Wadkins used to call it The House that Job Built. Quite a sense of humor Mae used to have until her arthritis. You should see her hands, poor thing, all twisted up like an old piece of rope. Can hardly walk anymore."

"What does it say about the place, Mrs. Bailey? Is there anything else?"

The woman fixed Erica with a killing stare. "Always impatient, you youngsters. No time to breathe. Let me see . . . That was number eleven thirty-two Stone Hollow, right by the Boltons. Theresa Bricklin sole owner, it says. Had a run of bad luck at that place for a long, long time. Started soon as it was built. Rich family those Garretts but money can't buy happiness, you know. Sure, it doesn't hurt but those folks would've been better off with a little less money and a little more luck.

"The first Garretts move in and right away the whole lot of them come down with scarlet fever. Two of their children died from it right then. A year or two later, the woman died of an embolism. Something just exploded in her head. Pop. Just like that . . . Nice girl she was, pity.

"Then the old man dies and the house is left to his son. Smart young fellow. Not stuck up or anything the way those rich folks can be. Anyway, he goes out for a ride on one of those yachts. Big fancy things with a crew and all. Storm comes up. Freak thing, you know. And he's drowned. Never found the body.

"So the place is left to Bertram Garrett and his wife Nell. Good-looking young couple, nice little girl they had. Sweetest blonde curls, you'd think they put her hair up in pin curls and touched it up with a little peroxide. Anyhow, the wife gets pregnant right away and we're all, you know, sort of nervous about how things are going to turn out.

"Nell Garrett just laughed it off. She wasn't worried at all. Had a real fine pregnancy and all, no problems. Then bang. The baby's born and rumor has it he's a real mess. Not normal at all. Doctors told the Garretts the boy would be a hopeless case. They had to send him off to an institution.

"Nell was never the same after that. Cried all the time. Even made her husband bring the baby home for a time but it didn't work out. You know, they had the little girl to think of and all. Couldn't have that other one around without disturbing everyone. Real problem he was. Some kind of mental case I think. So they sent him back.

"Nell couldn't cope, you know. She just cried and cried for days. Felt guilty, I guess. Finally, she stopped crying and just sat staring at nothing. Something snapped inside. She'd just sit there with her arms folded like she was still holding a baby. Sad . . . real pitiful."

"Those things happen," Erica said placing a protective arm over Horatio.

"True, true. But that wasn't the end of it. Not by a long shot. After a few years, Nell died. Heart attack, they thought. Broken heart if you ask me. And a few years later still Mr. Garrett married a lovely young New York girl name of Marion. They had twins after a time, all fine and normal. Two little boys. Dearest things. Smart, full of the dickens. Marion used to bring them around to my Isabel's from time to time. Marion and Isabel were good friends, you know. And Isabel took a real shine to the boys. Never could have children of her own, poor thing. Something about her tubes. And John, that's Isabel's husband, wouldn't hear of adoption. There's no reasoning with John once his mind is made up, I'll tell you.

"Anyway, just when we all thought the bad streak was over, one of the twins is found dead in his crib. Suffocated by one of those little lace pillows you put in for decoration. Can you believe it? Sweetest little pillow with his name embroidered and all. Sarah Pritzker made it for a birth gift. Sarah's got golden hands. Makes most of the crafts for our Christmas fair. You know those wreaths made of woven scraps of fabric? Like that.

"The other boy is okay till he's just a few years old. Then he drowns out by the pond. Wasn't supposed to be swimming by himself, you know. Went down to catch sunnies was all and must've gotten warm and wanted a dip. Found the little pole by the shore. Pitiful.

"Marion was so torn up by it she shot herself right in the head with Bertram's rifle. Found her with her pretty face about blown off, he did.

"None of us could understand how Bert held up through it all. He was about the strongest man you ever wanted to meet. I mean it took its toll but he wouldn't be beaten. Still believed the house wasn't to blame or anything. Just bad luck."

"Some people can deal with an awful lot," Erica said.

"True. But it finally got too much, even for a tough customer like Bert. His little girl, all he had left in the world, had grown to be a real pretty young woman. Real nice too. She was maybe twenty-three. Engaged to a real nice young man. A doctor, I think. Someone with a real bright future.

"Right before the wedding, it was. Invitations were out

and everything. Wasn't a thing anyone could do. Found the poor thing with her head crushed in. Must've tripped and landed on a rock or something. Bertram went wild after that—drinking, gambling, running with a fast crowd. Never showed his face in church again I'll tell you. Wouldn't have anything to do with God anymore. Guess he just stopped believing."

Erica peered over Mrs. Bailey's shoulder at the ledger. Vague charts and statistics on faded parchment. There was no hint of the intricate weave of lives and histories for an outsider to see. "So Bertram let the place go and it was sold for taxes?"

The old woman squinted at Erica, then bent to read further. "Nope. Nothing like that anywhere. Went right from Bert Garrett to this Bricklin woman."

Erica frowned. "Funny. I guess it was just a misunderstanding. I thought it was sold for taxes. The place was in pretty bad shape . . ."

"Sure. I imagine. Bertram was in no mood to worry about his property the last few years. Too busy raising Cain with his fast friends, he was. In the bag more time than out. You should've seen his eyeballs, pink as a rabbit's most of the time. And breath you could light with a match. Bert was in no condition to worry about any house. Could hardly take care of himself, poor fellow. Looked a fright. Bert was a real dandy in his heyday. Then his hair turned all white and ratted almost overnight. Face got all sunken and yellow. Like you read about. Man became a whole different person."

Why would Goody lie about the estate being sold for taxes? No, Erica. Don't be foolish. It was all an innocent mistake. Someone had given him the wrong information. Or, there was some misunderstanding. There was nothing to gain by a lie like that. Sold, auctioned. What difference did it make? All that had to do with strangers. Nothing to do with her. With any of them. "This Garrett person must have been in really bad shape. I mean, to let everything deteriorate that way, to lose all his money."

Eunice Bailey shook her head. "Never came to that. Bert had more money than the Lord, bad luck or no. Couldn't have lost it all in a lifetime of foolish living. He left the place to this Bricklin woman in his will." She clicked her tongue. "Must've been quite an item, those two."

Erica felt a wave of dizziness. "No. That can't be. It doesn't make sense."

The old woman placed her bony hand on Erica's shoulder. "Hardly anything ever does, missy. Believe me, I know."

Why did it have to be this way? One question is erased and another, more disturbing one crops up to take its place. Easy, Erica. There could be a simple, logical explanation for all this too.

There had to be.

CHAPTER
30

Mel arrived early and unannounced. Erica was still asleep after an exhausting night filled with doubts and dark images. Mrs. Oh clucked over Mel's obvious agitation. She led him to the solarium and tried to relax him with weak tea and "Music of Your Life" played over the local radio station. "You lissen to old blue eyes," she told him. "He'll lower your blood pressure for sure. Whenever my Philly's had a really awful aggravating day I fix him some nice tea with honey and put Frankie on the Victrola. Works like magic."

Mel waved the woman away. He was in no mood for annoying good intentions. What right did Erica have to be sleeping when he felt as if some mad fiend had spent the night sandpapering his nerves?

Mrs. Oh was not one to surrender without a fight. "Look how jittery you are. Now you sip that tea and relax before you have a regular fit or something," Mrs. Oh said. "I remember when Philly's mother got like that. High strung that woman was. And mean . . ."

Erica appeared just as Mel was considering whether to throw the Royal Copenhagen ashtray or the Wedgewood candy dish—directly at Mrs. Ohringer's mouth, he thought. Perfect target. A big one in perpetual motion. Pull . . . fire . . . smash. Like shooting clay pigeons. He smiled for the first time in days.

Erica was accustomed to the deliberate, controlled Mel Underwood, not this pudgy ball of frayed nerves who paced the solarium like a caged bear. He seemed so out of place at Bramble Farm. She knew his pulses were tuned to a more frenetic pace, his brain pitched to the tones and tempos of the city. "This is an interesting surprise," she said. "Is there a problem?"

He stopped his pacing and shot her a look of pure exasperation. "This is not a good situation, Erica. Psychologically, it's not good at all. Here, the big numbers are flying around like plastic Frisbees and I can't even stick my hand out for a simple catch. Prescott can't firm anything up without a script in hand, a story line, a contract, something. All I have are oral promises from your Mr. Strangelove. Worst of all, the whole furor over another Bricklin book is likely to cool before I ever get anything in print. It's not just for me, for Prescott. You have a stake in this too. Get your name associated with a successful Theresa Bricklin novel and you can call your shots for future projects. You know this business. Everyone wants to ride with a winner. Can't you give me something? A few chapters?"

She turned her palms up. "Goody won't budge, Mel. You know that. You've tried yourself, right? He won't let a page leave Bramble Farm until the whole book is found."

"But he wouldn't know, would he, sweetie? A few chapters could simply drop in my little briefcase over there and no one would be the wiser. If the Lord wanted information kept secret, he wouldn't have invented copy machines."

"Unethical, my friend. You taught me to be ethical, honest."

"So I made a mistake. I take it back. Be a ruthless opportunist. Honest doesn't make profits."

She held out the crystal candy dish. "Want a mint, Mel? That's all you're going to get from me."

He sat beside her on the couch, hitching his pants to make room for his ample thighs. "Tell me, at least. What is it—mystery, horror, fantasy? What hasn't Bricklin tried?"

"It doesn't fit neatly into any of the standard genres. That much I can tell you. And it's nothing like any of her previous work. In fact, the critics will have to go to great lengths to compare this one to any of the others." Erica frowned. At Bramble Farm, there was no opportunity to discuss the book. Simple truths, like the enormous difference between this manuscript and Theresa's other books, hadn't fully occurred to her, until now. "It really is very different . . . almost too different."

"Nothing is too different, Erica. Not anything from a writer like Bricklin—consistent, proven. She has the perfect combination of literary credibility and commercial appeal. This book could make Prescott's year all by itself. And yours. You know Hemphill even intends to give you a piece of the profits. He's determined to have you stick with the manuscript until it's published. It's unprecedented."

Erica looked past Mel out the solarium window. Work on Bramble Farm was proceeding with a vengeance, a race against the weather. Each garden had a separate character, a distinct personality that she found vaguely disturbing. The formal topiary stands overlooked a playful profusion of bold color in the cutting garden. A cedar walk lined with antique brick chevrons and carved stone benches stood beside a natural rock garden thick with mosses and lichens. Hemphill had so many disparate demands, the place seemed a study in confusion.

"It's odd, Mel. At some point in this book, I almost have the feeling Theresa Bricklin changed to something, someone else. I think parts of this work come from a part of her that didn't exist before."

"You mean you think she wrote it with a few cracks in the ceiling?"

"It's possible, isn't it? Her psychological state could have been affected before the stroke. She might have had some mental changes, right?"

"Anything is possible, Erica. Are you trying to tell me the book is a bomb?"

"No, not a bomb. Most of the book is wonderful. As good, maybe better, than anything else Miss Bricklin has ever done. Then, the work seems to change, deteriorate." She shivered. "Reading the latest chapters Goody found, I couldn't help thinking she wrote them when some damage had already been done."

"Swell." Mel took a handful of mints and tossed them, one at a time, into his mouth. "The entire industry is buzzing about the latest Bricklin blockbuster, and the end of the book is sewage. Encouraging."

"I haven't seen the end, Mel. And it's not sewage. It just doesn't exactly work."

"Can it be made to work?"

"I don't know. I won't know for sure until I see the rest of the manuscript, if I ever see it."

"Swell, swell." He was stuffing his mouth with a vengeance now, chewing his words. "No big deal. So what if the book stinks? So what if Prescott loses its credibility? Why didn't you tell me about this little turn of events, Erica? You owed me that much."

His anger stung. "I'm sorry, Mel. I'm sorry you feel that way. I just couldn't believe the book was going downhill that way. I didn't admit it to myself until now. And . . . it may work out fine if the ending turns up, and ties things together."

"Those are some pretty big ifs to hang my professional reputation on. I'm going to have to go home and do some serious backpedalling."

Horatio poked her in the side. "Please, Mel. Don't do anything yet. Give it some more time. Maybe I can convince Goody to search a little harder for the last chapter or two. If we find them, everything might look different."

His argument was interrupted by Mrs. Ohringer's knock. "You two mind if I vacuum in here? Mr. Hemphill asked me to be sure the solarium was shipshape. I hate to interrupt, but he doesn't like it when I don't do what he asks. You understand?"

"It's okay, Mrs. Oh. We were about finished talking anyway. Come on, Mel. I'll show you the rest of the place."

"Good. Get some air, Miss Phillips. You could use it," Mrs. Oh said. "Take a nice long walk. Works wonders for the bowels, the complexion, the whole bit. When I was pregnant with Lynnie, I used to walk two, three miles a day, every day. Kept the old pipes chugging just fine. And you, Mister, if you don't mind my saying so, a walk is good for the nerves. A little exercise and you'll wind right down. You'll see."

As they walked, Mel whistled under his breath. "This is some little place. Seems a bit much for one old, sick woman and her husband. What do they need all this for?"

"Good question. I suppose it's a mentality I'll never understand. Goody seems to think perfect surroundings will help Theresa's recovery. He wants so desperately for her to get well."

"If I were Bricklin, I'd have another stroke just thinking of the cost of all this."

"I don't think money is an issue," Erica said, thinking of Mark Bloomway, who had blessed them with his absence for the last few weeks. "They both have plenty."

"Don't be so sure. From what I've heard, Miss Bricklin was in the habit of spending faster than she earned. And Hemphill?"

"He sold a successful import business a few years ago. From what he told me, I gather he did very well."

"Doesn't seem the type," Mel said. "But then, you never know. He doesn't seem the type to be lord of the manor either."

They were in front of the stables. "It's a mistake to judge by appearances, Mel." A horse whinnied in fright. Erica took an involuntary step backward. "That's Goody's pride and joy," she said as she walked quickly past. "They own several prize Arabians."

"Interesting. I have a friend who invests in Arabians. He's been trying to sell me a piece of the action for years. Good tax shelter. I'd like to see them."

She shook her head. "I'm afraid this part of the tour is by invitation only. Goody says the place is climate-controlled, very delicate systems. He doesn't allow anyone to visit without him."

"That's ridiculous," Mel said. He pushed against the door. "Locked?"

"And alarmed." She pointed to the key pad at the side of the door. "I told you those animals are extremely valuable."

"That may be, but Joe Bledsoe, the guy I told you about who invests, says the risk is minimal. These animals are always insured. There's no reason to keep them in a vault like this, especially in broad daylight when the whole damned place is like a fortress anyway."

"Look, Mel. That's Goody. What can I say? He's a little . . ."

"Paranoid?"

"That too. Come on. Let's forget the horses. Okay? I'll show you the hydroponic, solar-powered, state-of-the-art greenhouse if you're a good boy." Her feet were starting to ache but she wanted Mel to see Bramble Farm, didn't want him to leave. Having him there added a welcome touch of normalcy.

"No. I want to see the Arabians. Didn't you say Goody has his studio in the back? Let's knock."

"He doesn't like to be disturbed. I wouldn't . . ."

"But I would." Mel raised his fist to knock but the door swung open before he could make contact.

"My, my. What a lovely surprise. Our dear Mummy and Mr. . . . ?"

"Underwood, Mel Underwood from Prescott Press. We've spoken on the phone."

"A pleasure," Goody gushed. "I'm delighted to meet you. Erica, I trust you are giving Mr. Underwood a proper tour of our home?"

"Quite a place," Mel said. "Very nice job you've done fixing it up. Erica tells me you have some top-notch Arabians. I was thinking of investing in a syndicate. Can I have a look?"

Goody pursed his lips. "Unfortunately, Mr. Underwood, this is not the most propitious of times. Four times each day, a rather potent insecticide is circulated through the stable air ducts. The chemical composition is quite harmless to the horses but can cause severe lung damage in humans. That is why I was leaving myself, in fact. Perhaps another time."

"One little peek couldn't hurt," Mel said. "I'll hold my breath."

"I'm afraid I cannot allow it, Mr. Underwood. Now, why don't I see you to your car?"

Erica watched Mel pull away in his steel grey BMW. His bald spot had grown from quarter size to a shiny skull cap. Good old Mel. With Hemphill, he sank into the professional guise reserved for temperamental artists—calm, reasonable, conciliatory. The real Mel would have stood his ground, stayed as long as he liked, seen his fill of the Arabians.

"Your Mr. Underwood is most eager to launch this latest manuscript, I gather. I fear he shares your impatient nature. Art cannot be hurried nor creativity urged beyond its natural progress."

"When art is big business, other pressures are inevitable, Goody. Publishing is a fickle industry with a very short attention span. If Miss Bricklin's novel misses the rush of enthusiasm it's already created, I don't know if there will be another one."

"Certainly there will. How could there not? Who is a greater novelist than Theresa Bricklin? Whose work more richly praised or appreciated? Every one of her works has been a critical and commercial event! This latest shall be no exception."

"Yes, but . . ."

"No buts, my dear. No vain doubts or petty eventualities. This work will be dear Tessa's most successful creative effort—duly and justly rewarded. I will not entertain another possibility.

Erica held her tongue. She was tempted to tell him about the novel's flagging conclusion. But this was not the time to try to tell him anything. Anyway, there was still a chance for a firm, redeeming final chapter. A good chance, she told herself.

There had to be.

CHAPTER

31

"Michael, I'm so glad you called. I've been looking for you everywhere. I must've spoken to Kathy a thousand times. Did she finally track you down?"

"She didn't have to. I always check in with her once a week, wherever I am."

"Once a week? What if someone needs you sooner? What if there's an emergency?"

"You're right, Wick. I can see that. From now on I'll be sure never to go anywhere until I leave you a complete itinerary."

She frowned into the phone. "I'm not being entirely rational, am I?"

"I guess you're rational enough, for you."

Her voice dropped to a harsh whisper and her eyes darted from the study door to the open window. It seemed paranoia was contagious. "This is serious, Mike. I need your help."

His voice trailed hers in a husky parody. "Sounds serious. Are you feeling all right? Any problems with the baby?"

"No . . . none that I know of. My doctor, Jim Wellings, says everything is in order. It's about this place, Bramble Farm. I was hoping you were still an incurable snoop."

"I'll try not to take that personally. I'm not a snoop. Just professionally curious."

"Good. Then you won't object to using your 'professional curiosity' to find out a few things about a man named Garrett, Bertram Garrett. He died a few years ago and it seems he willed Brabble Farm to Theresa Bricklin."

"Hmm. Interesting. What exactly do you want me to find out?"

For some reason, she kept expecting the door to swing open. An insistent pulse was hammering in her head. "I want to know about his relationship with Miss Bricklin mostly. Was it romantic or what? And about his family. I hear he was married twice. Had four or five kids. I was wondering whether there were any living relatives. Why the place was left to Miss Bricklin and not someone in the family. That sort of thing."

"Oh, is that all?" She could picture the laugh lines tugging at the corners of Michael's dark eyes. No matter. She would sign on for more than a little brotherly teasing is she could clear up this final mystery.

"Well, no. Actually, I was hoping you could dig a little into Miss Bricklin's background as well. Information that might have been left out of the magazine pieces and the authorized biographies. And find out whatever you can about Goody Hemphill's past. Though that may not be so easy. To listen to him, he might have landed here full-grown from another planet. He never talks about family, school, nothing."

"What's going on there, sister dear? You're not the suspicious type."

"Who said I'm not. Anyway, I'm not suspicious. Just personally curious. If you can't help, just say so. I'll understand."

"Whoa, take it easy. Of course I'll help. In fact, by a stroke of incredible coincidence, L.C. Kipness and I have been digging up information on your Bramble Farm and its principals for the past few weeks."

"Michael! I told you there was no way Goody would ever agree to a photo shoot of the estate."

"I have not gotten where I am today by listening to reason, Erica. There is no percentage in it. Tell me what you know and I'll see what I can piece together. You'll have your answer in a couple of days."

Still speaking in a strained whisper, she told him what she had already learned, bits and pieces picked up from conversations with Goody and Mrs. Oh, the information from the Historical Society, what she remembered about Theresa's background and the meager information she had about Goody.

"Where are you now, Michael? In case I have to reach you."

He cleared his throat. "Well, in fact, Wicka, since you ask, I'm not far away from you at all. As I mentioned, we've been doing some preliminary investigating that's almost finished and . . ."

"No, Michael. Please. You can't continue with this one. Goody will never permit it. He'll be furious. Please!"

"What is it, Wicka? I don't like the way you sound. If that Hemphill character has you spooked, you get out of there. I'll come and get you out."

She measured her words and managed to smooth the hysterical edge in her voice. "No. It's nothing like that. It's just . . . well, your timing is lousy. Give me a few weeks and I'll talk to Goody. Once the book is done, he'll be much more receptive, more relaxed."

"You mean it? A few weeks?"

"I mean it. In the meantime, please promise me you'll lay off. Promise you won't do anything foolish."

"I'm wounded. Don't you trust me, Wicka? Aren't I a reasonable person?"

She replaced the receiver soundlessly and released some of her unbearable tension with a slow deep breath. Asking Michael was the most sensible way to proceed. With his resources, he would be able to come up with the answer—a simple, logical explanation. Couldn't Goody be ashamed of the house's past? Theresa's past? Simple as that. He was ashamed so he left out the part about Theresa and Bertram Garrett, rewrote the past just a little bit.

Possible. It was all possible. Michael would call back in a day or two and they would have a good laugh at her foolishness.

Just a few more days.

CHAPTER

32

"All right, Miss Bricklin. Let's try it one more time." Erica sat opposite the old woman on the rear patio. The autumn chill had surrendered to a fierce midday sun and she held the communication board at a calculated angle to avoid the glare. "I know it's hard but please try."

"Beckah . . . mmup!" Theresa raised her good hand and rapped a gnarled finger on the edge of the board.

"That's right. You're supposed to point." Erica's demonstration was slow and exaggerated. "Like this. Point to Erica."

"Muppuh." Her lip quivered with concentration but the response was clean, direct. The old woman scanned the board and placed her finger on the correct picture.

"Yes, yes! That's it!" Erica worked to rein in her enthusiasm. She didn't want to break the woman's concentration. "Now . . . try 'eat.' Point to 'eat.'" With sweeping gestures, Erica brought some imaginary food to her mouth and chewed with large rolling motions. "Eat, Miss Bricklin. You point to 'eat.'"

With a triumphant glint in her eye, Miss Bricklin found the word and set her finger on it. "Berakuh!"

"Yes, you wonderful, brilliant woman. We are getting somewhere at last. Now try 'Goody.' Point to 'Goody.' Won't he be thrilled when he sees what you can do? Point, please."

She found his picture with ease and pounded on it with an eager fist. "Eppuk . . . becka."

"That's right. That's wonderful. Now, let's move on. Point to your name. Point to 'Theresa.' "

The gauze curtain dropped back over the old woman's eyes. Erica knew the look only too well. She had managed to steal a few solitary minutes each day to work with Theresa on the word board. And every session ended this way, with the old woman's sudden lapse into an impenetrable fog. Defeated, Erica hid the board under the table, slumped back in her chair and tipped her face to the sun. There was no way to speed the process. The neurologist had warned Jim about that. Miss Bricklin might learn to use the board to communicate her thoughts but it would be a slow, labored undertaking. It would take time Erica simply did not have.

Mel's deadline hung over her like a guillotine. Two weeks. If she didn't find the rest of the book in two weeks, Prescott would pull out of the project. His professional reputation was too valuable to be spent on shaky ifs and possibilities. No novel was worth that. Not even Bricklin's.

If Mel pulled out, Erica would be left . . . nowhere. Goody would take the book to another publisher and a new editor would be assigned. She realized now how much she had been counting on this project. She had no alternative plan, nowhere else she cared to turn.

She should have known better. What was it Goody said? "Fortune is crafted of firm desire and due diligence." He was right. She had two weeks to fight for the future. Two weeks to find and finish the book.

If only she could get past the stubborn sentinels guarding Theresa's memory. So much was hidden behind those cobwebbed eyes. The house. Her past. Erica reassured herself again and again that there were simple answers, easy solutions to all of the Bramble Farm puzzles locked behind that warped expression and beneath that unruly mass of flaming hair. Above all, there was the possibility that Theresa would be able to tell Erica where the last chapters were hidden.

On the other side of the board, Erica had drawn a sketchy map of the main house, a labelled box for each room, the furniture reproduced in rough miniature. If only Miss Bricklin could get to the point where she could raise her finger and point to the hiding place.

Then, there was the manuscript itself. By now, she could recite the words in her sleep. Still, she might have missed something, some clue to the whereabouts of the book's ending. How many times had she searched for something only to find it waiting patiently in the most obvious of all places?

Finally, she would make a thorough search of the house. No matter how risky the undertaking, she could not surrender without a proper struggle. Finishing the book meant financial security, a professional future. Yes, she had skills, experience, determination. She would manage without it if she had to. But it would be so much easier and nicer to manage with it.

Last night was a good start. She lay awake in her room, waiting for the others to go to bed.

First, Mrs. Oh helped Theresa to her room to the tune of her ceaseless, senseless monologue. "Damned stairs, how many? A hundred, I bet. Maybe two hundred. You know, Miss Bricklin, this kind of house was really built for those goats who like mountains. You know the ones . . . what are they called again? Mountain goats? Heh, heh. Always the simple ones I forget. My Lynnie's the same way. Couldn't remember the capital of Nebraska to save her life. Drove her teacher, Mrs. Whatserface, crazy. She called Philly and me in for one of those conferences teachers have so they can tell you all the ways your kid isn't perfect. Well, this time I had to stick up for Lynnie. I said, lissen, who cares about the capital of Nebraska anyway? Problem is the brain is only so big, right? They fill it up with all that dumb stuff there isn't room left for the really important things. My cousin Lester's girl had her head so full of capital cities she had no space left for any common sense. Went to that hotsy totsy school, whatchamacallit? Big deal. Girl didn't know which end was up, you know what I mean? Got herself in more trouble. Capital of Nebraska was no help then."

Later, she heard Goody's door brush the carpet and close. Predictable sounds in familiar order: rushing water in the sink, drawers sliding in the antique armoire, the closet door, the squeak of the casement window as he slowly cranked it shut.

For an hour, she waited in the darkness, watching the soft black breeze that rippled the cloud canopy overhead, measuring the deliberate rhythms of her breathing. Horatio's foot rapped lightly against her abdomen.

When enough time had finally elapsed, she moved in elaborate slow motion. She tried to think past the fear that thumped against her chest and buzzed in her head like a swarm of angry bees. If Goody caught her, she would plead restlessness but she knew her voice would be an unconvincing tremor. Why was she so afraid of him? Foolish fear. Harmless little man. Still, she wished she could silence the cacophonous tree locusts outside and the plaintive neighing of the Arabians.

For the search, she had divided the house into ten logical sectors, eliminating the areas she already searched that night with Theresa. The kitchen and pantry were first. There, she knew, she had the best excuse. "I was hungry, Goody," she practiced over and over. "Want to join me in a snack?"

She made her way down the corridor, holding her breath as she passed Hemphill's door. He was snoring heavily and she matched her pace to the stertorous backbeat. Easy. Careful. Almost to the stairs. Three more steps.

A floorboard creaked. She stood frozen in terror, as Goody snorted in somnolent protest, not daring to move again until his breathing settled in the even symphonies of sleep.

The small vent light above the eight-burner stove cast the large room in eerie shadow. It was a cold, utilitarian kitchen, all shimmering steel and ice-white tile. Several large pots hung from an oversized rack like heads from a gallows. Erica shivered and wrapped herself deeper in her blue terry robe.

Deftly, she slid open the drawers and felt beneath the divided cutlery racks and under the stacks of place mats and table linens.

Breath held, she explored the back corners and dark spaces in the cabinets, willing the cookware and appliances to keep still. The blessed silence was only broken by the thunder of her own pulsebeats. But she found nothing.

The pantry was lined with provisions, enough to feed an army. Broad stacks of cans and paper boxes. Hundred-pound bags of flour and grains. Large canisters of sugar, powdered milk, coffee and tea. Strange, all this for such a small household. She imagined an army under siege, well fixed for the duration.

Sector one complete, she assured herself as she flicked off the pantry light. Only nine more to go. Nine nights of terror. No big deal, right, Erica? A little terror builds what? Character? Ulcers were more likely but she was determined to find the manuscript in time.

Something moved overhead.

Paralyzed, she waited for the footsteps, the angry accusations. Straining to listen past the painful stabbing of her heart, she waited for what seemed a smothering mass of time. But the house settled back in stillness.

Stiff with fear, she made her way back through the maze of corridors to the Fallen Angel room and slipped between the cool softness of her sheets. Little by little, the ropes of tension uncoiled and the first prickles of numb weariness climbed up her legs.

Absently, she patted the taut mound of her abdomen. Horatio was still, oblivious. Just as it should be. "I'll take care of everything, kid," she whispered. "Don't you worry."

Closing her eyes, she could almost feel the silken warmth of a sleeping infant against her chest, the peace of perfect trust.

She drifted along the edge of sleep where dream and reality form a seamless whole. Night sounds bounced lightly around her: an owl's shrill query, the angry barking of a dog.

A warm wave of sleep washed over her at last, and, as she sank beneath it, she thought she heard a laugh. A chill, evil, inhuman sound. But it was so far away . . . She stilled the frantic hammering in her chest. Far, far away, she repeated to herself in a soothing mantra. Far, far. Nothing to do with me.

And then it stopped.

CHAPTER

33

She recognized the dream from a foggy distance and tried to turn back but she could not struggle free from the paralyzing ropes of sleep.

She had to get away. Please! Please, no. No! A scream bubbled up in her throat and caught there, sharp as a razor blade. A sharp blue pain that spread behind her tongue and up through her head until her temples pounded and hot sparklers flashed in her eyes. She was trapped.

And then it came. Always the same beginning. The day a crisp apple. Flame and lemon leaves shimmering against a polished sky. A lazy fly walking a slow, pleasant tickle up her forearm as she toed a shiny boot into the stirrup and hoisted herself over Heather's solid middle.

Firm and erect in the saddle, the cool leather of the reins settled in a steady hand. The old chestnut was acting up. Snorting in contempt and shaking her head. Temperamental old nag. "You're in a mood, girl. Aren't you?"

Holding firm to the reins, she jerked Heather's head upright, away from the hay pile, and led her out of the barn. This was a job, after all. A real job and a stroke of incredible good luck. The stables were just down the road from Erica's house. Mr. Brady, the owner, had watched her ride a couple of times and offered her a dollar an hour to exercise the horses. Amazing. She would have done it for nothing. In fact, she had saved every cent for her occasional ride. And now they were paying her. She was the luckiest girl in the world.

Heather's tail slapped a nosy fly and she issued a petulant whine. As they rode, a vague breeze ruffled Erica's hair so a thick wave fell across her eyes. She brushed it back, thinking she needed a haircut.

This was the filth animal she rode around the paddock, trotting and cantering until the surface of the dry ring rose in grainy clouds of dust, burning her eyes and leaving her throat parched and sore. Mr. Brady hadn't given her permission to take any drinks from the ancient refrigerator in the office. And she knew the old fountain behind the stable only too well. The water was warm and bitter with rust.

She could go home for just a few minutes. No harm in it, she thought, as she turned the horse out through Brady's creaky gate and down the road to her house. Mom would be home now, waiting for the bus to deliver Michael from his first day in second grade. It was fun to have her home all the time now that she quit teaching to wait for the new baby.

Heather kept stalling at the edge of the road, nibbling at the scrub grasses and wild flowers. Erica tugged sharply at the reins. Gotta show 'em who's boss, Mr. Brady had warned her. Gotta get that across right from the beginning.

"Stop that, Heather," she said crossly. "C'mon girl, walk on!" She kicked the broad flanks lightly for emphasis.

The ride was halting, frustrating. The horse, still unconvinced of Erica's authority, continued her defiant grazing, but they finally reached the head of Erica's driveway. Turning in, she adjusted her seat and felt a broad grin spread over her face. She was a working girl now, grown-up. Responsible. Sitting bolt upright, she slowed Heather to a walk and felt the gravel crunch like celery under the heavy hooves.

"Mom!" she called, wanting to show off her proud seat and obedient charge. "Mom, how about a glass of juice for a working girl!"

In a few minutes, the screen door slammed and her mother appeared carrying a large glass of pink lemonade, the ice clinking against the sides. She looked so young and pretty, her hair tied back, the puff of her stomach firm under a red gingham maternity dress. "I didn't know you were going to get a coffee break, Erica. I'm impressed."

"Is Michael home yet?" Erica asked. "Who did he get?"

"Not yet. He'll be here soon. In a few minutes."

Always the same. Erica sitting astride the horse. The breeze ruffling her hair. Mom smiling. The whole scene a slice of fresh baked Americana.

Then, in a blink, a page turned. A pulse of change too small to detect unless you tuned your whole mind to it. Erica much too busy feeling important, too full of self-pride.

The horse shied. Nothing to it. A quick click of reaction in her body—pulling here, holding fast, adjusting to avoid a fall. Nothing to it. It was fun. Almost fun.

Over in a second, a snap. But when she looked back to find her mother, there was a blank place, an inky void. Even when she called. Nothing. She stared at the emptiness, thinking enough will could bring her mother back. Staring until her eyes ached.

A move. A flicker. And Erica knew her mom had just been playing along. A silly game. "You had me worried," she said. Her voice was scratchy and slow but it grew as she watched. Grew to a siren scream.

Her mother falling. Falling in a deep black hole. No end to it. Falling and falling and Erica screaming for her to stop. But she kept falling, getting smaller and smaller until Erica knew she was gone. Lost.

She turned Heather back up the path, out through the gate. The terror was boiling in her gut but she had to find her mother, find the bottom of the hole. Riding, riding until her eyes were burning dry and the reins left bloody creases in her palms. Screaming for her mother, over and over again. Ready to drop from exhaustion but she couldn't stop.

Riding until the horse was stumbling lame and struggling

against her lead. "Come on, girl. Just a little more. Just over there."

She knew before they climbed the rise. They had reached the end. She could feel it before she saw her mother lying there. Lying cold, rubbery dead with a grimace of a smile pasted where the life had been. Big holes like Swiss cheese all over her body. No blood. Just clean cut holes filled with black empty despair.

As Erica watched, a tiny creature swaggered out from behind her mother's inert body. Baby-sized, simian, pink and toothless but it walked like a grown man and its little thumbs were hitched in the pockets of a pair of baggy brown corduroy pants. It wore an ugly green shirt and a horrid little tie with diagonal stripes the colors of dirt and dried blood. And there was a scrub of grey-brown whiskers you wanted to rub at with a soapy cloth. The voice was the low growl of a cornered animal. "You killed her," it said over and over. "You killed her—killed, killed."

"No. No, I didn't. It wasn't me. Not me."

Over and over. The words stabbing at her. "You killed her . . . you killed . . . killed . . . killed!"

"No!" Finally, she broke free, pulled away from the chains of sleep and lay awake, drenched with sweat. Cold beads of it stood out on her face and ran in warm rivulets between her breasts and down her sides. Her chest was heaving and a dizzy wave washed through her head.

Why now? She had been free of the dream for years. She had spent so many hours pulling out the pain, examining it until the slicing blades were dull and innocent, until she could sleep without the horror. So much time going over and over it. An accident. She knew it was a solitary event set off by some quirk of a mindless fate. No fault of hers, of anyone's. And there was no guarantee that was the reason for her mother's death. It could have happened anyway, without the fall. Nobody knew the reason for sure. Just one of those things. Over and over it until she thought she believed her own blamelessness.

So she wasn't finished with it after all. The useless, sense-less guilt.

Why now? Why?

"All right, Erica. No more of that," she told herself, re-peating an ancient refrain. "No more . . . no more. Nothing is solved, nothing changed by all the guilt and self-punish-ment."

It was early, so early. She slid quietly out of bed and stood at the window, staring out at the soft blanket of silver shadow, trying to absorb the stillness. Nothing stirred. Nothing broke the soothing pulse of the sleeping universe. If only it could be like this for a while, a few days.

Her white cabled cardigan still lay on the chair from last night. Without thinking, she pulled it on over her long flannel nightgown and padded soundlessly out of her room. Something moved her with a sure, even hand and held away the fear of detection. Sooner or later, she had to do it.

Her shadow stretched down the long, narrow corridors and cushioned her footfalls as she fled down the short flights of stairs.

In the foyer, the grandfather clock hissed and sounded six somber tones. She turned the heavy deadbolt and let herself out into the dim chill.

Bramble Farm had been swallowed by a dense cottony mist. Nothing left but smudged silhouettes. But she knew the place well enough to find her way.

Down the walk, she felt the cool brick chevrons under-foot. Soon she would pass the topiary garden. A few more steps. There it was. Her mind filled in the vague outline of a proud Arabian, the elephant trumpeting in majestic si-lence, the eagle poised for flight. She circled widely to avoid a collison with the stone bench and made her way to the cutting garden.

Erica ran her hand along the top of the wire fence. Cold, so cold. The blackened head of a dahlia fell away as she touched it and settled in the crisp carpet of winter mulch.

The rock garden was next. Moving slowly, she made her

way over slick stone formations and craggy boulders that bit her feet through the thin soles of her slippers. Something slithered across her path.

Shivering now, she ducked beneath a low-hanging limb of the ancient maple and arrived at last at a long, flat, grassy expanse. She raced across the frozen ground, trying to keep ahead of the frigid wind of fear breathing down her neck. Too close to turn back. This had to be done, sooner or later.

Her breath came in short, bitter gasps as she neared the stables. Blood roared in her temples. What had possessed her?

When she reached the sleek, low building, Erica ran her hand across the rough siding and found the keypad beside the door. Down the middle, she told her trembling fingers. That's how Goody had done it. Down the middle.

What if there were something else to do? She wouldn't consider that. Too late to worry about that. A musky animal scent filled her frozen nostrils.

She was about to push the door but something held her immobile. Some sound? A warning? There it was. Footsteps in the distance. And the rhythm. Goody's footsteps. The unmistakable lurching pattern, ta-dum, ta-dum. He was coming toward her. He would find her standing there.

She willed her wooden legs to move. A few steps. Around the corner she would be out of sight. If she could only make it in time!

Slowly, carefully. A single misstep and he would hear. So close now but still a part of the mist. Three more steps. Two.

As she turned the corner, her foot came down in a hillock of dried leaves. Crunch. The sound deafening to her. No choice now. She ducked behind a low privet hedge in back of the stables and croched low, waiting for him to come, to find her.

Kneeling, her legs trembling, a sledge hammer pounding at her head, she waited as the sounds of his uneven gait came closer and closer. Dawn was sifting through the night's ashes, shaking out the mist. Closer and closer. Soon it would be light enough for him to find her.

Closer still. So near she could feel his feet coming down in erratic rhythm on the frozen earth. Each step shot through her.

What would she say? What would he do? Her heart was leaping like an eager puppy, tearing at her chest. Crazy sparks of fear burned the backs of her arms. A lead fist of pain punched her womb.

The steps went on, past the stable door. Coming closer to her. She was trembling violently, trying to find words. An excuse. Something.

There, in the lightening shadow, his face so close the cloud of his warm breath settled over her. "Here, kitty, kitty," he said. "Here, kitty."

Then he turned away, muttering something Erica could not hear. Her relief was a warm liquid rush. Why was she so afraid of Goody? Foolish little man.

Why?

CHAPTER

34

She lay shivering under the covers, trying to collect the scattered splinters of her sanity. Finally, her heart slowed to a walk, the terror receded and she felt capable of confronting the world. Using all her reserves, she managed to pull her brick of a body out of bed. The night demons had left her sore and exhausted, her legs knotted with tension.

She splashed cool water on her face and ran a comb through the snarled mess of her hair. That was the best she could do. No energy to bother with makeup or the cameo that still lay on her dresser. If she saved every bit of extra strength, maybe she could somehow get through the day.

Mrs. Oh was bustling about the kitchen, mouth running in high gear. "Don't know what gets into these kids. Only thirteen she is and wants to go to parties with boys. Thirteen, mind you. And a young thirteen at that. You know, not sophisticated like some, thank goodness. So I told her, look, Lynnie. When I was your age I was still playing with dolls, still skipping rope. What's the big hurry? I turned out all right, didn't I? Remember you got your whole life ahead of you. You don't want to start too young, I told her. A girl gets herself in trouble that way, you know what I mean? First thing it's parties. Before you know it . . ." She snapped her fingers. "Pregnant. Just like that." Looking at Erica, she clapped a hand over her mouth. "Sorry. I didn't mean anything about you. Sometimes I just don't know what gets into me. I swear, Philly's right. 'Watch that mouth Lorraine,' he tells me. That tongue keeps on hanging out like that and one day you're going to trip over it."

Erica managed a smile. "It's okay, Mrs. Oh, I'm not thirteen."

"No. True. Even so. You gotta watch these kids every minute. So I told her, look, Lynnie, as long as you're living here with us, it's our way, simple as that. You're ready when we say you're ready. Not before. And I don't care what all the other kids are doing. You're the only one matters to me, I told her. Philly was behind me all the way. Parties, he says. Hah!"

"Sure, sure," Erica said, stifling a yawn. "You have to do what you think is right."

Mrs. Oh held up a finger and frowned. "Now where did I put that note he left you? My memory's going, I swear it. First it's the eyes, then the brain. Used to have a real good memory. It's true. Philly said I had a mind like a steel trap. Used to know everyone's birthday, anniversary, you name it. Now I hardly remember what I had for breakfast this morning." She looked around the room and shook her head. "Mr. Hemphill told me to make sure you got it. Usually he's gone before I ever get here but he got a late start today, I guess. Waited to make sure you got the message. Now where in the hell did I put it? I swear I'd lose my teeth if they wasn't glued in." She looked around again and shrugged. "Oh well, at least I remember what it said. Seems your doctor's office had to cancel your appointment. An emergency or something. They'll call to reschedule."

"Okay. Thanks." Interesting that Goody went to the studio and came back to the house, all so early. Interesting but she was too weary to do much thinking about anything. She was simply glad to hear the appointment was cancelled. Glad and relieved. The last thing she needed today was a trip downtown and a lecture from Jim about taking better care of herself, getting more rest.

"And I wanted to know if you need me to do anything for you before I go. If there's anything you want?"

"Go?" Erica said. "Where are you going?"

"Didn't Mr. Hemphill tell you? I'm supposed to be out before one. Crew's coming in to pave the road. Two, three days no one can ride on it. In or out, he told me, so I said out. Philly's just been at this new job a couple of weeks. Can't exactly have him taking off now. And Lynnie's got school. And cheerleading practice. Heaven forbid she had to miss that. Whole world would come to an end for sure. Nothing's more important than cheerleading, you know. Not even breathing, to listen to Lynnie. We're going to stay with Philly's cousin Ruth in White Plains. Can't stand her boy, Larry. Real wise ass, he is. Thinks, he knows everything about everything. You know the type. Always wisecracking at Lynnie too. Drives her crazy. But what can I do?"

Erica followed Flumacher as he wheeled Theresa into the dining room. She was dressed in a white ruffled blouse, a flowered dirndl skirt and a long black crocheted shawl. Smudges of charcoal shadow hovered above her eyes like storm clouds and the warped bow of her mouth was painted a bloody red. Flumacher positioned her chair in place at the table and locked the brakes before leaving.

Mrs. Oh brought a soft-boiled egg in a porcelain cozy, a slice of dry wheat toast and a cup of pale tea for Theresa's breakfast. "You two be okay in here? Got a lot to do this morning. Vacuuming, dusting. Have to straighten up in the kitchen and run a couple of loads of wash. Busy, busy. Don't want to leave the place a mess. I got my pride."

"Sure, we'll be fine. I'll help Miss Bricklin. You go on and do what you have to." Erica waited until the footsteps retreated to a safe distance and spoke to no one in particular. "I don't know why Goody didn't mention a little thing like the road being paved, two or three days of imprisonment. I'm afraid I have some arrangements to make myself. If it's in or out, I had better be out also. Maybe he didn't realize it but I could deliver any time. There's nothing unusual about being a week or two early."

"Enguk . . . mmmupuh!" Theresa was leaning toward Erica, straining to make herself understood. "Aruguk!"

"Don't worry about it. I'm sure he just didn't think it through. After all, he's never had children of his own. He probably thinks it's like a bus schedule. You don't bother to go to the terminal until an hour before arrival time."

"Ack . . . kukk." She cupped the fingers of her good hand and tapped them over and over again on the table. "Kukk."

"You want to tell me something? What? What is it?"

Theresa's eyebrow shot upward, then settled in a gentle twitch. She looked at Erica again, her eyes pleading for understanding and tapped the air above her lap.

"Something important, Miss Bricklin?" Maybe important enough to get her to communicate at last, she thought. "I'll be right back."

Erica went to her room, retrieved the word board from its hiding place in the bottom of a drawer and hurried back to the waiting Theresa. She looked around, furtive as a thief. Flumacher was nowhere in sight and Mrs. Oh's vacuum was droning at a reassuring distance. "Tell me, Miss Bricklin. What is it? Point and tell me."

The old woman stared deep into Erica's eyes, her expression pleading, desperate. Slowly, she looked down and scanned the board, staring at each word in turn. "Pebuck . . . bim . . ."

"Try, Miss Bricklin. Try to show me. You remember. Point with your finger. Point . . . like this."

Theresa fixed her gaze on Erica's mouth and took a deep breath. "Muggibuk . . . Piddum."

"Use the board, Miss Bricklin. Tell me with the board." Erica pointed again in demonstration.

The old woman tapped the board and smacked her lips. "Peckah . . . bmmm." She fisted her good hand and slowly raised her index finger. Pausing, she looked at Erica as if to be sure she was watching. "Bemmup?"

"Go ahead, Miss Bricklin. Tell me."

Theresa shook her head as if to clear it and turned her attention back to the board. Her movements were labored, her face twisted in concentration. Her finger settled on 'Goody.'

"Goody," Erica repeated. "What about him?"

The gnarled finger searched and stopped at 'cold.'

"Cold?" Erica frowned. "Goody cold? Doesn't make any sense. Cold? Is it your breakfast? Stupid me . . . I'm sorry. Let me fix that egg for you." She buttered the toast and cracked the egg into the flowered bowl. "The whole thing with the road is really no big problem. I'll manage. I could always call Jim . . ."

"Bamupuh . . ." Theresa's face was tight with effort. Her fist a tremor of struggle. "Gannh!"

"There. You eat your breakfast, Miss Bricklin. Then we can try again." Erica settled back in her chair. "And don't worry about me. If worse came to worse, I could take a room in a hotel. There are plenty nearby: the Holiday Inn, the Marriott. I'm not crazy about the idea right now, but I'll manage. It's not as if I'll deliver in a big hurry. Twelve, fourteen hours is the average for first-time mothers, I'm told."

"Kikkub . . . pekkam." The old woman shook her head and pounded her fist in frustration. She pushed her food away and her finger stabbed at the board. Goody . . . cold . . . love . . . hate . . . sleep. A mottled flush rose up her neck. "Mahbuk."

Erica softened her tone and stroked the withered hand. "Don't worry. Everything will be fine. I promise."

"Kikkik . . . kkkk!" The sound caught in her throat. Erica watched in horror as the old woman pulled at the invisible coils closing around her throat. Her color deepened to the dusky purple of a bruise and her eyes bulged.

"Miss Bricklin! Take it easy. Please!" Erica loosened the ruffled collar and pressed a dampened napkin on the old woman's brow. "Mrs. Oh, call an ambulance. Quick!"

Mrs. Ohringer ran into the dining room, took a look at Theresa who was now steeped in a cold sweat and pale as bleached muslin, and hurried back to the kitchen phone.

Erica kept a finger on the meager pulse in Theresa's neck and petted her with reassurances. "Ssh. Take a deep breath. Just take it easy, Miss Bricklin. Ssh."

It was another stroke. Erica was sure of it. The neurologist had warned Jim that she might well be at risk for another one. Often happens that way, he said. They get better and there's a second stroke.

"Emmup." Theresa was pale as death, her voice a kitten whimper. "Mmupuh."

"Ssh. You just take it easy. Help will be here in a few minutes." Erica took the board away, held the limp hand, and strained to listen for approaching sirens.

Mrs. Oh bustled in buttoning her plaid coat, her purse tucked under an arm. "They're on their way. We got lucky. The ambulance corps was having a meeting at Pepino's, right down on Glenville. They'll be here in half the time." She fussed over Theresa, smoothing her hair, arranging her skirt demurely over her knees. "Don't suppose she needs a coat. They'll put her on one of those whatchamacallits and cover her up with blankets, won't they?"

"Yes. I guess so. See, Miss Bricklin. They'll be right here. You're going to be all right. Just take it easy."

"There. Hear that? Hear the siren, Miss Bricklin? Like music, isn't it?"

A shrill pusling scream announced the ambulance. Two burly attendants raced in with a gurney, lifted the old woman like a sack of laundry, and strapped her in place. "I'll go along," Mrs. Oh said. "You go get Mr. Hemphill and tell him to meet us at the hospital."

They were gone in a breath. Erica fought back a wave of nausea and walked out through the gardens to the stables. Bramble Farm was frozen still. Her feet clacked against the frigid ground and her breath came in smoky puffs.

Last night was drowning in the sea of events. So dim and

distant now. No harm or consequence. Now all that mattered was Miss Bricklin. Saving her. It was important to get Goody there in a hurry. Theresa would be so frightened without him.

Shivering, Erica pounded on the stable door. A horse whinnied in response but no Goody. She kept on until her fist ached.

Disgusted, she tapped down the center row of buttons on the keypad and pushed the door open. The exhaust fans whirred and a spent fluorescent tube sizzled overhead. One horse bumped the side of his stall and another whinnied in complaint. It was too noisy for Goody to hear the knocking.

She trained her eyes past the long row of stalls. His studio was in one of the rear tack rooms. On the left, she thought, trying to remember where he had pointed, trying not to think about the horses, the dream or anything else.

The first two rooms were empty. And the third. She was trembling. Cold, she thought. She should have stopped to put on something heavier. And still nauseated. Don't think about it, Erica. It's just the strain, the worry.

The last door was locked. She hammered on it and called. "Goody. Goody, it's Erica. Please, you have to hear me." Why didn't he come? Why didn't he answer? What was taking so long? "Goody, please! It's Theresa. She's . . ."

With a startling lurch, he flung the door open and stepped out, shutting it again behind him. His expression was grim, menacing. "What, may I ask, are you doing here? And how did you breach the security?"

"Goody. It's Theresa. I think she's had another stroke."

He leaned closer to her as if straining to hear a dim sound. "I see. Well, then. You were correct to come for me. That was precisely the thing to do. I shall take care of everything."

"No, you don't understand. It's all right, all taken care of. We called an ambulance. She's on her way to the hospital."

"Hospital. No, that cannot be. You foolish woman! How could you do such a thing? What gave you the right?"

"But," she sputtered. "Please. Just call the car and go to her. I'm sure she'll want you to be there. I'll come along . . ."

"No, you will not! You have done quite enough, I assure you. How could you take such an action upon yourself? Who gave you the right? Petty insensitive creature!"

"Please, Goody. I'm sorry if you're angry for some reason but now is not the time to argue. Please. Just go to her. Go to the hospital."

Muttering under his breath, he used his beeper to call the car and waited at the stable door, tapping his foot in angry impatience. When the Bentley finally arrived, he turned to Erica. "You have breathed the fire of malicious destruction and you shall live to taste its bitter ash."

She watched him limp to the car and drive away. Strange man. Angry. Why should he be angry? What had she done?

No matter. There were more important concerns. Her teeth were chattering and she hugged herself in a vain attempt to battle the chill. Warmer clothes beckoned and she hurried back to her room to put on soft argyle socks, a thick fisherman-knit sweater and the insulated mittens she had worn for skiing in another lifetime.

The mirror had nothing pleasant to report. Her eyes were vague and puffy, her face drawn. She would see Miss Bricklin later and in deference to the old woman's morale, she brushed on a trace of cheek color and lip gloss. As she was about to leave the room, she spotted the cameo and fastened it around her neck. Miss Bricklin had wanted her to wear it always and she felt a pang of guilt at the betrayal.

In the foyer, she stopped to sort through her confusion. What was the right thing to do? She knew she wanted to see Miss Bricklin but she didn't want to upset Goody any more. For the first hour or two, they would be busy with admissions procedures: forms, X rays, the slow grinding of the bureaucracy of illness. It seemed sensible to wait until the old woman was comfortably settled in a room. By then, Erica's presence might be welcome. She could stay with Theresa while Goody went to the coffee shop for lunch.

"They won't start paving the road until this afternoon. So I've got a couple of hours to kill," she told herself. "Okay, Erica. What's a good way to kill a couple of hours? No, Erica. That's not a good idea, not a good idea at all. If you go poking around the stables again, you'll probably just find yourself in another mess, won't you? This time, you'll probably step in a mountain of manure or set off the alarm or . . ."

The clock hissed the advancing minutes. "Erica, my friend. You are talking to yourself. I hate to mention it but that is not a good sign when you start talking to yourself. Not a good sign at all . . ." A wave of nausea overtook her and she grimaced in disgust.

"Why don't you just go back upstairs like a sensible, mature individual and lie down for an hour or two. After all, you did not have a good night and you need your rest. C'mon, Erica. Be a sensible person and stop playing detective."

She walked to the closet and put on her coat. "All right." She shook her head. "If you refuse to listen to reason, I simply will not be responsible. Go ahead and check out Goody's studio if you insist. It's your foolishness. Your funeral."

Walking out through the gardens again she hummed a slim, little tune. A few deep breaths had quelled the nausea and she felt a surge of well-being. Really it was the perfect time, the perfect opportunity to satisfy herself, once and for all. If the end of the manuscript was in the studio, she would never forgive herself for not looking. Horatio kicked her a playful reminder of his impending arrival. Now or never.

The sky was heavy with snow but the greyness was no match for her soaring spirit. As she walked past the topiary garden, she winked at the somber owl and shushed the leafy horse. "Don't tell Goody. Okay? Theresa will be fine and he'll come back to find the manuscript complete. The last chapter will be wonderful, as masterful as Theresa Bricklin has ever been and Mel will be overjoyed and the Momma bear and the baby bear will live happily ever after . . ." She grinned at the neat scenario. "Has a ring to it."

The studio was such a logical hiding place. Goody spent so much of his time there. And more chapters had been found there than anywhere else. All of Erica's instincts pulled in that direction. She could close her eyes and see the crisp stack of pages, the clear characters of Theresa's typing. The final benediction—"the end." It had to be there. Erica could feel it.

The book was no help. After weeks of examination, Erica isolated the sole passage that might have some relevance to the search.

My will begs for surrender, my soul for swift relief. But deliverance eludes my failing grasp. Chained as I am, bonded to the madness of Xanthippus, chiselled in the cold granite of my personal epiphany, I must endure . . .

The part about the "cold granite" of her "personal epiphany" was obvious to Erica. Having studied Bricklin's work, she knew that the deadly permanence of the written word was a recurrent theme. Theresa suffered from the author's plague, self-doubt about the quality and integrity of her work. Each word was a commitment, a revelation, her thoughts laid open so she was naked and vulnerable. Yet she needed to write. Writing was an incurable obsession.

But what was the "madness of Xanthippus"? She knew it was more than one of Theresa's poetic inventions. Something familiar about the name but not familiar enough. She pored over dozens of volumes: mythology, early history, science, anthropology. Xanthippus?

Under ordinary circumstances, she loved a challenge. But these were not ordinary circumstances and she was sick of this particular challenge. Xanthippus was tossed somewhere in her rubble pile of casual memories. So many places to search. A mundane event. Or one book in a flood of books, from the days when books, words, were someplace to crawl, someplace to hide from herself.

Xanthippus? Her foot skated over a glossy patch of ice and, after regaining her balance, she trained her eyes to the ground. The last thing she needed was a fall. In her present state, she might fall to pieces like Humpty Dumpty or leave a deep chasm in the frozen earth like a fallen chunk of cosmic debris.

The stable door was still ajar. She pushed it open and stepped inside, blinking away the glare. At a near run, she passed the row of stalls and walked directly to the fourth tack room.

The door wouldn't open and she noticed a key pad, identical to the one outside, partially hidden behind a wooden stool. Hoping Goody was a creature of habit, she tapped down the center row of buttons. Breath held, she placed her hand on the door knob and turned.

As the door slowly yielded, she felt a tremor of fear. "Don't be ridiculous, Erica," she told herself. "There's nothing to be afraid of."

She pushed slowly, tentatively, fighting with herself over the wisdom of the whole adventure.

Nothing to be afraid of, she thought.

Famous last words.

CHAPTER

35

The room was black as a cave. Nothing but thick, syrupy darkness. How could anyone see here, much less paint? As her eyes adjusted, she made out the faint silhouette of the windows covered by thick, black drapes. The walls were lined with hundreds of books and the entire room was cluttered with a jumble of cartons and sheets-wrapped furniture. Much more like a store room than a studio, she thought. Nothing like a studio.

Stepping over several large, taped boxes, she went to the window and tried to pull open the drapes but they were nailed in place. Serious, moon-faced nails held the shrouds of dark fabric against the heavy wood frames.

Searching in vain for a light, a lamp, she tripped and toppled a pile of boxes. They fell with an enormous crash and she giggled nervously, glad Goody was all the way downtown at the hospital. "Just a few miles away, he might have heard that," she quipped to hide her nervousness.

None of it made sense. Where were the paintings? The brushes and palettes and tubes of pigment? The tipped easel with the perfect light? She climbed over several more cartons looking . . . for what?

There. A door to another room. Naturally, Erica. There was another room after this one. Always a simple explanation. Always.

Relieved, she turned the handle. Locked. Groping along the door frame, she found the expected keypad and tapped down the middle. Bless consistency.

The door was heavy, surprisingly heavy. Like a vault door, she thought as she pushed the force of her whole body against it. It yielded slowly, creaking in protest.

Goody Hemphill was a card-carrying paranoid. That was clear. She pushed until firm beads of sweat stood out on her face and her heart was doing the varsity drag. Open at last.

Her mind raced as she looked around. Damp and airless. Lights too bright, sharp pins poking at her eyes. Squinting, she took in the tiny living room.

Amazed, she walked slowly about until her eyes adjusted again. All the comforts: bright upholstered furnishings, a TV and video recorder, knickknacks, magazines, framed photographs of smiling strangers, chocolate candies in crystal dishes.

There was a noise, so low she more felt than heard it, from beyond the room. Out through yet another closed door.

The sound came again. A low, pitiful moan. Erica forced herself to walk toward it. Trembling, she opened the door a crack and peered into the darkness. A bedroom, black as ink. She could barely discern the outline of a single bed, a small nightstand, a childsized chest of drawers. And a chair, a rocker.

"Please." The voice was so tiny, so powerless, Erica almost charged it to her own imagination. "Please, help me . . ."

She groped for a light switch. Then she spotted the silhouette of a small lamp and found the pull cord.

"Please . . ."

In the pale wash of yellow light, she saw an old woman, sitting in the rocker, body held rigid, head cocked at an odd angle like a flower on a broken stem. "What happened?" Erica blithered. "Who are you? What are you doing here?"

The woman coughed a dry, bloodless cough. "Air," she rasped. "So hard to breathe."

Erica leaned and helped the old woman to her feet. No
substance there. Her legs were boneless rubber like a doll's.
As they stumbled the few steps to the bed, the woman's
slack flesh slid under Erica's fingers like flimsy cloth. So
frail. Frail as death.

Lying on the chenille spread, limp and ghostly pale, the
old woman breathed in several greedy gulps before she
spoke. "That's better. So much better. Thank you. Could
you scratch above my nose? I would be grateful. I can't
move. The medicine." Her hair stood out in fine white puffs
and deep lines of fear and exhaustion creased her hollowed
cheeks. As she breatheed, her chest rose in a pillow of effort
and collapsed like a spent balloon.

"I don't understand. Who are you? Why are you here?"
The woman lay inert, limbs thrown about like old clothes.
"Let me call for help. Is there a phone?"

"Not here. Back at the house. Hurry. Before Goodwin
returns."

"He . . . Goody kept you here? Why? I don't understand.
Why would he . . . ?"

"Not now. Please. Go. Call the police."

"Will you be okay here? Can you come with me?"

The woman strained to move but her body would not
respond. "I can't. Can't move. He's given me something,
some medicine. Please. You go. If he returns . . ."

"Don't worry. He won't be back. Not for the rest of the
day. I'm sure of it. His wife had another stroke. He took her
to the hospital."

The old woman's voice was shrill with desperation.
"Please. We must get away from here. Now!"

"All right. I'll go. I'll call from the house." She left the
apartment and stumbled through the dark, cluttered storeroom. The roar of blood in her head made it hard to think.
This was crazy. Insane.

The horses seemed so still, expectant. She hurried past
the row of stalls, eyes riveted ahead. Don't look. Don't.

Outside, a bitter wind had risen. She ducked her head
against it and hurried toward the house.

Past the field, through the maze of gardens she raced as quickly as she could. Fists of terror pummeled her temples.

Insane. He was insane.

Had she always suspected? Known? He was crazy. That woman, that poor old woman. Why?

The house was visible in the vague distance, a giant shadow muted by the biting gusts. She strained to be there, warm. Safe. The police would come and they would be all right. Everything would be all right.

She managed a stiff run past the orchard, the rock garden, over the frozen soil to the circle of topiary. The elephant trumpeted in silence through a frost-heavy trunk. Everything still, innocent.

She stopped for an instant. Stopped to catch her breath, to still the crazy tremor in her heart. One second. One second she'd be fine. Fine.

Then, as she stood, there was a flutter. Something moved. A deep shadow crossed her intended path. And she heard the sharp blade of a voice.

"There you are, my dear Mummy. Tsk, tsk. You shouldn't be out in such inclement conditions. I fear you'll catch your death."

Goody stepped out from behind the leafy horse. Through the bitter squalls, she saw the tight smile on his face and the glinting metal of a pistol. Terror was a vicious wave in her ears. "I was just . . ."

Still smiling, he shook his head. "Explanations are most irrelevant, my dear, I assure you. I would advise you to reserve your energies. You will have need of them, I suspect."

She felt the cold gun metal biting into her back as he forced her back toward the stables. "Curiosities. How I have warned you of the destructive force of your vain curiosities. But you would not listen. Stubborn, foolish child."

Her legs felt wooden and violent tremors assailed her as they walked, the gun lurching with Goody's uneven gait. "I don't know what you're talking about," she managed. "Please put the gun away."

"Hurry along!" he rasped. "Do you take me for a fool? I have monitored your every word, every movement. At first, your snooping was an amusement. You believed so ardently in your ability to find the remainder of the book. Childish delusions of omnipotence, I presumed. But I underestimated your stubborness. Now, you have forced me to act precipitously. You shall pay for this, Erica. You shall pay dearly."

"Please, Goody. I don't know what you mean. I haven't done anything." Her mind raced to calculate her chances for escape but she could not predict his reactions. He was crazy, insane. If only she could get away, get to a phone. "Why don't we go to the house? It's warm there. We can talk."

"Oh, we shall talk, my dear. You shall have a surfeit of words, I assure you. Now move!"

She walked stiffly on the numb blocks of her feet. There was no way out now. She would have to play for time until there was some chance, an opportunity to get away. They were approaching the stables. Inside now, the gun pushing her, threatening.

He led her along the row of stalls, passing his hand over the dividing walls, and stopped in front of one of the Arabians. This stall was larger than the others and fronted by a heavy wooden gate. "Here we are. Before we go further, I want you to view this magnificient beast, my dear Mummy. See how tranquil she appears. How docile. Do you recall my admonitions against blind faith in appearances? This proud beauty is a perfect example of appearance as deceit."

Erica turned away from the horse but Goody clutched her jaw and forced her to look. The gun's frozen muzzle cut into her neck.

"She was merely a foal, newly weaned, when she had her first taste of killing. Small creatures at first. Squirrels. Rabbits. I remember one pathetic, little dog, a terrier of some sort, vile little animal. How the creatures bellowed when they confronted their imminent demise. Quite an indescribable sound—the crackling of bone and sinew, the death knell. A melody unparalleled.

"The training was painstaking, requiring the noose of discipline and the spur of mortal determination. As she grew, the prey were larger and more challenging. Her appetite for death has been cultivated, carefully nurtured. One need only step inside and she will rear. Rear and crush the intruder with the full weight of her devilish fury. Her name is Xanthippus. Horse of Death." The bile rose in Erica's throat as she looked into the horse's eyes. They were glazed with tortured madness.

"Please, Goody . . ."

"Spare me the entreaties, my dear. This is but one of the many faces of the glorious queen of deliverance. So many guises, so many paths to the place of final retribution. I shall introduce you, my dear. Come!"

He pressed the gun into the small of her back as she groped her way through the dark, cluttered storeroom, through the massive door to the apartment. The old woman still lay on the bed, eyes dropped shut. "Did you call?" she whispered. "Are they coming?"

"I fear your savior was forced to revise her plans, my dear lady. Such is the fickle nature of circumstance."

"No, please." The old woman began to sob in desperation.

Erica placed a soothing hand on the frail arm. "I'm sorry. So sorry."

"How touching. How very touching, my dear. I'm certain your reassurances are of great comfort."

The woman was sobbing hysterically now. Goody eyed her with an expression of smug contempt and slapped her hard across the cheek. "Stop that!"

A flash of rage broke through Erica's fear. She gripped Goody's wrist. "You leave her alone!"

Pulling free, he pressed the gun hard against her throat, gagging her. "How touching," he rasped. "To think you would risk your personal welfare for the sake of a stranger. You two have not even been formally introduced, have you? In fact, I have been unforgivably rude . . . Erica Phillips, allow me to present the great Theresa Bricklin."

CHAPTER

36

The room was suddenly askew, wrenched out of focus.
Erica took a deep breath and looked from Goody to the old
woman. Her mind raced in dizzying circles. "I don't understand. You're Theresa Bricklin?"

"I am what is left of her." She lay inert, eyes wide and
vacant, a solitary tear trickling down her sunken cheek. "I'm
so terribly sorry. You shouldn't have come, shouldn't have
involved yourself in this wretched business. I'm an old
woman at the end of a long, satisfying life. It doesn't matter
for me . . ."

Goody snickered. "An attitude of surrender, my dear
Tessa? I am appalled. Truly. Who is more courageous and
determined than the great Theresa Bricklin? Who more cel-
ebrated and revered? Hah. Imagine if your fawning, adoring
public could see you now, wallowing in self-pity, mewling
like a pathetic, little animal."

She lifted her head, trembling with rage and effort. "You
have what you want, you lunatic. Now go and leave us
alone!"

He crossed to the night table and lifted the neat stack of
papers. "The manuscript is complete at long last, my dear.
Isn't that marvelous news? A tedious wait but most worthwhile in the end. I shall deliver this valuable property to
your Mr. Underwood personally as soon as I have fulfilled

my currect obligations. He is, as you know, most anxious to receive the completed book. Perhaps you would like me to convey your regards."

Erica struggled to focus, to think past the fear. There had to be a way out, some way. She needed time . . . to think. "Why, Goody? Why all this?"

His mouth curled in a vicious sneer. "Still encumbered by vain curiosities, my dear? An incurable affliction, it seems. Perhaps a terminal affliction, I fear. Pity. Well, then, I shall enlighten you. You shall have a feast of enlightenment.

"It's all quite simple actually. My father was not a well man, not fully in command of his senses at the end. This vile slattern took advantage of his condition, insinuated herself into his affections like a cunning reptile."

"It was not that way, Goodwin," Theresa sighed. "Not that way at all. Bertram was my friend. We met many years ago and remained close throughout his personal tragedies. For years, he managed to keep above them but all those dire circumstances seemed finally to defeat him. He was suffering the most dreadful emotional pain. I listened to his difficulties, helped him through his time of trial. That's all."

Hemphill held a finger aloft and spat his words. "Liar! It was theft. Theft at its most malignant, a birthright wrested from the deserving hands of an innocent heir. Calculating, deliberate, vicious theft! The brutal murder of a legacy!"

His voice had risen to a petulant shriek. Now he leaned toward Erica and dropped his tone to a grainy whisper. "There was no other way, you see. The estate was mine, by right. It belonged to me from the first, from the first breath of my accursed existence. And I was forced to protect my heritage against the greedy plunderings of one odious creature after another, to assert my rights against wave after wave of insidious affectionate assault. I have been chosen to satisfy the powerful cravings of justice, bound to bear the weightiest burden."

"He killed them all," Theresa said dully. "His mother.

His stepmother. All his sisters and brothers. Bertram always had the feeling it was him but he couldn't prove it, couldn't bring himself to make accusations without absolute proof. It was only the last one he knew for sure, the daughter. And then, it was too late. Bertram blamed himself for all of it . . . That's what finally killed him too. The guilt."

"I am dismayed by your doltish simplicity, Tessa dear. A woman of such presumed depth and insight. Genius, they call her. Hah! No one was 'killed,' as you so childishly put it. There were debts to pay, precious gifts of retribution to deliver. As a messenger, I merely distributed the proper offerings to the proper parties. This here, that there, and so on. I merely fulfilled an obligation from a higher order. I was a vessel, no more. Just as I am now, in your case. In the case of you two dear ladies. A vessel of moral right and justice."

He clasped his hands like an obedient school child. "We must tarry no longer . . . So much to do. So little time." He pursed his lips. "Now let me see. I must determine the proper sequence of events? Hmm. I imagine you should be next, my dear Mummy." He slid open a cabinet in the closet and made several adjustments on a timing device. "One hour will be ample, I should think."

He stood and turned to face them, his mouth set in a satisfied smirk. "So, dear Erica. The glorious moment has arrived at long last. Tessa has already known the sweet irony of proper retribution, have you not? You see, she had a terror of paralysis. It seems her dear father was afflicted with a degenerative disease that rendered him wholly immobile at the end. Incapable of sustaining his own pitiable existence without the aid of pumps and motors. Poor pathetic creature could not breathe independently or take sustenance or even blink after a time. But Tessa solved his predicament, did you not, my dear? You put the poor fellow out of his misery. What an unselfish, loving act. What more could a parent ask of a devoted daughter?"

Theresa's eyes bulged with shock. "How did you know? Who told you?"

"You told me yourself, my dear. Just as Erica has revealed her darkest apprehensions and foulest deeds. My ears are attuned to the web of cracks in the human surface, my nose sensitive to the barest hint of decay in the fiber of the soul."

"I don't understand," Erica said.

He dismissed her with a wave. "Mine is a humble talent, I admit. I simply listen and the secrets of the soul are laid bare. Nothing is sacred, nothing held in private counsel. All petty cowardice is revealed to those who wait in watchful silence."

Erica thought of all the times she had sensed his presence, felt herself watched by some unseen eyes, overheard. She shivered at the thought of what he might know about her.

He clapped. "So. We shall begin with you, my dear Mummy." He crossed to the closet and retrieved a covered carton. Setting the box next to Erica, he grinned in childish delight. "Give me your hand, my dear."

Her mind registered the horror inside. The squeals, the flutter. Erica was frozen in terrified disgust. "No, please, Goody. Please!"

"You must not refuse my most heartfelt offerings, my dear. I have labored too long on your behalf. Give me your hand!" He grabbed her wrist in a grip of iron fury and plunged her hand into the box. She felt the slimy backs of the rodents, the flicking tails, the pulsing whiskers against her trembling fingers, the darting tongues, the bite of vicious teeth. Rats! "No!" In a reflex of terror she managed to pull her hand away.

Goody laughed in a mad rumble of appreciation. "How lovely to see how well you respond to my humble arrangements, Erica." He lifted a fat, squirming rodent from the box and held it up to her face. The animal's scent made her gag and a frantic claw scratched her cheek.

"There, there, dear Mummy. Quite a graceful creature, don't you think? Nothing to fear, is there now?"

Erica closed her eyes and swallowed back the sour lump

in her throat. She would not scream, would not. The rat scampered across her scalp and caught its darting foot in a tangle of hair. A sick warmth crept up her neck.

"Tsk, tsk. You are looking unwell, my dear. Perhaps we should move on to another activity." He put the rat back in the box and stroked its slimy back. "There now, you have served nobly, little fellow."

Goody chewed thoughtfully on his lower lip. "Now let me see. How shall we proceed? There is so much to do. So many amusements, so little time.

"Perhaps this is the moment for Xanthippus, magnificent creature. My dear sister was most taken with him. Most taken, heh heh." He bowed his head in concentration and muttered to himself. "But first, you must visit my special museum, Erica. True, it is not fully completed, not entirely ready for public viewing but you are practically a member of the family, are you not? Tessa will excuse us, won't you, my dear? We shall return in short order. I needn't warn you of the futility of escape, must I, my dear ladies? You are both aware of my fervent determination to have you with us for a long, long stay. Heh, heh."

Once again, they traversed the frozen path between house and stable. Goody prodded Erica's leaden body with the sharp muzzle of the gun. She was oblivious to the icy, frostladen gales buffeting her on the way. All she could do was stare ahead and place one dead foot in front of another. This could not be. It was a dream. A vicious, black dream.

The house was cold and silent. Inside, he urged her past the main rooms and through the maze of stairs and corridors to the closed east wing. He stopped at the boarded wall and pried loose several strategic planks. They came away with ease to reveal a gaping black hole in the corridor wall. Finished, he ordered her to crawl through the opening.

She scraped her arm on the rough planks and stumbled on something inside. There was no pain. Her mind was too numb with the weight of hopelessness, too desperate to find a shred of salvation. There had to be a way out. Some way.

The scent of musty disuse filled her head and her eyes watered from the acrid mingling of mold and decay.

Goody crept through the opening behind her. When he flipped on the light, she was faced with a sight too hideous to absorb. The walls were covered with grossly enlarged photographs of corpses, dead women and small children with tortured grimaces and wide, empty eyes. A small boy stared at her through death-glazed eyes, his little mouth twisted in a final grin of failed mischief. A lovely young woman, her hair a spill of flaxen silk, held a delicate hand to the remains of her forehead, crushed and bloodied by a murderous fit of evil. One blue eye bulged from her face like a pod about to burst. The other winked for all eternity at some sick private joke.

Beside each picture was a small table holding the instruments of death: razor-sharp knives, hypodermic syringes fitted with huge needles, snub-nosed guns and grim bludgeons encrusted with blackened blood and fragments of dried bone and flesh. Erica felt an overwhelming rush of revulsion. And a blessed black curtain of unconsciousness began to descend.

Goody gave her a violent shake and smacked her hard across the face. "Now, now, dear Mummy. You mustn't be overwhelmed. That will not do, not at all. I am so pleased to see you are impressed with my modest display, truly delighted. But our remaining moments are to be scrupulously husbanded and I fear we are being most rude to dear Tessa. We have left her long enough."

Time was suspended in a frozen void as they made their way back to the stables and Theresa's prison. Erica struggled to find a plan. Some possibility. But escape seemed somewhere beyond her fading resolve.

Theresa lay as they left her but a tiny hint of strength had crept into her voice. Her words were measured and calm. "Goodwin, I know all this is not your fault. You act on irresistible impulse, anyone would understand that. And you can be helped. I know you can. There are methods, medications. New approaches to rehabilitation that might change the course of your life. Allow us to get you the assistance you need."

"Help? Oh no, dear Tessa. It is I who shall assist you in restoring the ultimate balance. We near the coronation of the right queen of justice. You two ladies will be properly recompensed for your repugnant deeds and abhorrent frailties. All is arranged. When the time comes, you need only sit here until the air fills with a deadly gas. Quite simple you'll find. Simple and painless."

"Bertram blamed himself for everything. That's why he could not go on any longer," Theresa sighed.

"Suicide?" Erica said.

"In a manner of speaking. A long painful course of personal ruin, degradation, self-punishment. But for a time, I thought it could be otherwise. I was able to ease the burden by taking the stories from him. Somehow, my writing them made it easier for him to bear."

"*The Fallen Angel?*" Erica said. "*The Debtor? Belinda?* All those stories were based on Bertram's family?"

"All of them," Theresa said. "And *Child of Eternity.* But that was too late. All the damage was done by then. There was no one left to save. No one but Bertram and he was beyond salvation." She bit her lip and shut her eyes to dismiss a painful image. "Still, Goodwin's story had to be told as well. That was my reason for agreeing to write this latest book. Goodwin wanted the money and I allowed him to think I was writing the novel under duress. In fact, I would have finished his woeful history in any event. That was the only way to chronicle his tragic evil, to make certain such evil is never permitted to go unchecked in the lives of other innocents. The authorities never suspected him. No one thought he had the capacity for such deeds. No one, that is, except Bertram. And he was blinded by a parent's guilt and devotion."

"Why must you go on and on, words and words and words. Stupid words with no blood or substance. You are a stupid, stupid woman. It shall be my pleasure to see to your particular penance, knowing how you have deceived, how you have duped an ignorant, adoring public. How you plotted and calculated, you wretched crone. You malevolent shrew." Cloudy spittle collected at the corners of his mouth and his head bobbled as he spoke.

"For all your gift of word and imagination, you are unable to grasp the most fundamental equation. Each deed, each ounce of cosmic undertaking, exacts a particular price. Payment may be deferred but never avoided. Never!"

Theresa was drifting, letting go, a mournful song drowned in a howling wind of despair. "You have what you want. I gave you what you want. Let her go at least, Goodwin. Let her have her child . . . her future. With all you've had, you don't need her destruction."

"Now you wax sentimental, Theresa? My word. You never cease to astonish, do you? I know you possess all the sentiments of a slab of granite. Did you think I would be swayed by the doe-eyed persuasions of a withered avaricious witch? Do you take me for a fool?"

Erica's mind raced past the words, past the seeming impossibility of her predicament. There had to be a way. Something. A notion crept into her consciousness. A chance. "The road . . ." she said more to herself than anyone.

Goody stopped his ranting and turned to face her. Deep frown lines furrowed his milky brow and his lips were drawn thin in concentration. They could hear the vague clatter of heavy machinery in the distance. He passed his fingers over the face of his watch and began mumbling to himself in agitated bursts. "Not yet. Those incompetent boobs . . . I told them one-thirty. One-thirty, not before. By then she would have been dispatched. Both of you. That was the plan. The plan is all, everything. But now . . ."

He was trembling, frightened, muttering to himself. The gas? Erica spotted a small circular vent in the ceiling. The road crew was drawing closer, the sounds growing more distinct. She needed time, a few more minutes. "You still haven't answered all my questions. What about the other Theresa? Who is she? And how did you hope to get away with all this?"

He waved her away. "Ssh. Not now. No time for idle queries and vain curiosities. The timer. I must reset the timer. Nothing is going as planned. Nothing. Must stop the crew. Start them later. All to the second. Precision is imperative . . ."

Erica caught Theresa's eye and passed a silent question. The old woman nodded in almost imperceptible agreement. Her eyes directed Erica to a cabinet opposite the bed.

Still wielding the gun, Goody edged toward the living room. "My education. Have I described my education? Quite an astonishing accomplishment if I may be so immodest." He removed a small square metal plate from the wall and revealed the complex of electronic circuitry behind the timing device. Carefully, he began manipulating the dials. Fingers poised, ear cocked to detect the sensitive meshing of the cylinders.

"I was discarded shortly after birth, tossed aside for the heinous sin of imperfection. They placed me in a vile asylum teeming with inhuman rubbish: drooling idiots, crippled morons, brainless monsters reeking of their own fetid wastes. I can still summon the wretchedness of the so-called infant ward—the stench of inhumanity, the seeking fat tongues extending from the mouths of living gargoyles, the grovelling of greedy, mindless hands, the cruel poisonous touch of foul, mercenary caretakers. They were hardly more competent than their pathetic charges. Ordering, abusing. My innocent soul drowning in the base poison of unthinkable injustice!"

Slowly, he adjusted one dial, felt for its perfect placement and moved to the next. "Mine were mere physical anomalies—a club foot, a disorder in the skin pigmentations, some visual deficits. An aesthetic dilemma, to be sure. I was not a fit subject for the delicate mind's eye. But I was a precocious child, possessed of a particular genius. An absorptive mind, the psychologist said. Knowledge of events and circumstances that far exceeded their expectations for one well past my age and experience. I am gifted with total retention of visual and auditory events. One glance at a printed page, one hearing of a recitation, and it is indelibly imprinted on my consciousness for all eterntiy.

"They didn't know, Goodwin. They only did what the doctors said . . ." Theresa sounded better, stronger. "You were unique. A singular case of such severe anomaly mixed with those particular abilities. It was a different era. The doctors were not enlightened about the whims of nature as they are today."

"Am I to be comforted by their ignorance!" he screamed. "Does that return my childhood? My life? My human dignity and opportunity?"

Erica was inching toward the cabinet. She could hear the wheezing rasp of his breath as he struggled for control. "I am a self-educated man, completely self-actualized. Before my sight dimmed beyond a useful level, I read the works of the world's noblest thinkers. I remember every word, integrate and restructure, advance and resurrect, combine and reformulate in purer, more intricate form. My thoughts, my efforts, my contributions could place me above them, all of them. All!"

The medicine was beginning to wear off. Theresa raised an arm experimentally. Her voice was gentle, soothing. "Your mother and father loved you, Goodwin. They took you home again as soon as they knew. But you weren't right . . . emotionally. There was more to your condition than the doctors recognized at the time. A quirk of emotional imbalance that left you with irrepressible violent impulses. You suffered from fits during which you harmed small animals, acted in unpredictable, destructive ways. When your sister was born, you came within inches of seriously harming her on several occasions. You needed constant supervision. Your parents managed you for as long as it was humanly possible. They tried. You know that."

His face was tight with fury and concentration. One of
the dials was confounding him. He turned to Theresa in
disgust. "I know nothing of the sort. They were vile, pusillanimous egoists. Again and again they sought to replace
me, to install some brash, insipid infant in my rightful place.
Fortunately, I was able to serve justice with the help of my
firmest ally."

"Death," Theresa whispered. "Bertram's final words
haunt me, Goodwin. I can see his eyes, vacant with hopelessness. He was the strongest, finest man, reduced to a
fragment by your deeds. 'You must stop him, Theresa,' he
told me. 'He thrives on killing.' "

"I am appalled by your simple-mindedness, Tessa. Appalled." He frowned and returned to his adjustments. "Genius indeed. You masquerade as intelligence, you wretched
heap of decaying human debris."

Erica's hand was on the cabinet door. Slowly, she inched
it open. A crack, a finger space. She nodded at Theresa,
urging her to continue.

"I suppose I am not very intelligent, Goodwin. You are
correct in that. Otherwise I would not have come here
alone. Even after Bertram's warning, I thought I could
somehow convince you to commit yourself voluntarily. I
thought I could make you see the futility of your course.
Foolish of me to think you would spare me, knowing how
much I cared about your father. And you . . ."

"It would not have made the slightest difference, I assure
you, Tessa. If you had not arrived of your own volition, I
would have found a way to bring you here. After all, I
needed you, your work, the royalties from this new book, to
sustain me in comfort. The comfort I so richly deserve. You
were merely kind enough to ease the undertaking. Dear
considerate Tessa."

Erica kept pushing. Two fingers open. Three. Theresa
spoke in a conspiratorial hush, as if Erica were right next to
the bed. "He took the old woman from a nursing home,
pretended she was me, that he and I were married and I

had suffered a stroke. Her appearance was so distorted, he knew no one would question the substitution. A clever plan. Audacious enough to succeed. After we were both gone, the book would have been his. That and the proceeds from my other works."

"Not would have been, my dear. Shall be. I have seen to that. Nothing shall be permitted to stand in the path of my grand design."

Erica could see inside the cabinet now. There was a row of hypodermic syringes and several small vials of medication. Theresa nodded.

"He killed them all. The children. His mother and stepmother. My nephew and his wife."

"Mark Bloomway?" Erica asked. Then she cupped a hand over her mouth. Stupid! Would he notice her change of position? Please no!

He paused for an instant and cocked his head. She held her breath until he leaned toward the dials again and continued his work.

"Yes," Theresa said. "Mark and Sharon. He was afraid they would manage to get involved in my inheritance."

"Not afraid. Never afraid. Fear is a useless, senseless indulgence. For every malady, there is a remedy. The Bloomways were a pox, a plague. I simply effected a cure." He snapped his fingers and snickered at some private joke.

Silently, Erica withdrew a syringe and filled it through the porous stopper on the vial. The clear fluid bubbled into the glass reservoir as she drew back the plunger. "What about the old woman?" Theresa asked. "Erica told me she had another stroke. What happened? Is she . . . ?"

"Dead. Unfortunately, not as yet. But I shall rectify that in due course. Naturally, it would have been simpler had she remained at Bramble Farm. A simple dose of medication and the poor, wasted creature would have been spared the further trial of her uselessness. But Erica insisted on meddling. Didn't you, my dear? You have been a trial since your arrival. Always intruding, poking about."

She was close, just a few feet away from him in the shadow of the door, sliding her feet soundlessly along the plank floor. "Didn't you?" His voice rose in impatience, his head lashed side to side as if he knew, as if he felt her presence. "Erica!"

A board creaked under her foot. He stepped toward the noise and raised the gun.

She was still in shadow. Ducking, she lunged toward him and stuck the needle deep in his thigh. He groaned, trying to shake loose the pain but she managed to push home the plunger.

Stunned, he dropped the weapon. In an instant, his fingers curled, twitching into dead fists and his legs trembled and crumpled beneath him. In seconds, he was locked in a paralyzed heap. Helpless. "The gas," he whimpered. "I haven't finished. Just moments and the gas will start. It will kill us all."

Erica went back to Theresa. "Can you walk? We have to get out of here."

"I can't. You go and get help."

"There isn't time. Here. Lean on me." Erica helped the old woman to her feet. She was trembling with weakness, barely able to take a step.

"Come on, Miss Bricklin. You can do it."

Together, they managed to stumble out of the bedroom, through the living room, past Goody's stricken body. "You can't just leave me here," he whined. "You can't do that. What manner of foul beings are you? Dear ladies, please. I entreat you. Mummy? Dear Tessa. You cannot leave me like this. You must not!"

Each step a monumental effort. Erica felt cold beads of sweat on her face and searing thrust of pain in her belly. "That's it, Miss Bricklin. We're getting there." They were outside the apartment now. Erica struggled to help Theresa over the jumble of cartons, through the maze of stored furniture. The pain hit again, harder this time. She breathed deeply and trained her eyes on the door. Nearly there.

"I can't, Erica. I'm too weak. You go on without me."

"No. We're getting out of here together." She was dragging Theresa now, pulling her toward the door. "Both of us."

Through the vicious pulsing in her head, she heard something. A faint whirring sound. The fan starting. The gas. Goody's voice rose in a childlike whimper. "Tessa . . . Mummy . . . dear ladies, I implore you. Help me . . . Help!"

"Now!" With all her might, she dragged Theresa through the door and out of the storeroom. She closed the door behind them and slumped down next to the old woman on the cold, dirt floor.

"Thank you," Theresa managed. "Are you all right?"

Erica winced as another pain hit her. She was still breathless from her efforts. "Fine," she gasped. "I'm all right. You?"

"No strength," she said. "He had me on that drug so long my body has forgotten how to operate. Please. You go on by yourself. Lethal gas will not be contained by a wooden door, I'm afraid. Not for long."

"Then we have to get out of here. Now. Come on, Miss Bricklin. We'll make it." Another pain hit. She bit her lip.

"You go alone, Erica. Go quickly. It's our best chance. Our only chance. Please. There is no time to argue."

Time. Erica could smell the first acrid traces of the gas. No time. She had to reach the road crew. Had to bring help for Theresa.

No time. She walked to the first stall, unlatched the wooden gate, and freed the giant Arabian from his tether. Trembling, she maneuvered him out of the stall and managed to hoist herself over his back. With a sharp tap of her heels, she set the beast in motion.

No reins, no saddle. No time. Her fingers clutched coarse fistfuls of his white mane as she urged the horse to a trot, a gallop.

Over the field, throught the maze of gardens. Terror squeezing at her throat, choking her. Another pain, a burning sword of pain.

The horse was approaching the cutting garden. Too late she remembered the fence. The sharp wire spikes rushed up at her, she could see herself ripped to bloody shreds. Closer. A blinding blur.

Then she felt the muscular ripple beneath her. The horse bounding effortlessly over the barrier. They hung suspended in air for what seemed an eternity of terror. Then, the dizzying rush of ground came up from below. Too fast. The horse struggling. Stumbling.

Then the pain.

And the blackness.

CHAPTER

37

The sun was a lemon square, shining in her eyes. Polished metal sun suspended from a dotted silver sky. Strange.

And the voice was so soft. Warm and soft as fresh tapioca. Jim's voice.

"That's good, Erica. You're doing fine. Just fine." He stroked her hand.

"Jim?"

"That's it. Not much longer now."

A sharp wave of pain lifted her and carried her back toward the blackness.

"Breathe, Erica!"

He caught her, stopped her in time. "Jim, I . . ."

"Look. There it is! The baby's crowning." He pointed toward the mirror. Following his direction, she spotted the back of her baby's head.

"Just a few more seconds, Erica. You're doing great. Just great."

This time she rode the crest of the pain, strained against it.

"That's it . . . push!"

She pushed with every fiber of her being and felt a warm glorious rush of power.

"Good. Great. Now breathe for a minute. Don't push again until I deliver the shoulders."

His eyes were so blue and serious. "Now?"

"Now . . . push!"

Again she felt the surge of power, the warmth. She could see Jim's eyes over the mask. Smiling.

She heard the weak kitten cry of new life. And then Jim. His voice was full of joy and wonder. "Congratulations, Miss Phillips. You have a daughter. A beautiful, wonderful daughter."

He took the infant to be weighed and washed, then gently swaddled her and placed her in the crook of Erica's arm. "She's fine. You're both fine."

"How did I get here? Who found me?"

"Your brother, Michael, called me this morning. He was trying to reach you at Bramble Farm but the phones were out of order. You must have mentioned my name and he called the office to see if you might be in labor or something. I checked with Connie and she told me you cancelled your appointment. We decided to meet at Bramble Farm and make sure you were okay. Michael got there first and the men working on the road told him the place would be impassable for a few days. He didn't like the idea of you being out of reach like that so he went in to drag you out. He saw the horse throw you. The timing was incredible."

"Yes. Amazing. What happened to Miss Bricklin? Is she okay?"

"Ssh. Yes. She's going to be fine, thanks to you. No more questions now. Let me finish up here and get you back to your room."

"Jim? I can't believe it, all of it. I guess after this everything is going to be easy."

He leaned over and kissed her, a sweet gentle breeze of a kiss. "I hope so, Erica. And I hope I'm around to see it."

Her eyes filled with tears. "I don't know what to say, Jim. I can't think right now about that or anything. For now, all I know is that I'm very, very happy."

He stroked her hair and patted the sleeping infant on the back. "That, my friend, is a big step in the right direction."

CHAPTER

38

Back in her room, Erica lay in a dream state of relieved exhaustion. There was so much to absorb, so many new realities to sort into the packed cubicles of her mind. The past few months, the future, all crowded in on her and clamored for attention.

One at a time, Erica. First she would memorize the baby—the boneless warmth of her daughter as she slept in perfect innocence and curled her tiny fingers around Erica's. Her little girl.

And Jim's smiling eyes, blue as the sea in a child's painting, Crayola blue.

She was drifting in a sea of contentment . . . Mom, I need a new box of crayons, Mikey melted them in the sun . . .

Guess what, Aunt Meggy Muggins? You can buy that little pink snowsuit with the rabbit ears after all . . .

Precious nonsense. Delicious mindless pleasure. She thought she imagined the enormous blue teddy bear walking across the room bearing a basket of pink roses in a furry paw.

Michael appeared from behind the bear, set the basket on the window sill and offered Erica a satisfied grin. "Nice work, old girl. My niece is a little beat up but beautiful. What are we going to call her?"

"Rachel."

"After Mom. Nice. She would have liked that."

"I hear you rescued me, Michael. And Miss Bricklin."

He shrugged. "That was pretty dumb, Wicka. Playing Pony Express in your condition. Lucky you have the famous Phillips hard head or you might have really hurt yourself. As it was, you had enough energy left to give me hell for showing up. And you were able to tell me where Miss Bricklin was before you passed out. I got to her just in time. She had already lost consciousness. The gas was even starting to get to the horses.

"Anyway, your Doctor Wellings showed up with the ambulance a few minutes later and helped me cart the wreckage to the hospital. It was all very neat and tidy."

"Jim said Miss Bricklin will be all right. I'm glad."

"Me too," Michael nodded. "The doctor said she'll need some therapy. Her muscles were severely atrophied from months of being on some medication that left her immobile. But she's a tough old bird. I went to see her before you got back from delivery and despite everything, she still had the strength to spin a few priceless yarns for me. She's some story teller. I can see why her books are second only to Doctor Spock and the *Bible*. She'll be fine."

"And the other Theresa? Have you heard anything?"

"Fine too," he nodded. "It wasn't another stroke, it seems. Just a stress reaction. Funny thing. A doctor named Magida is treating her and he recognized her from some nursing home he used to work in. She used to be a patient of his."

Erica smiled, remembering. "Dirty Bertie Boyargin. Interesting how all the pieces fall into place. And . . . Goody?"

He shook his head. "The gas was really potent. It must have killed him immediately."

"You mean I killed him," Erica said.

"He killed himself, Wicka. You know that. Some people are just beyond help."

There was a vague knock on the door and a soft, insubstantial voice. "May I come in?"

A brusque uniformed nurse with a cupcake cap and a large, humorless face wheeled Theresa into the room. "Just a short visit, Miss Bricklin. The doctor was very clear about that. Five minutes at most. You need to get your rest if you want to get well."

Theresa waved her away. "Please leave us then. Let us visit in peace." She turned to Erica and winked. "They have transferred me from one prison to another, I'm afraid." With a trembling hand, she smoothed the white wisps of hair back from her forehead. "Forgive my appearance, I must look a fright. But I had to see you. I was able to thank Michael earlier, Erica, but I could not rest until I offered my thanks to you . . ."

"I'll leave you two and go call the family," Michael said. "I think everyone in the world knows about the baby except them. Your old boss, Underwood, is waiting to see you with his wife. He brought what looks like the whole editorial staff from Prescott Press. And there's this real character, a Mrs. Orange?"

"Ohringer," Erica said.

"Whatever. She can't wait to get in here and chew your ear off. She said I should be sure and tell you to drink plenty of water. Said that will keep the old pipes chugging."

"I think I'm all chugged out for a while."

After he left, Theresa turned to Erica with a kindly smile. "How can I begin to thank you for what you have done? How can I ever repay you?"

"You don't owe me anything, Miss Bricklin. In fact, I feel indebted to you. It was a great honor to work on your manuscript, whatever the circumstances."

"Then you must continue as soon as you feel ready."

Erica shook her head. "I don't know where I'll be living. What I'll be doing. I have some decisions to make."

"By all means. You have given me the gift of time and it will be my pleasure to share it with you. I want you to continue with the project. Whenever you're ready, wherever. You let me know."

"Of course, I would love to work on the book. If you're sure . . ."

She sighed. "I'm afraid we have some considerable revisions to make. For a time, I tried to scuttle the manuscript, tried to make it unacceptable in the hope that might postpone Goodwin's plans to execute me. In any event, the story's ending was not exactly as I anticipated."

"Endings rarely are," Erica mused.

Theresa cleared her throat. "Doctor James Wellings was in to see me this morning. Quite an unusual young man."

"Yes, he is something. Isn't he?"

"It appears the admiration is mutual. I suspect he would be willing to pay me handsomely if I could somehow persuade you to remain in the area." Theresa folded her hands. "Forgive me if I overstep my bounds, Erica. But I hope you will consider your options carefully. When I was a young woman, I allowed several excellent relationships to slip away. I was intoxicated by adventure, unwilling to invest in a long-term commitment. True, I had my little flings and dalliances, but I ran from the threat of permanence.

"One morning, I woke up and found that, despite my plans never to do so, I had become an old woman. A solitary old woman. Needless to say, it's difficult to snuggle up to book contracts or promotional budgets when the wind howls."

Erica looked into the soft grey eyes. With all she had been through, there was still the fire of intelligence, the strength. "I understand, Miss Bricklin. And thanks for the advice."

"I would just hate to think you might have regrets. Later on that is," Theresa said.

"Regrets?" Erica said. "Did you say regrets?" She started to laugh. A light giggle that grew to a bout of teary-eyed hilarity.

"Are you all right, Erica? Is everything all right?" Theresa sounded alarmed. "Shall I call the nurse?"

Erica wiped her eyes on the sleeve of her plaid flannel

robe and composed herself with a deep breath. "I'm sorry, Miss Bricklin. It's just that you really do have an incredible way with words. Regrets. Perfect."

Theresa took Erica's hand and held it between hers. "You know, Erica, getting old has its advantages. I can speak as freely and act as foolishly as I please. My age is ample excuse for anything.

"And I no longer bear the burden of the world and its woes. I feel I am ready to step aside, to review and recollect. It's your world now, yours and your little girl's. And I so want to know it will go well for you."

Erica could feel the weight of age in Theresa's frail fingers and the warmth of her concern. No matter how long you waited, how carefully you searched, there were no definite answers, no guarantees. In the end, Erica knew, feelings were as good a path to follow as any.

"Things will turn out the way they're supposed to, Miss Bricklin," she said at last. "The way they're meant to be."

"Yes, Erica," Theresa nodded. "They always do."

The nurse came and wheeled Theresa back to her room. As the door closed, Erica lay back and stared out the window. A light snow was falling, soft flakes drifting on a gentle cushion of crisp air. One after another, the bounty of fresh possibilities danced in her imagination. A new life equipped with top-of-the-line accessories. "Lucky, Erica. Very lucky," she mumbled. Contentment settled over her like a feather quilt. And she drifted off to sleep.

ABOUT THE AUTHOR

JUDITH KELMAN is the author of nine novels, including *MORE THAN YOU KNOW, ONE LAST KISS,* and *THE HOUSE ON THE HILL.* In addition she's written articles for major magazines, including *Redbook, Glamour, Ladies' Home Journal,* and *McCall's,* and for the *New York Times.* She lives in Connecticut with her husband and two sons, where she is at work on her next novel, *FLY AWAY HOME.*